PRAISE FOR LAMAR GILES

"My twin, Lamar, is a phenomenal, innovative storyteller. His thrillers have laid the groundwork for us all. A true king!"
—Tiffany D. Jackson, *New York Times* bestselling author of *Grown* and *The Weight of Blood*

"Lamar Giles's work always has something to say, and it's well worth your while to listen." —Barry Lyga, *New York Times* bestselling author of *I Hunt Killers*

RUIN ROAD

"*Ruin Road* brims with malice, each page sure to drag readers into a community's—and boy's—fight against the greedy forces preying on them. Exceptional and not to be missed!"
—Trang Thanh Tran, *New York Times* bestselling author of *She Is a Haunting*

"Lamar Giles's latest thriller is filled with chilling haunts and horrors, not just in the magical curse that burdens the main character, but in the authentic real-life struggles and stigmas that plague him. A brilliant concept, deftly executed!"
—Neal Shusterman, *New York Times* bestselling author of the Arc of a Scythe series

"Riveting, grounded horror tinged with characters who leap to life. Lamar Giles writes with imagination and urgency that will appeal to all horror fans, as *Ruin Road* raises an intriguing question with surprising answers: What would we be like if we had no fear?" —Tananarive Due, American Book Award winner and author of *The Reformatory*

"A refreshing tale with twists you'll never see coming. Giles crafts an action-packed story, filled with both real-life and supernatural terrors. *Ruin Road* pulls your heartstrings tight and keeps you on your toes!" —Erin E. Adams, author of *Jackal*

"From the first line, *Ruin Road* lets you know you're in the hands of a master. The story moves with the knowing swagger of its main character, Cade Webster, fascinating, charismatic, and layered. With elements of Stephen King and a double helping of that Giles magic that makes his work so unforgettable, *Ruin Road* is a mix of terror, heart, and intelligence, with a dash of social commentary. Giles is in peak form, and you don't want to miss out!" —Maurice Broaddus, author of *Unfadeable*

THE GETAWAY

"Timely, thrilling, and gripping from start to finish. An absolute page-turner." —Karen M. McManus, #1 *New York Times* bestselling author of *One of Us Is Lying*

"*The Getaway* grabbed me from page one and didn't let go. I was immediately fascinated and disturbed by the fictional Karloff Country. You too will be lured in and then horrified by the truth behind those perfect customer service smiles . . ." —Malinda Lo, *New York Times* bestselling author of *Last Night at the Telegraph Club*

★ "With hints of Cory Doctorow, Jordan Peele, and Richard Matheson, this book stands on its own as a dystopian adventure, but the deeper metaphors around servitude, privilege, class, and solidarity mean that there's a lot to think about as the characters reckon with their proximity to and complicity in violence both

local and far-flung. Hold tight: You'll want to stay on this
nightmarish roller coaster till the end."
—*Kirkus Reviews*, starred review

★ "This arresting and engaging dystopian thriller interrogates
the horrors of racism, classism, unregulated capitalism,
and eco-fascism." —*Shelf Awareness*, starred review

"Giles's harrowing dystopian novel combines an exploration of
capitalistic greed and systemic racism and oppression with
gripping psychological horror, resulting in a read that is
guaranteed to terrify." —*Publishers Weekly*

"With elements of adventure, science fiction, horror,
and even a bit of romance in a broken world, Giles keeps
readers wondering who can and cannot be trusted
throughout this page-turning novel."
—*Horn Book*

SPIN

"The first test of a whodunit is how heart-stopping and strange
a thing has actually been dun. In *Spin*, Lamar Giles nails the
murder . . . What's even more impressive is the subtle stuff you
almost don't notice because Giles wears his intellect so lightly:
the masterly knowledge of hip-hop and R&B; the command of
technology's uses and abuses; the discerning ear for the way high
schoolers talk . . . A two-time nominee for an Edgar award, Giles
is a terrific plotter . . . *Spin* champions the resourcefulness of
teenagers and pities the grown-ups—villainous or just clueless—
who underestimate them."
—*New York Times Book Review* (Editor's Choice)

★ "Not to be missed." —*Kirkus Reviews*, starred review

★ "*Spin* delivers everything you could want in a book: lush, complex characters; a spine-chilling plot; a vividly drawn world; and, best of all, hip-hop." —*Booklist*, starred review

★ "This novel transcends its genre."
—*School Library Journal*, starred review

★ "This fast-paced tale seizes attention from the first thrown punch to the final curtain call." —*Publishers Weekly*, starred review

OVERTURNED

"Giles, a founding member of We Need Diverse Books and two-time Edgar Award finalist, is in top form, weaving together the threads of his whodunit-and-why and resonantly depicting his characters' home and school lives. As a poker genius Nikki may be a singular sort of teenager, but she's grounded in desires and motivations that make her story as moving as it is thrilling."
—*New York Times Book Review*

★ "An utterly compelling whodunit."
—*Kirkus Reviews*, starred review

"Another Giles winner." —*BCCB*

"A fast-paced, endlessly intriguing mystery." —*Booklist*

RUIN
ROAD

RUIN ROAD

LAMAR GILES

SCHOLASTIC PRESS / NEW YORK

Names: Giles, Lamar, 1979– author.
Title: Ruin road / Lamar Giles.
Description: First edition. | New York : Scholastic Press, 2024. | Audience: Ages 12 and up. | Audience: Grades 7–9. | Summary: High school football player Cade Webster buys a ring in a pawnshop, but when his wish that people stop acting scared of him seems to be coming true, he remembers the ring came with a warning—"When the strangeness begins, come back"—and suddenly people seem to have lost their fear of everything.
Identifiers: LCCN 2024003753 (print) | LCCN 2024003754 (ebook) | ISBN 9781338894134 (hardcover) | ISBN 9781338894141 (ebook)
Subjects: LCSH: African American teenagers—Juvenile fiction. | African American families—Juvenile fiction. | Good and evil—Juvenile fiction. | Wishes—Juvenile fiction. | Fear—Juvenile fiction. | Horror tales. | CYAC: African Americans—Fiction. | African American families—Fiction. | Good and evil—Fiction. | Wishes—Fiction. | Fear—Fiction. | Horror stories. | BISAC: YOUNG ADULT FICTION / Horror | YOUNG ADULT FICTION / Social Themes / Prejudice & Racism | LCGFT: Horror fiction.
Classification: LCC PZ7.G39235 Ru 2024 (print) | LCC PZ7.G39235 (ebook) | DDC 813.6 [Fic]—dc23/eng/20240208

10 9 8 7 6 5 4 3 2 1   24 25 26 27 28

Printed in Italy   183
First edition, September 2024

Book design by Maeve Norton

For Jamie, my most fearless teammate,
&
Brandon, the first to let me hang up my
shingle and open shop

1

You carry your people with you even when you ride alone.

Pop first told me that when I was six years old, then when I was seven. A bunch of times when I was eight, nine, and ten. When I hit my first growth spurt and was suddenly as tall as him, he said it again, along with a bunch of other Kincade Webster III's Nuggets of Wisdom™, so much it made me mad. *I know, man, I know.*

Lately he'd slowed down beating me over the head with common sense. There wasn't much time left; no need to waste it on repeats. Plus, he accomplished the mission. I remembered stuff he said even when I didn't want to. Right now, smiling for this camera, having never reached true comfort at Neeson Preparatory Academy after all this time, I felt every bit of that "ride alone" part.

There was this other thing he said, too: Every smart man is a con man.

It was best to run a long con when it came to this stupid, stilted script I'd been reciting. I acted like it was incredible, best thing ever written. It was the right thing to do. The *smart* thing. Especially if I wanted to get out of here in time to catch my bus.

1

I finished my second take and said, "We good?"

Sheila, the blonde, leathery-faced director of communications, said, "Cade, I'm afraid to be the bearer of bad news, but you're a natural."

"So we're good?"

"Coach Gibson told me you were camera shy, and, if I'm being honest, shooting athletes tends to be the more labor-intensive part of the boosters video. You might be the best we've ever had, though! Makes my job so much easier."

"Oh. Cool. I can go?" I was already moving when Sheila held up her hand, halting me.

She glanced at the cameraman. He touched two fingers to his headphones, listening to the playback. "Audio's good."

Sheila said, "You're so well-spoken, Cade."

I bristled. Bet Sheila'd be impressed I knew that word and many others.

She said, "Let's go again. Get an extra take to be safe."

We were in the school's TV studio, which still felt weird because most of my life, a school and a TV studio meant two separate buildings. Not so at Neeson Prep. (Go, Sparks!) This school had a test kitchen for kids in culinary classes. A robotics lab for kids who knew how to do that. An Olympic-sized pool. There were even a couple of curling lanes, that sport where they slide a big rock across some ice while guys sweep the path. (It's kind of intense, though I wouldn't admit that to anyone back in the Court.) At my old school, we had to share books and didn't always have heat in the winter.

Settling back in front of a green screen on a stool constructed for a much tinier person, spending my Saturday spouting off nonsense Sheila probably wrote herself, I wrestled impatience. Sheila was wrong about me being camera shy. I loved a camera. Loved showing off on the football field—my YouTube mixtape was disgusting! Loved photobombing baddies. Loved repping Jacobs Court. I didn't love this smile-for-the-boosters mess. This was an obligation. Part of the unspoken requirements of my athletic scholarship.

Don't get me wrong, I understood and appreciated the opportunities I'd been granted. Getting the call to bring my talents to Neeson's football program three years ago was life-changing. When it became clear that I was much faster than the guys in my neighborhood, stronger than most of my competition across Virginia, and as big as the recruits I went up against in the national invite-only football camps and combines, Neeson was the next best step toward a future in the pros. My whole family agreed. We were going to do the work, and make the sacrifices, to change not only my future but future *generations*. Sometimes that meant sitting your butt down and smiling when you don't feel like it! (Another Nugget of Wisdom™.)

Sheila said, "Reset. Go on my count."

My phone was face down on my thigh, out of frame. I flipped it to check the time—11:16 a.m.—and calculated my chances of catching the 91 bus across town. If this was the last take, I could probably be out of here by 11:30. It was a fifteen-minute walk to the bus stop if I was lazy about it, but I could cut that to seven minutes easy. Either way, I'm there before noon, which was imperative (give me my vocabulary points, Sheila) because the next bus didn't come till 2:00.

"Three . . ." Sheila said.

The teleprompter scrolled to the top of the script.

"Two . . ."

I smoothed my navy-blue Neeson Prep polo shirt.

"One . . ."

"Hi, I'm Cade Webster, wide receiver for the Neeson Sparks. If things go according to plan, we're going to have an explosive season—"

Sheila insisted on *two more* takes "to be safe," bringing us to 11:35. And I was leaving.

"Ummmm," she said.

"I have to go." I stood and plucked the lavalier microphone from my collar.

The room felt charged. It was low. Not the worst I'd experienced, but I'd moved too fast and unpredictably. Sheila and the cameraman tensed like I'd shape-shifted.

Sheila cleared her throat. "Yes. I'm sorry. I was told we'd have you as long as we needed you."

Another of Pop's nuggets dropped: You want to see how people feel about you, set a boundary.

I said, "The first take was clean, so you should be able to edit around that. I have to catch my bus."

The cameraman shuffled his feet and inspected some overhead lights that worked fine.

Sheila's mouth twitched into a position just north of a scowl, then she revealed a new rule. "Six to seven solid takes are mandatory for each segment of the boosters video."

"I'm sorry, but I gotta be somewhere this afternoon. I can't be late." When I moved toward the door, Sheila stepped back, even though she was nowhere near the door. Instinctively I made sure my hands were open and visible. No fists. Nothing concealed or threatening. I hesitated reaching for the knob. "We're good, right?"

"Enjoy your weekend, Cade."

Outside the studio, the door was slow closing. If Sheila thought I spoke well, she didn't think my hearing was so great because her voice wasn't low when she said, "They don't know how good they have it here."

"They?" the cameraman asked.

"Athletes," Sheila confirmed quickly. "That's all I meant."

Then the door sealed the soundproof room, and I shook off the sting of what she really meant, kept it cool. I had to. Like Pop always said, doing what was necessary now was what would take care of my family later.

Made my bus with two minutes to spare.

2

Ma

You on your way?

Me

Yeah

Ma

Stop by Lim's and get more
paper plates and plastic utensils.
Gabby made a cake.

Me

Gabby's coming? Since when?

Ma

Since we invited her.

Me

Book too?

Ma

You know we didn't invite one
and not the other.

                                        Me

                              Be there in like 20.

Ma

Get some vanilla ice cream.
And a big bottle of Tylenol for
your pop.

I nearly responded with MORE?? because I'd gotten him a big bottle less than a week ago. Instead, I thought about Gabby coming with cake and how Book was a long shot these days but maybe. Then I focused on the city so as not to get my hopes up, the buildings and skyline scrolling by my bus window, getting grayer and gloomier the farther I got from Neeson. Whenever I got my first big NFL money, I was gonna find out how rich folks bought better skies.

Eventually suburban neighborhoods obscured by hedges and trees became my neighborhood, Jacobs Court.

The Court was a mix of low- and high-rise apartment buildings, row houses, restaurants, storefronts (fewer and fewer every year, though), and other stuff that made the Court, the Court. All staggered in a way that had narrow

7

streets with no parking, angled away from downtown toward what was supposed to be public recreation space that wasn't well maintained, made up of benches, rough shrubbery, and tennis courts that hadn't had nets at any point I could remember. Mostly that unused clay was a giant art board for taggers whose work ranged from curse words and gang shout-outs to museum-worthy portraiture honoring the famous and the dead. RIP Chadwick. Nipsey. DJ ParSec.

When the bus drew near my stop, I peeled off my Neeson Prep polo, exposing the plain white tee beneath, and stuffed the shirt in my back pocket so it dangled like a flag.

Air brakes hissed, and I stepped off into a fall breeze that smelled like oil and the sweet rot of a nearby trash can. I was four blocks from my building but needed to walk a block the opposite way to hit Mr. Lim's corner store.

Crossing the first street, I ran into neighborhood icon Corner Joe. Corner Joe was always on the corner—sometimes, a nickname's that simple. His brown head was completely bald and in complete contrast to his full white beard; in a different universe he could've played a serviceable Black Santa. His outfits alternated from old army surplus gear to slightly less old army surplus gear. He was known for one-on-one conversations with himself, and though the circumstances of his sleeping on the streets were no laughing matter, he often showed a sharp sense of humor in the signs he crafted asking for help. *Checks No Longer Accepted at This Location*, or *I'm Willing to Share My (Mom's) Netflix Password for $5.*

Pacing, his chin tucked to his chest and his cardboard sign pressed tight to his body, I couldn't see what he'd come up with for today's help request. He was upset.

He got like that sometimes. Shaking and tugging on his infamous fake-gold rope chain with the huge "Big Joe" medallion dangling like a two-pound plate from my school's weight room. Pop said it was best to leave him alone when he got like that. When I was younger, I asked if there was some way to help Joe that wasn't just giving him pocket change. Pop said maybe, but he didn't know how. I gave the man a wide berth and said, "Hey, Joe."

He responded with the thing he always said on his bad days. "Deal's a deal. Deal's a deal."

Farther down the block, I came across Mrs. Jefferson, who was my first-grade teacher and my ma's first-grade teacher way, way back. She was retired now, rocking a shiny black bobbed wig with a single streak of color—blue today—across the front strands. She balanced on her walker with a laundry sack on one shoulder.

"Good afternoon, Mrs. Jefferson."

"Afternoon, Cade. You gonna score a touchdown for me next week?"

"I got you. Can I help you with your bag?"

"Oh, naw, baby. Been carrying my own for thirty years, and I'm already here."

Still, I held the laundromat door for her. The cotton-fresh smell of suds overpowered a moist mushroom scent

9

of mildew. On her way in, she said the thing a lot of people around here say. "Look just like your daddy, I swear."

I kept it moving.

"Big Time!" shouted Mr. Stuart from his stool outside Fashionz & Passionz Barbershop, where he hung with his old-man crew. Mr. Brown with the chomped-down cigar. Mr. Epps with his bottle of whatever in a paper bag. Mr. Rapier doing tricky shuffles with a deck of cards. Mr. Stuart started the usual commentary that'd probably sound like them roasting me to anyone outside the Court, but it was all love, for real.

"Your mama gotta be spending a grip to feed you."

"Boy got hands like tennis rackets."

"Y'all know his daddy kept me from doing a twenty-year bid, don't you?"

"Yes, we know, Clarence!"

"Ay, ay, ay!" Mr. Epps said, loud because whatever he was sipping on had him thinking everyone had trouble hearing. "When y'all boys gonna play a real *Friday* game? I been telling my son we got to see you play before you blow up, but that rescheduling mess your school been doing make it so y'all playing when he working. Then I can't go! Messing up *the groove!*"

As loud as his annoyance sounded, it wasn't near what I felt over the same issue.

"I know, Mr. Epps," I said. "I wish we could get back to Friday nights, too. We keep getting these threats, though, and the school's saying it's safer if . . ."

I trailed off because no one was listening. Not anymore.

Mr. Epps screwed the cap back on his bottle. Mr. Brown stubbed out the cigar in the ashtray balanced on his thigh. Mr. Rapier dropped his deck of cards into his lapel pocket. And Mr. Stuart gripped his stool like he was afraid he'd tip over.

Following their eyelines, I craned my neck back the way I'd come. Corner Joe was not on the corner anymore. When I saw what I saw, I remembered this was the first of the month. Rent was due.

The old white man behind the wheel of the old white Cadillac creeping up the block had come to collect.

"You could set a watch by him," Mr. Brown said, disgusted.

Mr. Stuart nodded and spoke even quieter. "Little weasel don't play about his money."

Maybe it was the rough morning I'd had shooting my boosters video, maybe it was me thinking about how Pop was chewing through Tylenol like candy, maybe I was just fed up with the man in that car and the weird vibe he brought with him whenever he came to the Court. Arvin Skinner had no friends here.

"What's his deal?" I asked, like I had many times, knowing I'd get no great answer.

"He the devil." Mr. Epps uncapped his bottle again and took a long swig of liquid courage.

"I don't think so," I said, keeping my voice as smooth and nonthreatening as I did at school so as not to betray how stupid I thought that sounded.

"Well, he's mean as the devil," Mr. Rapier said.

11

Skinner's classic Cadillac cruised by like it did every month when someone either paid him or ended up with all their belongings on the curb. A 1959 Coupe deVille with paint like pearls, it purred while coasting and roared whenever Skinner tapped the gas. It rode smooth, contradicting the smoky smell off the engine, like it was burning oil, triggering coughs from those closest to it every trip up the block. The wrinkled pink face fixed in a near-permanent panic mode, his stringy gray hair dangling from beneath his black wide-brimmed hat like ghost vines, his eyes skipping across every single person he saw. I imagined him checking and rechecking his locks every time he hit a red light. He looked about a thousand years old and terrified. I seriously doubted the devil would be that afraid of Black folks.

Skinner was a slumlord and a cheat. The owner of property all over the city, including the worst buildings in Jacobs Court. A local legend known for how bad his buildings were and how much he didn't care. Most of the apartments, row houses, and businesses in our neighborhood were managed by other people or companies. But everyone knew the Skinner buildings and knew someone in them. Those people were viewed with pity like they'd lost some game. I always thought it was strange that he'd come to the block in person to collect, but he did, and when it happened, the entire Court watched his car pass with the attention of fishermen tracking a shark's fin.

Then the Cadillac turned the corner. The block unfroze.

I kept it moving.

3

"Hey, Mr. Lim!" I said, speaking over the chimes announcing my entrance into the corner store.

"Kincade, hello." He waved at me from inside the bulletproof, plexiglass cage where he conducted transactions now. "How's your father?"

"Excellent," I lied.

"Tell him I asked about him, please. Let him know I'd like to catch up soon."

Nodding, I descended onto the aisle where most of Ma's items were located. Pop would be happy for a good word from Mr. Lim. They'd been close when Pop's law office occupied the space above the store.

With Ma's plates and the utensils in hand, I kept on to the back wall for some orange juice, no pulp. Breaking the refrigerator's seal, the cold air hit like adrenaline. Or maybe that was some spider-sense type stuff, the sort of awareness that served me on the football field when I felt the danger of a defender I couldn't quite see yet closing in. I caught movement in the fish-eye security mirror mounted just over my head.

The main door swung inward, and the chimes sounded as

cheery as always, though they signaled bad news. The One-Eights, short for One-Eights Disciples, entered.

"Out!" Lim yelled. He'd plunged his hands under the counter for what we called the Court's worst-kept secret, his "hidden" shotgun. My stomach cinched.

In the last three years, Mr. Lim had been robbed twice, one time landing him in the hospital with a black eye from a pistol-whipping, and the second simply leaving him on the curb sobbing and cursing everyone until the cops showed. After that one, he'd installed the cage and told everyone who'd listen about what he kept under the counter.

He was a widower. Alone and afraid. The store was all he had, so the community took up a collection because that's what we did when someone was hurting. It ended up amounting to about three hundred bucks in a coffee can, delivered by Mr. Epps of the barbershop stoop. It wasn't much, but it was also everything for Mr. Lim, who was trying to get back on his feet. Maybe made him feel less alone.

Now, with four of the One-Eights crowding his checkout area, I wondered if Mr. Lim felt alone or if the weapon in reach evened the odds.

These particular bangers were young, and I didn't recognize them. I used to know them all. They flanked their leader, who I did know; everyone in the Court knew Treezy.

They had Lim's full attention. Rightfully so. Their gang was responsible for both of his robberies.

Treezy smiled at Lim, showing the canines on his gold

grill, curved into fangs with a tiny red gem beaded on one sharp point like blood. He tugged a wad of money from his hip pocket. "You don't take cash no more?"

Lim said nothing.

"If you don't let me spend my money here, ain't that discrimination?"

His crew laughed like he was a comedian.

Lim placed his hands flat on the counter, a mild surrender. Broad daylight with a witness in the store, it was best to let them do what they would do and leave. Smart for him, bad for me.

Treezy saw me in his periphery, still vampire grinning. He glided my way with his bumbling crew.

He was taller than me by two inches and lanky from all the time he spent hooping—when he wasn't up to much more problematic activities. He said, "This dude all swole up. Looking like you be absorbing weights. I remember when you was scrawny and I used to slap you around. Remember that?"

No. Because it never happened. He knew that. Maybe his little gremlins didn't, but he did. Above all else, Treezy wanted everyone in Jacobs Court to be yes-men. If he said the sky was purple, he wanted you to be like, *Yooo, how come I didn't see it before?*

It was a delicate balance living around predators like him; in Treezy's presence, I felt a bit of what the old people must've felt when they saw Skinner. Nobody messed with me in the Court. What my father did in the past, and what I was supposed to do in the future, held too much sway. Still, though . . . the Court was like those fault lines we learned about in science class. Always shifting, and every so often an unpredictably violent quake changed everything. Treezy was tectonic.

"Whatever, man." I was firm, but no extra bass in my voice.

In a better mood than most days, he took it well and said, "You know I'm just playing with you."

That was the thing about bullies: They thought everyone liked how they played.

Treezy switched tactics, always looking for an in, a weakness. "How is it up at the white school? Being a house slave as cool as I heard?"

I didn't let my hand curl into a fist or graze the Neeson shirt in my back pocket. "You know me, there for the football."

His wad of money was out again, waving back and forth like he wanted to hypnotize me. "You need anything, though? I got you if you do."

"Naw. I'm good."

"You better be. I bet a rack on your next game." He nibbled his bottom lip with his bloody fang. "I ain't worried, though. Twenty catches on the season already. You and that white boy the new Brady and Moss. Whew! It's good to be in the Cade Webster business. Ain't it?"

"Guess so."

Treezy knew sports. He was the original Great Hope of the neighborhood. A b-ball standout us kids looked at like a superhero—a Jacobs Court Avenger. D1 scouts at his games. NBA buzz in the air. Me and Pop watched him play plenty. Trouble got to him faster than the recruiters could, though. Now he was one of the villains.

Him paying this much attention to me, I didn't like it. Him calling me a personal commodity to my face I really didn't like. I made a mental note to cross the street if I saw him again.

I spun up my excuse of needing to get the plates to my mom. Before I could use it, Treezy shifted the ground again.

Grin gone, he said, "Where Book at? I been looking for him."

"Book" was Booker Payne. Gabby's brother, my best friend from since we were little-little. I said, "Don't know. Ain't seen him in a while."

"If and when you do, tell him to holler at me. Immediately."

I worked so my face wouldn't betray how much I hoped to see Book soon. At my apartment, within the hour. Light grumbling from the goon squad told me that intel was best kept to myself.

I said, "I gotta go. Moms need these plates."

I expected something disrespectful. Either about me being a mama's boy, or just something nasty about my mom because she looked younger than she was, and many dudes around here weren't shy about letting her know. But Treezy waved his minions along. They moved on to the beer fridge, Treezy's malicious glee dialed down several notches.

What have you gotten into this time, Book?

With my goods on the counter, I asked for the Tylenol that Mr. Lim kept on his side, paid, and got gone. Mr. Lim handled the transaction on autopilot, watching Treezy and them the whole time.

When he was done with me, his hands slipped beneath the counter again.

4

Apartment 217. Home. I jiggled my key and opened the door on cackling laughs and the low chuffs of Pop trying to control his coughs. The inspiration for the laughter was my eleven-year-old sister's exaggerated bad dancing, though my eyes darted to Pop pressing a clear plastic mask over his nose and mouth, taking a hit off that green oxygen tank in the sling bag next to him. I flicked my eyes away before he noticed me noticing, focusing on the off-beat gyrations Leek should have been ashamed of but wasn't.

"What is that supposed to be, Malika?" Ma asked, her hand pressed to her mouth so as not to spit-spray everyone with her chuckles.

"I'm doing the Roger Rabbit!" My sister bounced her weight on one leg, then the other.

"No, you're not!" Pop said, wheezy but cheerful.

Gabby had a reel on her phone and sang along with the music scoring the video. "Real Love" by Mary J. Blige. Gabby matched Mary's voice perfectly. I leaned in, watching a lady who looked about Ma's age working through a series of old-school hip-hop dance moves in quick succession. With each flawless transition, the dance's name flashed on the screen.

The Robocop. The Slick Rick. The Wop. I guessed the Roger Rabbit must've been earlier in the video, and I'd need Gabby to run it back if I wanted to see an accurate demonstration.

"This your idea?" I asked Gabby, like it hadn't been weeks since we'd spoken.

"I merely granted a request," she said, pushing her pink-tinted shades high on her nose. The skin between her eyebrows crinkled, the same look of pain from when we were kids and she banged her elbow or skinned her knee on the playground. She never ever cried, just got the look. I'd noticed it every time we got together lately. There in a flash, then gone. Gabby aimed her attention back toward Leek. "The children are our future, after all."

Leek got more off-beat trying to match the current dance in the video—the Flyy Girls. Mr. Gomez downstairs banged his ceiling with a broomstick, and we all scrambled, giggling, to stop the madness. Gabby swiped the video away, and I scooped Leek up in my arms with her legs still kicking. Mom glowed as she laughed, and it was all good until Pop began barking coughs.

The rattling hacks started dry but got moist, sounding like his insides were clawing their way from his chest. As if he could hock up a bloodred goblin at any moment and the creature would rise, hiss-scowl, then dive through a window to freedom while leaving my father's chest collapsed like a deflated balloon.

Ma slid next to him, patting his back with one hand and

sealing his mask over his convulsing mouth with the other. I put Leek down and reached for my phone, ready to dial 911 and thinking, Was this it? Was the evening he'd planned in vain?

Pop read me well and held up a halting hand. He said, "I'm"—three more coughs interrupted the lie—"fine."

No, he wasn't. That's what tonight was all about.

The coughs did subside, though. Enough for him to say to Gabby, "Is your brother coming?"

She dropped her gaze. "I'm not sure. Haven't seen Book in a few days."

I said, "I'll check, Pop. Let me put these plates in the kitchen."

I crossed the living room while Pop asked the ladies, "So, what we playing?"

Gabby said, "Since Leek performed, maybe she should pick?"

"You should perform, too," Leek prodded Gabby, "then we both pick."

I turned the corner as Gabby blushed, and I could just about guess her response. "Naw. All you, little one."

"Life!" Leek squealed.

"Game of Life it is," Pop said. "Set up the board."

I dropped my bags on the counter and thumbed a text to Book.

Me

WYA?

21

Then, to distance myself from nearly guaranteed disappointment:

Me
Pop is asking.

For five minutes, I stood against the counter, waiting for a reply. Not that I expected one from Book these days, but I wanted to—needed to—finish crying before I returned to my family. I bit down on my knuckles to dam up the sobs. I hunched over the sink so the tears dripped onto a plate dirty with Leek's discarded crust from a PB&J sandwich. Only when Ma called me did I start to pull it together.

"Be right there," I yelled, hoping the snot rattling in the back of my throat didn't betray me.

I splashed water on my face, and when I saw the paper towel roll was a bare cardboard post, I tugged my Neeson shirt from my back pocket and mopped my cheeks. At least it was good for something.

Rounding the corner, I ignored clearly concerned looks from Ma and Gabby. Leek and Pop were too busy spinning the game board wheel to notice, and I liked that.

Pop pinned me with a gaze. "Booker coming?"

"He's on the way," I said, sniffling and not thinking twice about the lie. "Let's start."

• • •

The history of Webster Game Night goes back nearly a decade, to one of those periodic times when things got a little too volatile in the Court. The One-Eights had been beefing with some other crew during the summer. Shots popped often. On one especially bad Saturday, a battle jumped off near the now-demolished playground. One of me, Gabby, and Book's classmates caught a stray and died.

For the rest of the season, outdoor play got severely limited. Ma was busy keeping baby Leek fed and not fussy, and Pop was desperate for some way to safely occupy my time. He was most comfortable with me close, so I got permission to invite Gabby and Book over every day, and since those days were long, the evenings became a recurring game night. We all looked forward to it.

Even when temps—temperature and tempers—on the block cooled, game night stayed a thing. Monopoly. Scrabble. Boggle. Pandemic (until we had an actual pandemic and Ma tossed that box in the garbage). It was only after I started commuting to Neeson that it began to fade. Between the long bus rides and long practices, I didn't have much energy for it. Gabby had her own schoolwork and her music. Book went another way. All the game boxes got dusty in the closet.

A week ago, Pop asked for a game night. It was after one of his regularly scheduled doctor's appointments. An appointment that must've gone differently from all the others, because he and Ma were acting like it didn't happen, like they hoped I'd forgotten it had been on the refrigerator calendar.

Now we were in it. We picked our pastel cars, plugged our tiny peg people behind the wheel, and set off on the twisty, hilly paths the board laid out for us. It was more fun than I'd imagined. Mom pulled the fashion designer career card. Pop had an option between being a lawyer or a video game designer and went with the latter.

"Why do the same thing twice?" he reasoned.

Leek got the singer card and immediately tried giving it to Gabby, but that's not how the game works, and Gabby ended up being a veterinarian. I had a choice between teacher and secret agent and went with secret agent because it paid more. We began our quick and competitive path through our pro-tracted lives, with my parents ending up childless while me, Leek, and Gabby somehow gained nine kids between us. Leek was the first of us to near the end of the game—retirement—when heavy knocks rattled the door, surprising everyone, but me the most when I heard the voice on the other side.

"Hey, it's Book. Can I come in, please?"

Ma said, "Leek, get the door."

I rose and nudged my sister back to the floor, even though she was closer. "I'll do it."

Maybe that came off strange, but with Treezy asking about him, strange it had to be.

I peered through the peephole first. All I could see was the back of Book's head. It was like he was leaning on the door and looking toward the stairs. He seemed alone.

I opened the door, and as it swung inward, so did he. He slumped at my feet, no longer having the benefit of a sturdy piece of wood as a brace. He lay moaning, with plum-colored bruises on his face, one eye swollen half-shut and a gash at his hairline dribbling blood.

All the players were present, but no one liked this game.

5

"Oh Lord." Gabby darted over, mumbling a small prayer.

Kneeling, I tucked a hand in his armpit and got him half up. Gabby wrapped her arms around his ribs to help, and he winced. Ma was behind me next, all three of us dragging Book fully into the apartment. With his legs clear of the threshold, Leek slammed the door and twisted the dead bolt. Pop never moved from the couch, and a quick glance in his direction confirmed how much that pained him. He no longer had the strength to do anything urgently.

Ma said, "I'm calling 911."

"No!" Book shouted through gritted teeth. Then, more softly, "I won't go to the hospital."

Gabby stood. "I'mma get Momma."

Book gripped her pant leg. "You know better."

We all did. Gabby and Book's mom wasn't a bad person, but her tolerance was nonexistent. Maybe for good reason. Book's activities over the last couple of years weren't something she'd allow in her home. Given a choice between his mother's wishes and the streets, the streets won. When Mrs. Payne saw her only son in passing, she looked the other way, the same as most people crossing paths with a member of the One-Eights.

Ma pushed anyway. "Your head. You could be concussed."

"It's just a beating." He nudged Gabby away and waved me off. Got his feet under him without help like that was proof he didn't have a concussion when it wasn't. "I'm fine," he said, though nothing in this demonstration proved that either.

Ma shook her head and disappeared into the kitchen. She returned with a towel that she pressed to Book's head wound without his permission. He didn't fight her.

Pop took a hit off his tank, then set his mask aside. "Who did this to you, Booker?"

"Some of the One-Eights caught me over by Randolph Avenue. I was able to get away and lose them at the train yard."

"So you're good?" I asked, staring at the door like I was expecting company. The question wasn't about him, but I couldn't ask if we—all of us—were good without betraying too much knowledge.

"I wouldn't lead them here," he said quietly.

"You wouldn't know until it was too late, though. Would you?" The room got tenser because I was using the voice I used on the football field when communicating with my teammates and rivals. The voice that scared people.

"We good," Book said, trying to meet my aggression but not quite getting there.

Pop asked, "Why was your own crew beating on you?"

Book shuffled his feet and scratched at the One-Eight ink peeking over his collar.

Pop pressed, fully in his lawyer cross-examination bag. "The local gang element doesn't make a habit of abusing their own people unless there's been a violation of some sort. Have you crossed them somehow?"

Book said, "Naw. I mean, I didn't snitch or nothing."

That did not sound reassuring.

"Tell us what happened, son," Pop said. "It's the only way we can help."

Gabby guided him to the couch beside Pop, and Book dabbed at the cut on his forehead even though the pressure from the towel seemed to have stopped the bleeding. "Y'all can't tell nobody else," he said.

"You're with family," Pop reassured him.

"Literally," Gabby said, some old sibling annoyance seeping in.

Ma said, "Leek, go to your room."

But as she rose, Pop said, "Wait. Stay."

Ma raised a questioning eyebrow. Pop squeezed her knee. "She'll need to get used to hearing hard things. Sooner than later."

Ma turned away, blinking too fast, then quick-stepped to the kitchen. Her voice was thick when she said, "Go on, Booker. I can hear you from here."

Book began. "Treezy wanted me in on this new way the One-Eights are getting money. I—I didn't show up."

28

My stomach twisted because the One-Eights never thought of good or legal ways to get money, so what *wasn't* he saying?

Squirming in the silence, Book finally spilled, the words running together. "That thing that went down with Dice and Speck and the cops, Treezy acting like it's my fault because I wasn't with them."

"Book. No," Gabby said, hugging herself.

The whole neighborhood knew about "that thing" with Deveon "Dice" Monroe and Steph "Speck" Garner. Anyone who watched the local news knew, too. They'd been out in Glen Allen, where the houses cost a million easy, following rich white housewives from the grocery store and robbing them in their own homes. They got caught because one lady hit some kind of silent alarm button on her security system before they tied her up. When the cops showed, they killed Dice and took a wounded Speck to the hospital, then eventually jail. Treezy wanted Book in on *that*?

Pop placed a hand on Book's shoulder. "Steph's going away for a while. A good lawyer might get him three to five on a plea, but he's not going to have a good lawyer. He's going to get twenty years, most likely. Deveon is never getting anything ever again. Not going with them was the smart thing, Booker."

Mom returned from the kitchen with eyes puffier and redder than when she went in. She had a Ziploc bag filled with ice wrapped in another towel. She passed it to Book, who touched it to a random bruise. No one knew what to say.

So, in true Book fashion, he said something unexpected. "The Checkered Game of Life."

I said, "Huh?"

He waved his ice bag in the direction of the game board I'd forgotten about. "The original version from the 1800s was called the Checkered Game of Life. It had"—he hesitated, maybe regretting showing off his trivia skills for once—"worse ways to lose."

Leek said, "Did getting jumped turn you into Eeyore?"

"Malika!" Ma snapped.

Leek went bug-eyed. "What? Y'all know that was depressing."

Pop laughed. So did Gabby. Then we all were giggling. Better to laugh than cry.

"Stay here *tonight*," Pop said with finality, indicating it wasn't a debate but also not long-term. "We'll figure out something."

Book said, "No offense, Mr. Webster, but I don't think you can write a note for Treezy excusing my absence from the home invasion."

"No. Not me," Pop said, cryptic.

We thought he might elaborate, but he began coughing again, that hard hacking kind that had Ma helping him to their bedroom, where it still wasn't under control.

If my father was going to be part of Book's solution, he'd better hurry up.

6

Around 5:00 a.m. the next morning, Book rolled off our couch, folded the blanket he'd slept under, placed his pillow on top of it, and left a hundred dollars in twenties on the coffee table before tiptoeing to the door.

I drained the last of the protein shake I'd been gulping and cleared my throat.

Book yelped like a baby. "Cade? Are you crazy?"

I set my cup down, joined him at the door, then waved for him to follow. We didn't speak until we were on the sidewalk, where the quietest part of the night dragged on and I felt safe. This was the hour before sunrise. All the monsters who'd feed on Book had scurried back to their holes.

I said, "You were gonna Batman vanish on us, huh?"

"*I'm* Batman? You were the one lurking in the shadows."

"'Cuz I'm Blade."

Book laughed and I could see how wide his grin was even from the corner of my eye. "Here we go again. Blade cannot beat Batman."

"Lies! It might also be a little bit racist, but I haven't figured exactly how yet."

"Bro, you can't win this. The gadgets alone."

"Blade got gadgets, too."

"For *vampires!*" Book clapped his hands, passionate now. "Batman got gadgets for anybody who want that smoke."

This has been a battle between me and Book for as long as there's been a me and Book. Blade's been my favorite superhero from the first time Pop showed us the old Wesley Snipes movies. Book been rocking with Batman ever since Mr. Lim gave him a bunch of the old comics that'd been sitting in his back room. We used to argue this kind of stuff for hours, and it was fun because I could tell how into it he was. Even if he made good points—he always did; he was the smartest guy I knew—me not giving in made him dig deeper in the funniest ways. Like the time he built a Batman-type grapple gun.

He used a Nerf gun, a compressed-air canister, some fishing reel, and wire clothes hangers. That thing really worked. Kinda. The grapple didn't shoot far, and the fishing line couldn't hold any real weight, but that's the way that big brain of his worked. Since I couldn't outsmart him, I had to finesse him in other ways.

I said, "A clown routinely beats him."

Book huffed. "Okay, that's a bar. But I'm saying, for real, Batman always comes back with some fire for whoever. That's his *whole thing*. Blade don't want it."

"Superstrength. Speed. Enhanced healing. Batman don't have none of that."

"Batman has the ultimate power that Blade can't touch. Money. Them rich kids at Neeson ain't taught you that yet?"

Annnnd . . . this suddenly wasn't fun anymore. Book's rebuttals didn't used to be so ruthless.

When the conversation lulled, I think he felt guilty about saying what he said. So he deflected. "Why you up?"

"Because some guy I need to outrun, outcatch, and out-score is up early, too."

He nodded, respecting what was only half-true.

Yeah, I trained. Might as well because I hadn't slept good in weeks. Between the creeping inevitability of my father's illness and Leek sneaking into my bed every night because she didn't want to be alone, who was sleeping in?

"How bad is he?" Book asked, as intuitive as ever. "He didn't sound good."

"Bad."

"Are y'all . . . I mean, are y'all doing okay with it?"

"Man who raised me, who threw me my first football, who never smoked a day in his life, gonna die of lung cancer before I graduate. Naw. Not doing okay with that."

We crossed to the next block in silence. Yet a light popped on, and a second-floor window slid open. "Hey!" Gabby whisper-screamed, loud enough to get our attention without getting the neighbors cussing. Guess I wasn't the only one having a tough time sleeping these days.

"Why *you* up?" Book called back.

She held up a wait-a-minute finger. "I'm coming down."

We waited, still silent. Book stared at Gabby's window, or maybe the one next to it, his old bedroom. I didn't know what he was thinking, but I took in the emptiness of the morning I maybe didn't appreciate like I should when my earbuds were in and I was sprinting blocks and blocks, chasing more stamina than I started with. Early traffic on 95 hummed. A garbage truck's hydraulic forks groaned against the weight of a dumpster. A distant dog ruff-ruff-ruffed.

Some country kid was probably up somewhere listening to roosters crowing or looking at a mountain on the horizon, but I'd take a sleepy-headed Jacobs Court over that every time.

Gabby shouldered her way through her building's front door with her hands stuffed in her coat pockets. "What y'all doing out here?"

"Schooling Cade," said Book. "He still think Blade can beat Batman."

Gabby said, "Rocket's better than both of them."

Me and Book groaned. Raquel "Rocket" Ervin was a secondary character in the Icon comics. A bunch of those were in the same box as the Batman comics Mr. Lim gave Book. This argument has been burning in our souls ever since.

He said, "She's a *sidekick*."

"Find me one other person in the Court who even knows who she is," I said.

As usual Gabby wasn't having it. "Doesn't matter. Her inertia belt makes it so neither of your guys can touch her. Because she can absorb kinetic energy, the more they try, the stronger she gets. Who's beating that?"

I said—and maybe I was still a little salty when I said it, "You gonna tell her about Batman's money?"

Book did not take the bait, stuffing his hands into his pockets.

Gabby picked up on my vibes, though. She said, "Rocket's Black and comes from a place like where we come from. Being rich and/or famous doesn't make those other characters better than her. After all, the Word says the love of money is the root of all evil."

Gabby was sharp-tongued, quick with a Bible verse or an insult, depending. Book's mind was as fast or faster, though he preferred action over words. Part of the reason he was no longer allowed in the apartment his mother and sister occupied. They weren't twins, but the eleven months between them never felt that wide. The sibling love-hate relationship flickered like flames, and lately taking shots at me was like something genetic they shared.

"Let's walk," I said, jaw clenched.

We strolled and Book asked Gabby, "For real, why you up so early?"

She shrugged.

"You writing?"

She shook her head. "No. I couldn't sleep, so I was praying. Mostly for your dad, Cade. Mostly."

The look she aimed at Book clarified who the other prayers were for, and I let that stay between them. If God

35

was putting up miracles, he must've been going for a buzzer beater on Pop.

Book's head bounced, not taking her confession for granted. "I hope you been writing, too. Have you?"

"A little," she said.

"Let's hear it, then. Hum something, at least. I mean, we're your fan club. All of it. Like, nobody else is your fan."

She acted like she was going to punch him.

I had his back, though. "You could sing us a little something. It's Sunday. Take us to church."

"Well, well!" Book shouted in an exaggerated preacher voice that sounded like *Whale-WHALE!*

She was bending. I could feel it. She inhaled sharply, preparing to belt something, when we were all jostled roughly aside.

Gabby got knocked into Book and he barely kept them from crashing into a row of foul-smelling trash cans. I stumbled off the curb into the empty street.

A jogger had shoved between us at speed. Thing was, nobody jogged in Jacobs Court.

It was Corner Joe, rushing away from us while shaking his chain and saying, "Need more time. We can work something out."

"Joe!" I shouted. "What you doing?"

"Need more time." He glanced back but seemed to be looking past us. *Through* us. The sense of it was so strong I checked behind us and expected someone chasing.

No one there. I thought I heard a car, though.

Joe sped up, turned the next corner nearly screaming, terrified. "Let's work something out! Please!"

When he was gone, the unsettling nature of whatever had him so scared remained.

We walked the next block silently until we crossed the street, and Book stopped us in front of a darkened, closed Lim's corner store. He hesitated. I knew what he was going to ask and my brain whirled around possible responses.

Book said, "Cade, fam, I hate to bother you . . ."

He didn't ask, though. I knew it was hard for him, and part of me would've preferred to leave the implied question hanging forever. I didn't really want to be mixed up in Book's mess. A beef with the One-Eights was nowhere near my pro football plans.

But him getting killed by those guys wasn't part of the plan either, so if he thought this was what he needed . . .

"You want the key?" I said for him.

Gabby said, "What key?"

I tugged the lanyard I kept my house keys on from beneath my sweatshirt. I worked the key that wasn't for my home off the ring and passed it to Book.

Gabby sneered. "What is that for?"

Book said, "If LeBron James can help with the fire escape, we'll show you."

I led us into the narrow alley beside the store and said, "You could just admit you can't reach stuff instead of calling me every tall guy's name when you need help."

37

"Whatever, Jayson Tatum."

On the back side of Lim's building was a rickety old fire escape with counterbalanced stairs. They're supposed to drop when you apply weight from above, thus the "escape" part, but if you can reach the bottom rung, which hovers about nine feet off the ground . . .

I got beneath the stairs and leapt, an easy jump for me, not so much for anyone who didn't have my kind of bounce, which was most people. With a grip on the step, my added weight dragged the stairs down while the boxy counter-weight that balanced the whole thing slid up on cables inside an iron track bolted to the wall like a mini-elevator. When my feet touched ground, I ducked beneath the step because I was on the wrong side, then brought it all the way down, where I held it in place with my foot.

The whole process was quick, smooth, and near-silent. The opposite of the screeching rusted metal horror from the first time me and Book tried it.

"The lubricant's still holding," I said to Book.

"Told you that silicone spray was better than that basic WD-40."

Gabby said, "We're breaking into your dad's old office?"

"It's not breaking in because we have a key," said Book.

"That's not true at all," I said, and climbed the stairs.

The escape went up to a window that didn't have a latch. We crowded on the little balcony, the whole thing wobbly. While Book muscled the window open, the motion alone

38

making the escape sway like there was a strong wind, I wedged the heavy-duty screwdriver we'd left behind into the counterweight system, preventing the stairs from retracting.

Book climbed into a short corridor leading to a frosted glass door that used to have *Kincade Webster III, Attorney at Law* stenciled on it. A door no one changed the lock on after Pop's lease ended. Book keyed the lock, swinging the door inward for a brief inspection. "This'll work."

Gabby deduced his intent. "You're not going to stay here."

"Not right now. Mr. Lim will be opening up shop soon, so I'll hit my usual spot during the day. After dark, though." He shrugged.

She grabbed him by the shoulders and made the balcony lurch. "Come. Home."

"Naw."

"You can stay a couple of nights at least. Momma's got a two-day trip midweek. She won't even know."

Their mother was a flight attendant who was gone several nights a month, allowing Gabby to make such an offer. Book accepting it . . . I wouldn't bet money. The history there was ugly. I descended the stairs to let them work it out privately.

I checked my smartwatch, the time, my steady heart rate, the miles I still needed to clock for today's training. This part, the high drama of my friends—of Jacobs Court—was the stuff I was running from when I strived to get a little better at what I did every day. For my family. For my friends. Everyone I planned to take with me—to rescue. It'd be their come up, too. That's why I didn't feel bad when I yelled, "I gotta get my run in, guys."

Their hushed debate ended abruptly, and they descended the stairs, not looking me in the eye.

Book said, "My bad, bro. I know how valuable your time is."

That "apology" felt real sharp. I didn't want to make it a thing. Except the way he said it, I couldn't let it go.

"You know it's not just about me, right? What I'm doing is for all of us."

Gabby said, "We know what you're trying to do, Cade."

My head jerked from her to Book like, *See, she gets it.*

Book stayed quiet. Whatever. He'd appreciate all this when I got to the pros and plucked him and Gabby out of the daily struggle of the Court.

They just had to do their part and keep their heads down until that time came.

7

Your football and your education, that's what YOU control.

That was at the top of the vision board, visible from where I lay in bed. In Pop's handwriting. I focused on that until I dozed off that night and barely noticed when Leek snuck into my room and nuzzled against me. Something she'd been doing more and more. Nightmares.

Your football and your education, that's what YOU control.

By the time rainy Monday rolled around and I was climbing on a bus at 6:00 a.m. in a dripping poncho for a crosstown trip, I was in the right headspace to swap Court drama for prep school silliness, because I couldn't bring myself to think of my classmates' concerns as anything but frivolous.

Who got drunk and had to go to the ER (that happened like every weekend)?

Who wrecked their mom's Range Rover?

Who smashed whose boyfriend?

Most of my teammates lived for it. Every weekend a movie that they took turns starring in. Most of them. When I stepped through the Neeson gates, I spotted the one teammate who merely tolerated the nonsense. Nate Donaldson, my quarterback. Honestly, it wasn't like I liked him better for it. If everyone else was into partying to the extreme, his intensity was the equal and opposite.

He jogged my way under a Gucci umbrella, yawning, and I already knew the general topic of conversation. He paced me into the building and said, "I'm *tired*, bro. Flew down to Miami this weekend to work with that quarterback coach I told you about, Bob Cunningham. Got some major reps in. More velocity on the ball for sure. Knocked one receiver's pinkie out the socket."

I was only half listening. Wondering if Book made it back to Pop's office okay last night. I said, "There was a camp?"

Nate perked up. "Naw, bro. Private plane. Private lesson. All private everything."

"Oh." You'd think I'd be used to these kinds of casual flexes after three years around these people, but not really.

We walked the wide, barely crowded corridor. Neeson was as big as the high school close to my neighborhood that I attended freshman year but with a quarter of the student population, so every moment in the sparsely populated halls felt like school had ended already.

How is it up at the white school?

Treezy's jab wasn't quite accurate—Neeson wasn't *all* white, obviously—but the white kids outnumbered every other group by a significant margin. As far as Black kids went, there were others at Neeson. More than I could count on both hands; not *much* more. As I walked with Nate I made eye contact with some of the others, quick connections

42

followed by respectful nods. We all knew each other. Some of them were cool, like the Bordeaux twins, who came from a big-deal political family. Or Jamal Lansing, whose mom was a famous composer. Some were not, like this one kid whose family was in construction—Grint or Leer, whatever—I never bothered to learn his name because on my first day he was like, *What kind of gat you got on you, dawg?* in front of a couple of his cackling white friends. I don't play like that.

Another Kincade Webster III's Nugget of Wisdom™: Being the Black person racists like is never worth it.

Anyhow, even with the cool Neeson Black folks, we vibed differently. That was my fault—I guess I could've made an effort to be closer with them. Maybe I should've. None of them came from places like Jacobs Court, though. Even the few other scholarship kids on the team were from out of state and boarding with rich white families while they did their time here, like if that old movie *The Blind Side* was a real true story.

They weren't Book and Gabby, and I wasn't looking for replacement friends. My plan was my plan and I stayed focused, cutting my way through the ancient main building, the stone columns holding it all up like a history lesson I was never meant to understand.

There were modern touches. Like the media center expansion that would put most public libraries to shame. And the ceiling-mounted flat-screens at staggered positions along the main halls for broadcasting announcements, the journalism club's daily news show, or the freshly edited boosters video featuring a beaming version of me I barely recognized.

"Hi, I'm Cade Webster, star receiver for the Neeson Sparks . . ."

Action photos of me on the field overlaid what had been a plain green screen when I recorded my part. Sheila had superimposed the corny nickname the boosters gave me over the bottom third of the screen, which simply read: *C-4, Wide Receiver, #4.*

"They got your good side," Nate said, trying to make a joke though he couldn't quite nail the delivery.

At six four, he was a little taller than me. Good at that game but not as good as he wanted to be. The booster's video clip ran on a loop. All me.

"I'm going to do another private training session in two weeks," Nate said. "You should come with."

I couldn't count how many yacht parties, country club dinners, and weekend shopping trips Neeson classmates wanted me at. I rarely went (had to make an exception for that Future concert at my lab partner's beach house that one time, though). I don't know. I didn't like accepting stuff from people who had so much more than my family and me. Didn't like feeling I might owe something I couldn't repay. For as long as I could remember, Pop said debt was slavery, and naw, we ain't doing that.

I shrugged off Nate's training weekend invite, noncommittal.

Nate grabbed me by the bicep, halting our progress. "You need to come."

I stared at his hand on my jacket, scrutinizing it like a difficult math problem. Something tricky with a missing variable. When I met his eyes for clarification, he released me. "I need you to come."

"Why?"

He leaned in, whispering things he didn't want our teammates to hear. "If I'm getting better throwing the ball, don't you want to get better catching my passes? Me and you, our timing, is going to take us to the next level, but we gotta be *here*." He traced fingers between our eyelines, indicating we needed to be one, a well-oiled football machine. He was wrong.

I was going to the next level regardless. I already had the offers. Everyone knew that, Nate included. His need wasn't about me.

He had offers to solid midtier programs. He wanted better. So he reminded me I wanted better, too. "You hear from Ohio State yet?"

I chewed the inside of my cheek and kept down the hall.

Your football and your education, that's what YOU control.

If that was true, why was I still waiting on the school I wanted most?

And why had I let Nate know anything I actually cared about?

He had caught up, on track to get really annoying, when Headmaster Sterling came our way. He was a barrel-shaped, bearded man who wore glasses too tiny for his face. He walked with his arms clasped behind his back like old dudes in movies did, kung-fu masters and Jedi Knights. He stopped in our path, exuberant. "Cade! Nate! It's a dynamite day! Can't you smell it?"

Nate said, "Yeah, sure can, sir."

"I don't know," I said, "I might have a cold or something."

The building was almost two hundred years old, a former mansion built by a man named Cormac Neeson who made a fortune manufacturing dynamite. On my Day One tour, Headmaster Sterling gave me a whole history of the Neeson family, but the dynamite part was all I could remember. Mainly because when that Cormac dude had the house built, he got the stonemasons to mix a little bit of blasting powder in the mortar. He wanted to honor what made such a grand home possible. I'd asked if the stonemasons thought that was dangerous.

Headmaster Sterling had said, "Cormac Neeson wasn't paying for their advice."

On damp mornings Sterling claimed you could still smell the acrid tang of gunpowder in the air, a scent like old fireworks. I hadn't smelled it yet but found it funny how literal explosive material in the building's foundation was a cool story to him while actual bomb threats had been keeping me from my current life goal. I didn't want to smell the dynamite in the air. Not ever.

Since I had his attention, I asked, "You think we'll have any problems with Friday's game, sir?"

"I certainly hope not. It would be easier for me to bet in our favor if we'd caught the misanthrope making the threats. But these things are more sophisticated than ever. Our security firm says the culprit could literally be on the other side of the globe and our school community had the misfortune of, essentially, having our name plucked from a hat and being targeted for these . . . these . . . psychological assaults."

"If we know it's some"—I caught myself before the curse slipped out, cleared my throat—"er, crap, can't we play no matter what?"

Sterling said, "We don't take those kinds of chances. Protecting the Neeson community means we have to make the right choice one hundred percent of the time, while a bad guy only has to get lucky once to thrust us into tragedy."

Nate shuffled his feet, his hands clenching and unclenching. "If you find out that guy isn't on the other side of the globe, don't bother turning him over to the cops. Just drop him off at our locker room. We'll take care of it. Ain't that right, C-4?"

He extended his hand for dap, but he knew I didn't like that name. So, naw.

The time Nate's hand levitated between us went from awkward to aggro because he wasn't letting this go. "You just going to leave me hanging, fam?"

Headmaster Sterling, perhaps fearing a have-to-be-right-one-hundred-percent-of-the-time moment right in his face, grasped Nate's hand and gave it a hearty pump. Then snatched free and did the same to me. "Off to class, young men. Gotta exercise the mind and the body."

I couldn't let him go yet. Word was an Ohio State scout was coming back to town this week for a *Friday* game. Headmaster Sterling would make the call if another threat came in. I said, "Friday's really important, is all. Don't you think the boosters would agree?"

Sterling clapped a hand on my shoulder. "We believe in the power of visualization here at Neeson. See yourself on that field, under those lights. Perhaps it will be so."

For the rest of the week, through school days and grueling practices, I visualized Friday going off with no issues. I saw myself settling behind the line of scrimmage, moving around defenders like they were standing still, catching Nate's passes with ease, and securing my spot as an Ohio State Buckeye.

Our mystery man must've been better at visualizing, because at five thirty on Friday, he issued a new threat and wiped all my glorious fantasies off the board.

To: Neeson Preparatory Academy Faculty, Neeson Preparatory Academy Staff, Neeson Preparatory Academy Students
From: J. Voorhees
Subject: Your Final Friday

I know how you E-Leets plan to deestroy our country but I will deestroy all you E-Leets and your E-Leets children tonight at your football game. I want to see your blood.

8

Disappointment in our locker room was thicker than the smell of old jock straps and Axe body spray. Brett, a real swole defensive lineman, stomped through the narrow paths between benches and lockers, face red. Without warning, he threw a haymaker into this year's Neeson Sparks promotional poster, the one prominently featuring my face. The punch dented the drywall beneath it. "Dude's got to pay."

Someone on the far side of the room said, "It's probably some old lady in Russia who gets paid a loaf of bread every time she screws up something American."

That got a few chuckles. Not from me. I was boiling inside.

Brett's outburst stirred up more loud and violent proclamations. Someone wanted to skin the culprit who'd ruined another Friday night for us. Someone else wanted to douse him in gas and light a match. It went from more gruesome (acid injected directly into his veins) to cartoonish (strap him to a catapult and fling him into the side of the Blue Ridge Mountains). That haymaker Brett threw had me wanting to throw one, too. Even as I imagined the momentary joy it might bring, I knew it was misplaced anger. And fear.

Had I missed my chance with Ohio State?

Our team manager, Brady, squeezed between the bench I was sitting on and my locker. "Sorry, Cade. Grabbing your jersey."

"All good, B."

He plucked my jersey from my locker, adding it to the dozen or so he had draped across his forearm to return to the "armory," where everything from uniforms to pads to tackle dummies were stored. He kept on to the next locker, undoing all the prep he took care of during his game-day lunch period.

Brady was a skinny, freckled junior who had an encyclopedic brain when it came to football, but whose asthmatic lungs and stature (the cheerleaders were taller than him) prevented him from suiting up and taking the field despite his valiant efforts at tryouts every year. He took it well, though, diligently assisting with all the grunt work. Laundry, steaming the helmets, making sure all the right equipment made it to away games. Brady was essential to the Neeson Sparks running smooth.

Not everyone noticed him. A lot of guys here had domestic help at home. Maids. Butlers. Stuff like that. They'd grown up comfortable without seeing the people who threw their backs out for that comfort. I liked Brady, though. He didn't come from money. His mother worked in the kitchen and a perk of the job was severely discounted tuition. Not quite a full scholarship guy like me, but close enough that it mattered when he walked the halls, mostly alone.

Here in the locker room, in some ways, he had more clout

than the second- and third-string guys. Particularly on a night like tonight where the circumstances had him working harder than all of us.

I tugged my phone from my gym bag to post about the game getting rescheduled. Maybe I'd tag the Ohio State account and show them how disappointed (enraged) I was about not hitting the field tonight. Somehow show them I got that dog in me no matter what. I don't know. Coach Gibson entered the room, patting his clipboard on his thigh in a steady rhythm, and I lowered my phone.

"Bring it in, Sparks," he said.

We drew closer, a wall of bodies. Nate stood next to Coach as if he was going to make some sort of statement, too—faux leader vibes.

Coach said, "Look, guys, you know the drill. You're disappointed, as am I. But we got Forestbrook on Monday afternoon, and the game plan doesn't change. To keep you sharp I want you back at nine tomorrow for a two-hour practice."

A few guys made the mistake of groaning. Stupid.

"That's a three-hour practice now," Coach said.

Silence. Thank God.

Coach nodded, satisfied. "Nate."

Nate started talking. A bunch of clichés about staying hungry and in beast mode because we're the best, and while it riled up the rest of them, it only made me madder because I had that kind of energy ready to go *right now*, for the future me and Pop plotted so meticulously on my vision board. Getting all hyped in the locker room with my teammates, who I couldn't unleash this fury on, left me more frustrated than I was used to. So frustrated that when Nate finished up to cheers and I tried getting back to the business of smoothing things over on my social media, I couldn't.

I'd crushed my phone.

In the parking lot my teammates divided themselves among several luxury vehicles. A Mercedes G-Wagon, a couple of Teslas, a Beamer, a Subaru that a bunch of them clowned and called basic. I wanted to think I couldn't imagine what they'd say about my daily bus commute, but that was a lie. It was easy to imagine, though none were bold enough to crack those jokes where I could hear.

Nate drove a Porsche that could comfortably seat one other person. He offered me shotgun. "We're going back to my place and calling some girls. You down?"

A head shake. "I'm good."

"You really going to be the priest of the team, huh?"

That got a small laugh from me, mostly because it was amazing how much Nate misunderstood me. The way I felt, I actually really wanted to party with the team and be around some girls—even if the vast majority of Neeson Prep co-eds weren't really my type. I wanted to feel better. My refusal wasn't rooted in righteousness but anxiety.

If I went to Nate's house, which was ten miles in the

opposite direction of Jacobs Court, how was I going to get home?

In two years of offering me a ride after school to get pizza, or offering me a ride after school to see a movie, or offering me a ride after school to whatever, no one—*not a single one* of my teammates—ever offered me a ride to my apartment.

Because they knew.

Or thought they did.

Jacobs Court was "The Hood"—capital letters—to them. Scary, gangsta. The place people got robbed, shot, and murdered. Where the morning news mug shots with the face tattoos came from. Sometimes they were right. Just like sometimes the same stuff (or worse) happened in their neighborhoods but got presented sympathetically in a *Dateline* special ten years after the fact. Anyway.

With my phone broken, I couldn't even attempt a rideshare, not that I had rideshare money. I said, "My sister's going to be expecting me since the game's canceled."

Nate nodded, his attention already elsewhere. "Cool, cool. See you at practice tomorrow."

He waved his second-string friend Brett to the Porsche while a swarm of headlights flicked on in rapid succession. The team motored from the lot, leaving me to my bus-stop walk as dusk settled.

I started the hike, humming a J. Cole song the whole way.

9

The 91 bus was packed with a cranky after-work crowd. I squeezed in, grabbed a handrail mid-bus, my crappy mood mixing with the generally bad vibes. The small redheaded white woman holding on to the pole next to me made a point to look everywhere but in my direction while squeezing her purse to her chest.

There were a lot of stops along this route. I hoped some seats would free up at each one, but more people piled on than got off, packing us in tighter. One guy in stained mechanic's coveralls climbed the steps, realized he'd lost his bus pass, and held us up arguing with the driver. When it got loud, folks pulled out their phones to record the encounter. When Coveralls clocked his audience, his frustration peaked and he spat at the driver, then fled. The bus driver simply sat a moment, her shoulders heaving with each breath.

A person in the back shouted, "Drive the freaking bus. I gotta get my kids."

The driver flicked the most rage-filled glance I'd ever seen our way, but with no other recourse, she lurched us back into traffic hard enough to sway me into the little white lady with the most valuable purse in the world. I muttered, "Sorry."

More stops, more lurches. At about the midpoint of my trip the seething bus driver turned a corner so hard that the little white lady lost her grip on her pole and fell sideways. Out of instinct, I looped an arm around her waist to keep her upright.

I should've let her fall.

"Let me go! Let me go!" She pounded her fists into my chest and dropped her purse, contents spilling between shoes and under seats.

"Help!" she screamed, even though I'd already released her and she was standing on her own. "He grabbed me. He— he tried to take my bag!"

"I was trying to keep you from falling."

A gray-bearded white man seated near my hip said, "He snatched her bag. I saw him."

Not gonna lie, my first instinct was to funnel every bit of stored frustration into my fist and dent the man's face like Brett did my poster in the Sparks locker room. But Pop's screaming voice overrode my anger. No Kincade Webster III's Nuggets of Wisdom™. Just a single word: *Look!*

Phones were out again. All aimed at me, all surely catching the woman's meltdown. She said, "He touched me and tried to take my bag. How is no one doing anything?"

That question was pointed directly at two young white dudes in Best Buy polo shirts who continued doing nothing. They were scared.

I was six foot two, and strong, and could easily handle

56

them, even in this confined space. So instead of just staying out of this, they looked to more men. One said, "Anybody down to help us?"

Help them do what?

The Best Buy bros were getting more support. Strength in numbers. And the woman who'd started all this had made the transition from afraid and violated to righteous. She'd tugged her own phone from a pocket, pawing at the screen. "I'm calling the cops."

"I didn't do anything to you."

No one was listening. We were beyond that.

The bus halted. The doors were open. I shoved through the crowd, overpowering any of the heroes attempting to stop me, and stepped off into the night. Running down the sidewalk and rounding the corner onto a street I'd never seen in a neighborhood I didn't know.

I'd made it a whole block, running toward a rising moon, before I slowed and became alarmed by the quiet.

There were mostly row houses with scattered shops up and down the street. Not so different from blocks in Jacobs Court. Until I took in the fine details.

There was a yarn store.

It was closed because its business hours were nine to five. But . . . yarn? A whole store? It was called the Knitmus Test.

I walked this block slowly, taking it all in. It felt like I'd portaled into a different universe. A vegan barbecue restaurant was coming soon. There was a business specializing in sensory deprivation. I didn't know what that was, but peering through the glass door I spotted something that looked like a giant egg—big enough to fit a person inside—and nope.

Some of the homes were occupied. One place with big windows but no blinds or drapes offered unobscured views into rooms with warm amber lighting and ghostly specters from flickering TVs dancing on the ceiling. Four families from my building in the Court could've fit inside comfortably. It had me thinking about where I might live one day.

My first place would be wholly dependent on what team drafted me. Maybe I'd go with a super nice apartment at first. If I got to play in a big city like New York, I'd get one with the tall windows that let you see the whole city at night, all the lights looking like the stars were beneath you.

If Ma and Leek wanted to live with me, I'd make sure to get something big. Then the three of us—

Oh. No.

No.

The three of us? Really, Cade. You out here imagining the good life without Pop? What is that? How could you—

An ice spider skittered up my neck.

I turned around and spotted a white couple across the street. One of the men startled when our eyes met, then he whispered something to his partner, who had a phone pressed to his ear. His lips moved urgently. They had a tiny dog in a canary-yellow sweater (probably made of yarn from the Knitmus Test); it fired off yipping barks and jerked at its leash.

Time to go.

A casual speed walk. Heel, toe. Heel, toe. I felt how bad this was going but knew running would make it worse. I turned a corner, walked a block, turned another corner. Tried to get far enough away from dude on the phone that he couldn't tell the cops which way I went.

Maybe that didn't matter because at the far end of the street I'd turned on sat a black-and-white cruiser.

It was parked at the curb in the glow of the corner store light. One officer in his dark blue uniform overlaid with a black tactical vest, puffed out by his belly and whatever those guys put in all those pouches, backpedaled from the store with a grease-spotted bag and a big bottle of yellow Gatorade. His shoulder radio squawked. The cop's smile fell away. He turned to the cruiser, communicating with his partner behind the wheel.

That couple and the world's tiniest, most aggravating hellhound rounded the corner like hunters chasing a duck. Walking toward the cops was not an option. The corner crosswalk sign displayed a red hand, indicating it wasn't safe to go yet. It wasn't safe to stay either. I crossed on red.

As I did, the officers noticed me.

I kept it cool, easy strides, until the cop tossed the bag in the cruiser and hopped in with urgency. As soon as I passed the first building on the block and was out of their line of sight, I ran.

The couple with the dog shouted, "That's him! He's getting away!"

Then their voices were secondary to a growling engine and tires screaming on the asphalt.

My speed ain't nothing to play with, so I was already at the end of the block and turning again. This time on a shadowy street where the entire row of merchant shops seemed abandoned. Every second or third streetlight was broken. Paper trash skipped over the road on a breeze that stank like rot. Without enough time to make it to another corner, I ducked into the shadowy doorway of what used to be a television repair shop, pressed my back against the plywood covering the entrance, and waited, chest heaving.

The police cruiser crept through the intersection slow now, the flashing lights on its roof splashing everything in blue-red, blue-red like silent fireworks. The dark was my best friend, and the cops didn't spot me. Yet.

I didn't think I was super far from Jacobs Court, maybe a mile or two. Maybe. Without my phone, and being unfamiliar with this part of the city, I couldn't say for sure. If I found another bus stop, I—

Across the street, diagonal from me, the interior lights of a shop I hadn't noticed flipped on, washing the previously black sidewalk in yellow. The windows were crowded with stuff, piles balanced in the windows like a barricade. Beyond that, shelves of more stuff. While I tried to figure it out, a sign sizzled on in sections.

Electricity hummed into each segment, neon-red light bled onto the sidewalk like a shallow cut, seeping and seeping, until the word *Open* was fully lit.

Abandoning my hiding spot cautiously, I crossed the street, hoping for a little bit of luck. Please, just a little.

From the sidewalk in front of the store I peeped a counter through a gap in the shelves. A man moved behind it. A Black man. Thank God.

When I reached for the door, another sign flipped on. It was high on the exterior wall, stretching as wide as the storefront. Gold-and-silver neon tubing revealed the kind of establishment I was entering.

It said: *Pawn & Loan.*

In I went.

10

Bells jingled over my head, and my stomach cramped like the time my family had gotten bad shrimp from the seafood market at the river. The sensation passed as quickly as it came a few steps into the pawnshop. My unease subsided. Sort of.

The junk-pile decor in the windows extended to packed shelves that had no discernible logic to them. This kind of disorder would've driven Book insane. I didn't mind, though. Strung from the rafters was an aged banner advertising *Whatever You Wish at a Price You Can't Dismiss*.

I had a hard time believing that.

Walking the center aisle and eyeing a random shelf, I spotted an old toaster next to a rust-speckled machete. Farther down was the stuffed head of a bear, its mouth fixed in an eternal roar. Next to it was the pristine front grille of some old truck.

Okay, okay. Not gonna lie. This weird place started feeling fun. Like, what other wild stuff was the owner pairing together? There was a set of old Mason jars that looked empty except for some weird blue dust in the bottom. Those were next to a sealed comic book I'd never heard of—*Timeline*—with a petite Black girl and tall Black boy in a basketball uniform superpunching a swarm of robots on the cover.

Farther on, something shiny on a low shelf caught my eye. I squatted and reached for it because it was partially wedged behind a sack of old dog food but snatched my hand back at the last second when I recognized it was a hospital bedpan. Why would anyone want *that*?

Standing, maybe too fast, I got dizzy and disoriented. I looked back toward the entrance and I couldn't see it. The shelves seemed to stretch miles and miles to a flat horizon, like when we practiced drawing a vanishing point in art class. I squeezed my eyes shut, shook my head to jostle things right again, and when I opened my eyes, I saw the door. Maybe twenty feet from me. Like it was supposed to be. I turned the other way and saw the man I'd spotted through the window behind the counter. Staring.

He was on the short side, thin, in a red-and-black lumberjack shirt, peering through black-framed glasses. His complexion was medium brown but looked sickly under the yellowish store light. His hands were flat on the countertop, and his lips barely parted when he said, "What are you looking for?"

Burying the bedpan disgust under exaggerated politeness, I said, "How are you, sir? Hope you're having a good evening. I'm just browsing."

His head cocked to the side. "Browsing," he said, the fingers on his right hand curled like a claw, a mini-convulsion, "for what?"

All my manners fell away. I was tired. "I don't know yet. That's what browsing is."

His left hand went to his stomach, pressing hard. He grimaced as if in pain.

I took a few steps forward, concerned, forgetting I was speaking to an adult. "Ay, bro. You good?"

"You can't be in here unless you're buying. No . . . browsing." He panted, his eyes wide, sweating. Afraid.

You too? I thought, mad and sad and disappointed. Mostly mad.

Forget this. I'm out. That's what I thought until I saw the police car I'd been avoiding slow cruising past the shop window. They'd turned off the emergency lights, but still.

I said, "You got anything cheap? Like, on sale?"

If he was in pain before, it passed when I asked that. He straightened up and said, "We can meet any price point. Just tell me what you're looking for."

I wasn't looking for anything. If he was going to be a jerk about a purchase, though . . . I walked the length of his counter, really a long display case with various goods under the scratched glass, little handwritten price tags attached to each one by a string. A silver bracelet was $109. A broken compass with a slow-spinning needle was $53. An Apple iPod—that I only recognized because Pop wouldn't give his up for his iPhone until I was almost thirteen—was $24. All out of my price range because I had maybe fourteen bucks in my pocket and less than that on my debit card. Leaving the "luxury" of the display case for a crowded wall, I eyed the various oddities there.

The shopkeeper, his voice strained, that pained look on his face again, said, "There may not be anything for you here."

So he thought I couldn't afford any of this trash. In some cases, he was right, but I didn't like him assuming.

The pained look flashed away when he said, "Bet you like fast cars. Zero to sixty in four seconds."

"Who doesn't?"

"There are some nice models on the shelf behind you."

Sure enough. The boxes were in rough shape, the images faded, but there was a Lamborghini and that stainless steel car with the wing doors from the time travel movie Pop liked. Both were $20.

"Bet you like a big house, too," the shopkeeper said. "The finer things in life."

I didn't like that he was calling out every single thing I'd been dreaming about when I'd been staring through the window of that fancy row house before the night took a turn. Not bothering to soften my annoyance, I said, "You sell houses?"

"No," said the shopkeeper. "Keys."

He motioned higher on the shelf, and there was a clear plastic candy dish half-filled with silver and brass keys. The label read *$2 Each*.

I scowled. "What I want with some random keys that won't open anything?"

"You can always dream." He had a silly grin on his face. "You can always *wish*. Who knows what doors might present themselves?"

"Man, whatever." Even though the price was right, I wasn't buying any keys.

There was another bowl next to the keys, though. Filled with a bunch of toy rings a step above the jewelry you'd see in a gum machine. Well, not *just* a step above—these rings looked good. They had to be toys, though, because the label on this bowl said *$5 Each*.

Some of them were meant to look like gold, you could see engravings in them. Others were slim, small, with tiny fake gems. But there was one that caught my eye immediately. A red-and-blue flash over fake platinum overlaid with fake diamonds. It wasn't so much the color but the shape—the face—they formed. I knew his name. "Pat the Patriot?"

Burrowing through the pile with the *clink-clink-clink* of metal bumping metal for that ring I saw—*wanted*—I managed to pinch it and found its surface warm. Comforting. I pulled it free for a closer look.

It was heavy. Great quality. And yeah, that was for sure Pat the Patriot, the New England Patriots mascot, represented in colorful "gems." This was a super sweet replica of the Patriots Super Bowl LI championship rings!

I watched that game with Pop when I was a kid. He got so mad because he'd bet on the Falcons, and it looked for sure like he'd be collecting on a win when the Patriots were down 28–3. But Tom Brady and James White went *off*, coming back to win the game 34–28. Biggest comeback in Super Bowl history.

I held it up for the shopkeeper. "This one five dollars, too?"

"If you like."

I didn't expect to like anything in this place, but I liked the ring. A lot. I brought it to the counter.

The cash register was vintage. Like a prop from a movie set in the 1940s. All round mechanical keys and a glass window at the top where dollars and cents popped up on little tabs. There was more modern tech situated next to it. A computer that looked like the *first* computer in its yellowed plastic housing that might've been white once, and a dark screen with green text emitting an ambient glow like a spotlight through slime.

The shopkeeper—Eddie, now that I was close enough to read his name tag—said, "Cash or trade, buddy?"

"Cash."

He grimaced. "Are you sure? You don't have to."

Through gritted teeth, I said, "Yes."

What was his deal? At that point, even the way he breathed felt like a veiled insult. One moment he seemed okay, the next it was like he wanted to throw me through the window. Pop had a saying about Black folks who treated other Black folks as less than: *Sometimes it's your own people, Cade.*

Eddie typed something into his ancient machine. Then more things. Then more. His fingers moved like a pianist playing a fast song, the notes from the keys a discordant *clackity-clack-clack-clack*.

While he wrote his novel or whatever, I dug into my pocket and retrieved a five. Before I handed it over, I held the ring up to the light. "You know where this came from? One of those *Sports Illustrated* commemorative package deals or something?"

He snatched his hands from the keyboard like it got hot. "If you're having second thoughts, you should leave right now."

Yo. It was really taking everything in me not to snap on this weirdo.

I said, "I'm not having second thoughts. I want to know if you got information on this."

I thrust the ring at him, within an inch of his nose, fast, and he flinched like I'd thrown a jab at his chin.

At that point, I was done. I laid the five on the counter gently, then squeezed my newly purchased ring hard in my fist. I don't know why I said what I said, I'm not sure I ever would've uttered it aloud any other time, but in that moment, I felt compelled to speak the words exactly as they came out. "I wish everyone would stop acting so scared around me."

Eddie's eyes widened. The ancient cash register dinged.

I didn't see Eddie touch it, but, like, he had to have done something, right?

Two tabs popped into the little window. One said $5. The other said, in small print, *All Sales Final.*

The cash drawer popped open. Eddie, looking like dudes on the football field who'd played hard in a loss, dragged my five-dollar bill over and placed it in the drawer.

"Can I get a receipt?"

He pulled a pad from beside the register and scribbled on

it fast. He tore it off, retaining a yellow carbon copy, then, before handing me the original, he flipped it over and scribbled something else. He slid it to me faceup.

Item #145,792
Authentic Super Bowl Ring
Qty: 1
Unit price: $5.00

"Authentic?" I said. "Okay, my guy."

"Hope to see you soon," Eddie said.

"I don't think so."

I walked down the aisle to the exit with the receipt in one hand and my new ring in the other, triggering the chime when I shouldered the door open. I was back on the street. Flickering light over my head caught my eye, halting me. The *Pawn & Loan* part of the sign made up only a portion of the neon tubing up there. Now the rest was lit, revealing a word that made my breath catch in my throat.

It said: *Skinner's* Pawn & Loan.

Wait. *What?*

Skinner. *The* Skinner? The old white slumlord who owned a quarter of the buildings in Jacobs Court owned this place, too? Naw. Couldn't be. Could it?

But a *whoop-whoop* burst from the police cruiser's siren as the car's spotlight fell on me, derailing my thoughts.

"Hey!" the officer in the passenger seat said. "You lost?"

THEN

Arvin Skinner first discovered the complex economics of souls and suffering in 1929, when he was sixteen years old.

Later, that time would be identified as the start of the Great Depression. Being there—living it—didn't feel like something you could ever sum up in such a broad title. In the moment, when everything good felt out of reach, when the hollow pit in his stomach was a combination of hunger *and* despair, young Arvin decided he'd have no doings with the earthly tribulations everyone he knew fell prey to.

There were old ways to correct problems.

Rituals his family abandoned generations before.

He sought abominable answers and only recognized his mistake when a demon stood over him, laughing.

It happened in the middle of his father's cotton field, where he'd dragged a young, muzzled calf that fought the whole way. A sharpened knife poked from a sheath on his belt, and in his satchel was a sealed glass jar containing the unmentionable contents detailed in the blasphemous book he'd unearthed from a locked chest Mama hid in the root cellar. From the same satchel he produced a pike that he drove into the ground with a mallet, then hitched the calf's leash to it so it couldn't get away. He removed the book next, and a candle, and matches so he could double-check the instructions by the flickering flame.

When his father's watch struck twenty and twelve, Arvin recited the words and drew the blade across the calf's throat. He'd never been skilled at butchering; he caught the artery so it sprayed his face and the surrounding cotton stalks with hot ichor, giving the budding cotton an appearance like black roses under the half-moon. He coughed and gagged and used his fingers to wipe liquid from his eyes. With his vision restored he saw he was no longer alone.

A man-shaped thing stood just beyond the nearest cotton stalks, obscured by shadow, its eyes glowing an eldritch green. It was tall, though it did not seem to be standing on the ground. The earth bunched around its ankles in a loose mound, as if the being was planted there, no different from the crops surrounding it.

"You're the—the Night Merchant," Arvin said in a stunned gasp.

"Some call me that." It grazed fingers over a nearby leaf and spoke in a high singer's voice. "What is this?"

Arvin knelt by his book and still lit candle, desperate to double-check the next incantation, for there were warnings about the perils of misspeaking. "I am Arvin, son of Ernest, and I bind you until you have—"

It rushed forward, the earth roiling at its feet, creating a wake as if it were wading in shallow water until it was face-to-face with Arvin. This close, Arvin understood it was not obscured by night. It *was* night. Pure black poured into a man shape. Except for the verdant eyes and gleaming white teeth.

An inky hand whipped forward, knocking the candle from Arvin's grasp. It hit the ground flame first and extinguished.

"Oh, stop," the Night Merchant said. "So pathetic."

"I—" Arvin had no idea how to respond. His first instinct was to check the book, but he'd read it cover to cover and already knew nothing in it addressed *this*.

The creature said, "Let me help you find your tongue. This book, the incantation, the sacrifice. You want, what . . . Women? Riches? The admiration of other pitiful men?"

Arvin remained quiet, though it felt like the creature had torn his clothes away.

It cackled. "Very well. What do you offer as trade?"

"M-m-my . . ." Arvin had practiced saying it, and meaning it, in the mirror. "My eternal soul."

The beast laughed louder. Laughed for a long time. Then it said, "I already have that."

It turned in the earth, bubbling the ground again, and waded away.

"You already—what?" Arvin, confused and panicked, chased the entity and stepped directly in its path, risking being run over, but the Night Merchant stopped.

"You can't leave!" Arvin was indignant now. "You're supposed to be bound until we've completed the transaction."

"Is that what your little book promised? So it must be true?"

"I must've performed the rites correctly or you wouldn't have come!"

"I came because it's been a long time since someone in your bloodline attempted this nonsense. I was curious what kind of fool believed mere words and a slaughtered cow were capital enough to deal with my kind." The Night Merchant gave a disgusted little head shake. "Goodbye. I'll see you again soon."

The Night Merchant attempted to wade around Arvin, but Arvin sidestepped. "Soon?"

"When you die and I collect your soul to rend until the sun burns away."

The Night Merchant tried to leave again, but Arvin grabbed his arm. It was like grabbing a hunk of ice off the pond in winter.

Arvin panicked, spoke fast. "We didn't make a deal. You don't have claim to my soul."

"Child, your incantation is nothing more than the final step over a cliff you were going to fall off anyway. Your sheer *willingness* to deal in this sort of magic to satiate your greed and ambition all but guaranteed your shriveled, putrid soul was coming to someone like me. Since I answered your call and made the long trip here, I'm staking my claim now. You're not a stellar addition to my portfolio, but more *is* more."

"No," Arvin screamed, defiant. "That's not right. It's not fair."

"You have roughly ten years. Your death will be horrible, and the horrors will not end after. Do try to enjoy the time you have left." The Night Merchant pried Arvin's hand off his arm and strolled into seeping mists that formed from nowhere.

Arvin, desperate, yelled, "What would be worth a deal for you?"

The Night Merchant stopped, listening.

Arvin was never much good at the rough farmwork, hated the toil of it. Instead, he'd always impressed his father when they traveled to the market and he haggled with other farmers. From the time he was twelve, he felt in his gut how far he could drive a deal, then went further. His father was a quiet man, swore all that good talking came from Arvin's mother. How good was it? "You said a cow and the spell weren't enough capital for your kind. What is?"

"Pain is profit for me. Suffering is the point. However, values shift with time, new currencies come en vogue. A cow's suffering is worth very little these days." The Night Merchant looked to the stars, contemplating. "It's complicated and I don't want to waste what little time a mayfly like you has getting into the intricacies of *my* economy. Goodbye."

"A person, then?" Arvin said, grasping.

"Arvin! Don't overtax yourself here. Yes, of course, a *single* person's suffering is greater than a cow's, but barely . . ."

"More than one!"

The Night Merchant's chin dipped, considering. "Perhaps a bargain could be struck over the value of several such sacrifices. But, Arvin, I don't have all night."

A discussion was had. A handshake deal struck.

Arvin returned home then. He woke up his mother, father, and younger brothers, then murdered them all with his father's ax. It was so much worse than slaughtering the calf, as it was meant to be.

For the effort, the Night Merchant honored their agreed-upon terms and rewarded Arvin with an additional five years on his estimated twenty-six-year life span and an ample sum of money for other pursuits.

Arvin wanted more.

11

If a cop stops you . . .

It's one of those things Pop said to me all the time. The kind of thing that annoyed me because of sheer repetition. My typical response: *I know, I know.*

Yet, here, with a flashlight beaming on me and a badge glistening behind it, I couldn't remember any of the instructions.

The officer said, "You don't live around here, do you?"

Or maybe he said, "You don't belong around here." With my pulse whoosh-whooshing in my ear, it was hard to tell.

The officer flicked off the spotlight since the streetlights were sufficient, forcing me into rapid blinking as my eyes adjusted. Then he opened the passenger door and stepped onto the sidewalk with me. I glanced back through the pawnshop window; the checkout counter was deserted. My buddy Eddie would be no help.

With the cop in my personal space now, I could read the officer's name tag: Boyd. He was young like a couple of our assistant coaches and tanned despite the last few weeks of cool weather. He came to my collarbone, with black shiny hair that looked as hard as a helmet from all the product he used. He looked me in the eye, his pupils reflecting a weird yellow shine. He grinned. "We got a call about someone fit-. ting your description casing houses around the block."

"*Casing houses?*" The insult unfroze me.

"Casing houses," he repeated, but with an eye roll.

His partner, an older white man with an almost-full head of gray hair, leaned over from the driver's seat so he was visible to me. "Did the call come from a 1930s private eye? Because who talks like that these days?"

Boyd chuckled. It sounded like tiny axes chopping wood. Then, to me, he said, "Were you?"

"No." My fist clenched around my newly purchased ring. It felt warm. Not uncomfortably, more like those things you stick in your gloves in dead winter to keep your fingers from going numb.

"What's your name?" Boyd said. "You got ID?"

Then Pop's instructions came to me as bullet points, and I avoided flinching when the word *BULLET* swelled to all caps in my head.

"My name is Kincade Webster IV. I do have ID but it's in my back pocket and I need to reach for it. May I do so, Officer?"

I watched Boyd closely. Specifically, his hands. His right thumb was hooked into his belt inches from his holstered weapon. He seemed steady. Relaxed. "Yeah, man. You can get your ID."

Before I reached, the officer in the car said, "Hold up. Hold up just a second."

Then he was out of the car, rounding the front bumper toward me in a jog, and my pulse doubled. He clapped his hands and pointed at my chest. "You're C-4!"

Boyd's gaze snapped to him. "Who?"

The old cop, whose name tag read Warner, said, "This guy might be the best wide receiver in the state right now. You've never seen him play?"

"More of a b-ball guy," Boyd said.

"He's got seventeen catches on the season already." Warner spoke to me instead of about me. "Right?"

"Twenty," I corrected him, confused by how surreal this was getting but sensing a safe way out. "Hey, I got off at the wrong bus stop and lost my phone. I have to call somebody."

Warner said, "You need to get home?"

"Yes."

"We can take you."

"I—" I had trouble responding because I didn't expect that offer. Didn't like it either.

There were too many stories of Black folks taking a ride with cops and becoming mysteriously paralyzed or worse. I maybe wasn't thinking when I said a very honest thing. "I don't want to ride in the back. My pop wouldn't like that."

Boyd and Warner glanced to the back of their cruiser like that section of the car was a new thing they'd just discovered. I could just about see them trying to understand my concern and only kind of getting it. Warner was a little quicker to a solution. "No problem. Boyd can ride in back."

"I can?" Boyd said, clearly not appreciating being "volun-told."

"You said you were tired earlier. Take a nap."

Boyd perked. "You're a gifted salesman, partner. Let's ride." He opened the passenger door.

Not gonna lie, I didn't feel much better getting in the front of the vehicle. Didn't see any other options here. I wanted to go home and this was the most feasible way that had been offered to me all night. I adjusted Boyd's seat so I didn't have to fold myself in half, then got in. He closed the door gently and threw himself in the back, lying across the seat like it was a couch.

Warner got behind the wheel, then put us in motion. "Where to, C-4?"

That nickname. I wanted to cringe at the way he was saying it. "I live in Jacobs Court."

Warner pointed us in the general direction. "Bet you can't wait to get out of that dump."

I cringed then, though neither of them noticed.

The moment passed. I unclenched my fist because my adrenaline was tapering off and it hurt. When I looked at my palm, Pat the Patriot's face had left a red impression in my flesh, dimpling blood.

Could've been the way the scrolling streetlights and shadows drifted over me as the car cruised, but the mascot looked like he was winking.

12

Warner was chatty with the mediocre football insights of someone who played the sport a long time ago, watched games through a beer-soaked haze on weekends, and thought that qualified them to coach a pro team. Somehow that felt . . . comforting. I could talk ball with anybody, even a cop, without much concern the conversation would go somewhere unwanted. Or dangerous. So, yeah, Warner, tell me how if you were the Philadelphia Eagles' offensive coordinator, you'd only use Hurts on half the snaps because you see the potential in his backup. Solid plan, bro.

Boyd dozed in the back seat, snoring lightly. I checked the dashboard clock, mentally counting down how much longer it'd take to get home. There was a backup because of roadwork, so maybe another ten minutes in the current traffic.

Warner said, "Your team off tonight or something? Figured you'd be adding to those impressive stats of yours on a Friday. That's how it was back in my day."

"That's the way it should be now," I said, Ohio State popping into my head, along with fresh irritation. "We keep getting these stupid threats that postpone our games."

Boyd roused to say, "Some coward been calling in bombs?"

"Yeah."

"What's the point of a threat?" Boyd sat all the way up. "If you're going to do something, do it. Don't play."

I shook my head. "Huh?"

He lay across the back seat like he might resume his nap. "Don't talk about it, be about it. Alls I'm saying."

Warner got us away from the surface-street gridlock and on the highway. A longer but potentially faster route. Especially the way he was driving. He pushed the cruiser to eighty, then ninety. He craned his neck for a glance into the back seat, and that instant of taking his eyes off the road made the car swerve from the left lane to the middle, cutting off another driver who might've laid on the horn if this weren't a police vehicle. He told Boyd, "I should say the same to you, right?"

"What's that mean?" Boyd said, eyes closed. Unbothered.

Warner still wasn't looking at the road, though the speed-ometer crept to ninety-five. I clutched my seat belt with one hand while grabbing the handle over my door with the other. "Sir, the road."

It was like he didn't hear me.

Warner said, "How many times have you talked about"— he hesitated, glanced to me with a sly smile—"*the thing*? Yap, yap, yap. No moves yet."

Boyd sat up again. "That's on me? You're the one who's always like, 'I don't know . . . Sarah and the kids.'"

"Because I can't tell if you're serious. I need to know if you're serious."

Boyd slapped his palms against the plexiglass partition. "I'm so serious. Just say when."

We were doing over a hundred, but at least Warner was watching the road again. The uncomfortable sensation of floating down a narrowing lane, with the slower cars ahead looking like still objects we were going to ram as we closed the gap, had me feeling nauseous. Terrified.

"Sir"—my voice was low, squeaky, embarrassing—"please slow down."

"For what? We're almost there."

The cops kept bickering about "their thing," whatever it was. I didn't care. I was into my own silent conversation with God. *Please let me get home. Please let me get home.* In the midst of my rare prayer I looked at the rearview mirror and saw someone (something?) in the back seat with Boyd.

A white-toothed smile split the inky shadows.

I twisted in my seat to see the thing dead on.

Boyd was by himself, still ranting to his partner.

Was it a trick of the light?

Our speed decreased. Gradually, then rapidly, as the cop took the exit like a reasonable driver. We merged onto the city street doing the posted speed limit. Almost home.

I tried to sound casual when I said, "If you let me out at the next corner, I'll walk."

Boyd laughed. "You don't want the homies to see you riding with po-po."

Everything he said sounded stupid and condescending. A

bad impersonation of an old-school gangster rapper. Though he wasn't wrong.

Also, every second spent in this car felt like pushing my luck.

Warner said, "Works for me. I don't want to get any closer to the animals down here anyway."

"What?" I snapped, forgetting who I was and who I was with.

Warner waved off my outburst. "I don't mean *you*. You've got a future."

Boyd added, "If you keep acting right."

Chewing my bottom lip, I pointed to the next corner. "There."

Warner pulled over, and I got out, taking a moment to open the back door for Boyd to reclaim his seat. "Thanks," I mumbled.

I started to walk away, my hands in my pockets, grazing my ring. Still warm.

"Thanks what?" Boyd called.

I observed him leaning on the cruiser. The hand that never made it to his holstered weapon when we first spoke now rested on the butt of his gun.

One last thing. Then I could go home. I tried to see it that way. "Thanks, Officer."

Boyd tipped his chin and reclaimed his rightful seat. "Have a good night, citizen."

Warner busted a U-turn and activated the siren for no reason before speeding away.

13

There was a full house when I turned the key to our apartment. Ma and Pop snuggled on the couch, with Leek stretched on the floor in front of the TV. Some animated dog movie was on, but Leek was occupied with the videos on her phone while our parents talked. I walked straight through the middle of the room without saying a word, thirsty, and just about inhaled a bottle of Deer Park from the fridge. Then a second. Drank them too fast, though, because I got a brain freeze that felt like a silver spike piercing my skull from one temple to another. Wincing until it subsided, I braced myself for the next bit of inevitable pain, delivering the bad news about my broken phone to my parents. By "bad news," I meant "lie," because no way was I telling them I broke it myself. Keeping this at the "vague accident" level should work unless they pressed for details.

"Excuse me, I'm sorry to interrupt y'all's movie." I was back in the living room, breaking out every bit of politeness because I really wanted a working phone before the end of the weekend. "Our game got postponed, and when I was leaving the locker room, I accidentally dropped—"

I gave the whole spiel I'd rehearsed in my head. Even framing it as an accident, I waited for Ma to go off. I gotta be more responsible. Money's tight. We can't afford those kinds of accidents, all without saying why we couldn't. Pop's medical bills.

When I finished, Ma looked a little annoyed but said, "Leek, get my purse."

The purse was on a chair that was closer to Ma than Leek, but Leek was minion-aged so she was duty-bound.

Leek never broke eye contact with her own phone as she passed the bag to Ma. Ma fished her bank card from inside and handed it to me. "I need to be able to reach you when you're at that school, so go online and order a replacement. The protection plan should cover it. If not, we still gotta do what we gotta do."

Pop said, "You okay, son?"

"Sure. Why you ask?"

He stared, scrutinized. With a quick hit from his oxygen mask, he shook his head like he'd misunderstood something. "It's almost eight. What you been doing since the game got postponed?"

"I—I got a burger with the team. Nate dropped me off a few minutes ago."

No way was I telling him what happened on the bus or that I got a ride home in a police cruiser. Pop kept staring, head cocked, looking like he used to when he was really into a case. Kincade Webster III ready to cross-examine.

I had the credit card, had permission to get my phone; time to exit before I got my lie twisted.

Exaggerating a yawn, I rubbed my eyes. "I'mma call it a night. Coach called an early practice tomorrow."

"What time?" Pop asked.

"Nine. I'll catch the seven thirty bus."

He nodded, still staring. I tried not to squirm under that gaze. "Good night, y'all."

On my way to my room I said, "Leek, don't sneak in with me tonight. I'm trying to get some real sleep."

She didn't look up from her phone. "Okay."

My request to have my too-small bed to myself for once definitely didn't get through the wall of reels. Her unwillingness to sleep alone has been a thing for a while. A cute family joke. It became more persistent in the last year, since Ma and Pop told us the cancer got worse. Most nights now she slid her little gangly body beneath my covers so we were wedged back to back until my too-early alarm went off. It was still dark when I had to get up, but she slept better just knowing I was near. I didn't love it—large guy/little bed already had its difficulties—but I'd come to expect it. Sometimes big brothers had to big brother.

I used Ma's work laptop to order my phone express; estimated delivery Monday. Then retreated to my room, where I emptied my pockets—the ring, the receipt for it, my school ID, debit card, bus pass, and some loose dollars—onto the nightstand. I traded the day's clothes for practice shorts and a tank top. When I flopped on my bed I *reached for my phone* . . . a move that ended in facepalm. No music. No scrolling. No texting. All I had was me and Pop's vision board on the wall and the shadows in the corner.

It felt darker than usual over there. I hesitated looking directly into that gloom in case I saw teeth.

Instead of focusing on my new unease, I admired the Patriots ring on the nightstand. Couldn't say it made all that happened tonight worth it, but it was a cool consolation prize for a series of trash events.

I grabbed the receipt and read it in the moonlight stabbing through my blinds—*Authentic Super Bowl Ring.* Yeah, right. The paper was from a generic receipt pad anyone could buy from an office store, so it didn't have the store name to confirm what seemed too wild to me, that Skinner—the Court's Skinner—owned that raggedly little shop. I'd have to ask Pop about that when it wouldn't risk clueing him to the falsehoods in tonight's story.

With my thumb, I felt the paper was crimped. Remembered that Eddie guy scribbling something on the back. When I flipped it, I squinted to make sure I read it right.

When the strangeness begins, come back.

What?

Yoooo. My man was a legit weirdo. I balled the receipt up and swished it in the wastebasket by the door. Whatever, Eddie.

Then I turned onto my side and looked at the fake gems in the ring until I began to doze off, still vaguely aware of the unsettling darkness around me. I could admit this to myself and no one else . . . when Leek eventually "snuck" in here later, her presence would be a comfort.

Sleep came slowly, then all at once. I didn't dream, didn't toss and turn. It felt more like blinking a new day into existence. When I opened my eyes, the sun was rising and I was alone.

Leek never came.

The Patriots ring, though, wasn't on my nightstand.

It was on my hand.

CORNER JOE

The sun would be up soon, and Corner Joe prayed he'd get to see it—the same prayer as every morning for the last week since his tab came due.

He'd kept on the move and stayed visible. Really putting his theory that Skinner couldn't collect him in front of witnesses to the test. So far, so good.

Nights were hard because most of Jacobs Court was inside, but he stuck to the underpasses where folks had tents and barrel fires going. He kept his eyes open, listened for that horrible Cadillac motor, and when he smelled the smoke, he went the other way. Mr. Skinner might be the hustler of all hustlers, but Joe wasn't going to roll over and let that ghoul have his soul now!

"If," Joe said to no one while he pounded the pavement under the slowly brightening sky, "if souls are even a thing."

He chuckled, back to some splintered reasoning that helped him sleep on hard nights, something about how maybe the deal he'd struck hadn't been a deal at all. Mr. Skinner might've been playing a joke.

Then Joe's thoughts splintered again, and he was thinking of Maxine with them pretty brown eyes and their little

LaTonya with that missing front tooth that never got a chance to grow in before—

That old grief pierced him like a spear because if souls weren't real, Maxine and LaTonya were lost forever, and it was his fault. He didn't believe they were up and gone, turned off like a TV that got its cord snatched from the outlet. No. So then it meant the other thing—the deal, the infernal bargain he'd struck—was real. Enforceable. Unless he found some kind of . . . what was it his lawyers used to call it? A loophole.

All he needed was a little more time.

Joe made his way to Butterbean's All-Night Diner, its ghostly white lights projecting rectangular islands of salvation across the sidewalk where he could post up until full day, when the city awoke, surged, and provided more cover from Skinner's relentless pursuit.

He tugged at his chain. A full pound of 24-karat gold, with an equally heavy medallion of pure platinum, forged into his name. Might as well have been a white-hot brand that seared his chest every second of every day he'd worn it. There was a story they'd read in school once, the one where the rich man got visited on Christmas Eve by his dead business partner, a condemned soul dragging heavy chains for eternity. Joe didn't like thinking about that one, but it'd come back to him more and more and more . . .

Stepping into a pool of diner light, rubbing his bare head and ignoring the dirty looks from the people eating an early breakfast inside, he contemplated what he'd try next. Maybe if—

A motor roared in the distance. A full-throttle beast that sounded less like combustion than a screaming choir. Reflexively, Joe set to run in the opposite direction, but instead of sucking down air, he took down a phantom cloud of tobacco smoke, stale and tarry. When he tried to recover, he could not, because his chest seized.

It felt like a punch to the sternum that didn't let up, followed by an internal silence Joe hadn't experienced before. Because from the moment he was born, his heart had beat at a steady rhythm. Now it wasn't beating at all. He had time to think that the silence was peaceful in a way he didn't know was possible, but the cement rushed toward him before he finished the thought, and an endless blackness swallowed him . . .

Until it didn't.

Joe's eyes snapped open. He scrambled to his feet, more nimble than he'd felt in a long time. He patted his chest, and arms, and legs. All functional. What just happened?

He glanced at the ground and understood.

There was him. His body. Sprawled and unmoving. Panicked people rushed from the diner, including the owner, Butterbean, himself.

Joe backed up and watched them gather. A woman dialed 911. Butterbean said, "Joe! Get up off that ground! Stop playing. This ain't—"

Butterbean didn't finish. His mouth was open, formed in the shape of the last word, frozen. As were the people who rushed from the diner to assist. As were the moths that fluttered in the sodium lights. All as still as a photograph.

One thing—the worst thing—still moved Joe's way. A Cadillac.

Not the infamous white one that Mr. Skinner rode around the neighborhood on rent day, that same one Joe had been avoiding all week every time he caught it from the corner of his eye. This Cadillac was black. Long. The kind no one drove for pleasure. Old, too. Joe hadn't seen one quite like it since he was a kid. A hearse meant for carrying the dead in coffins.

Joe sensed with every fiber of whatever he was now that this hearse had a similar purpose, and he despaired.

Its gleaming chrome grille was like the mouth of a metallic wolf, and behind the wheel, Skinner. As sketchy and panicked as ever.

He poked his head from the window, craning his neck like he was the one being chased before facing Joe. He said, "I'm really sorry about this, Joseph, but it's you or me. A deal's a deal."

Looking back to the small crowd paused around his body, Joe understood there had been something to his theory. Skinner never planned to collect him in front of witnesses because the living weren't meant to witness this side of death, were they? Joe ran for the nearest alley, not understanding that things were different now. The Cadillac's engine revved for a short chase, and there was no mistaking the anguished cries beneath its hood. Hundreds, maybe thousands, of tormented voices shrieked as the car accelerated.

A quick glance over his shoulder before turning the corner was enough to undo Joe. The car in pursuit was different from his last glance. It was still a black Cadillac—still a hearse. Yet the metallic hood bulged and stretched like fabric in the shapes of human bodies, a half dozen or so trying to break through, a futile attempt to escape untold suffering. The white-walled, steel-belted tires protruded from the rims in the shapes of arms and legs, the sounds of their bones snapping on each rotation louder than the screaming engine. And in the gleaming grille, the worst sight of all. Faces. Familiar ones.

His love, Maxine. His daughter, LaTonya. Their expressions accusing and hateful.

His careless—selfish—words and intentions did this. The recklessness of a wish. If he'd known—Lord, if he'd known—what would happen, he would've cut out his own tongue and never stepped foot in that pawnshop.

Then he saw his own face in that grille, the reflection of a liar. He stopped running then.

The hearse bore down on Corner Joe.

Eternity awaited. Let's get on with it.

14

My whole house was still asleep when I cooked eggs and bacon and shook up some protein powder in my thermos. I was dragging and would have to sprint to the bus stop, but there was still time. Only, when I left the kitchen, I found Pop adjusting the carry strap on his oxygen tank by the front door.

"What you doing up?" I asked.

"Getting you over to practice. You rush to catch that bus all week. We can take the car today. Your mama's sleeping in, so she won't miss it."

As my literary arts teacher would say, there's a lot to unpack here.

We had one car that Ma mostly used to get to work. We had two, but when Pop got sicker and let the law practice go, expenses needed to be cut. We all got more familiar with the city's mass transit. Aside from the expense, Pop having his own ride got more and more sketchy because he didn't want to drive much anymore. He'd had some dizzy spells since starting treatment. One time, it was so bad he had to pull over and call Ma to come get us. Me and Leek had been with him, and it left him shook.

Maybe this was a good sign, though. If he wanted to drive, it meant he was feeling okay.

Before I got too far down that road, he shoved the keys at me. "You're the wheelman."

I didn't take the keys because of the obvious question. "My practice is three hours. How you getting back?"

The old man laughed. "Boy, I'm fine to get back. I want to see how your driving is coming along. It's been a minute."

A door opened, and pattering footsteps rushed our way. Leek, dressed in sweats and a Chloe x Halle tee, skidded to a stop. "Where y'all going? I wanna come!"

I said, "How you know you wanna come if you don't know where we're going?"

"It's gotta be better than listening to Ma snore."

Pop laughed again. "Your mother *is* sawing some serious wood in there. Come on, let's not make Cade late."

We were off—something like old times. After locking up, I descended the stairs, twisting my ring around my finger, enjoying the comfort of it.

When not trapped in the torture of the city bus schedule, it took like twenty-five minutes to reach Neeson. During the first five of our drive, I was tense, gripping the wheel at the driver-manual-mandated nine-and-three positions, waiting for the first bit of terror-drenched feedback from Pop.

Slow down, and don't wait until you're right up on someone to hit the brake!

Speed up or get out of this lane. That truck's almost in our back seat.

You took that turn on two wheels, boy. I swear.

That's a stop sign. That means a full *stop.*

All those things, and many, many others, were Kincade Webster III's Nuggets of Driving Wisdom™. Not that I ever drove as badly as he made it sound—I didn't think—but Pop didn't like being helpless in the passenger seat. I got it. But it made me hate driving him anywhere. I always expected he'd tell me to do the opposite of whatever I was actually doing. When he got like that, it made the bus look good.

He didn't get like that, though. I waited, and it never happened. Instead, he rode quietly, messing with the radio until he found an oldies station. Only then did he speak. "When I was your age, I couldn't have imagined one day they'd consider something by Biggie an oldie. Sheesh."

"Did you say 'sheesh' when you were my age?" I asked.

"I did not."

"Things change."

"Point taken."

He decreased the radio volume by half. Did the oldie thing bother him that much? The songs weren't what he wanted to discuss. "Have you talked to Booker lately?"

"No. Why?"

"I made a few calls on his behalf, was able to get on the phone with Romeo. I don't have good news."

Romelo "Romeo" Mitchell was the leader of the One-Eights

when Book first joined up. Not a great guy, but he'd steered the gang more toward petty crimes. Not a lot of violence under his leadership; some of that was Book's doing—his planning—for sure. It was no secret that Book, who was never a tough guy in any sense, rose through the ranks of hardened gangsters by concocting ways to make their lives easier. His general "work smarter, not harder" philosophy meant staying out of jail and staying alive. Mostly. When they listened. Which wasn't often enough.

Romeo got knocked on a possession charge almost a year ago, which violated his probation from a different possession charge, so he'd be sleeping in a cell for his next few birthdays. I knew why Pop called him; he'd defended Romeo once, and that extremely generous probation ruling was Pop's doing.

I said, "Romeo can't get Book a pass."

"Not that he doesn't want to, but he says, and I quote, 'Treezy's wild and don't care.'"

"Incredible."

"So if you can get *a text* to him, tell him it might not be a bad idea to get gone for a while. Visit some out-of-town aunt. Something."

Book didn't have any out-of-town aunts, and Pop knew that. Message received, though: Book's troubles weren't going away fast or easy. I'd let him know.

I checked the rearview. Light traffic behind us. Then my gaze settled on Leek; she sat sideways with her legs across the back seat. It was the same mobile couch position Officer

Boyd had taken the night before, and that reminded me of the shadow smile I'd thought I'd seen back there with him. I shook off the memory, focused on something else disturbing. "Leek, put your seat belt on."

"Y'all are too tall, I can't sit up straight."

"That's cap. It might be uncomfortable, but you know how to sit right in the seat. Not wearing a belt ain't safe."

Three surprises. One, she listened. Two, even I noticed how much I sounded like Pop when he used to tell me to belt up. Three, actual Pop didn't say a word. He stared at the city passing us by.

To him, I said, "You good?"

"I . . . am." He faced front, his forehead creased—his deep concentration look.

"You thinking about something?"

"Your driving."

Uh-oh. Here we go. I waited for my one-star review.

"You're very good," Pop said. "That's a comfort. For a long time, I worried about stuff like this."

"I know. Believe me."

Pop said, "I don't mean only your driving. I was concerned about how heavy it'll be for you once I'm gone. Not that your mother and I haven't already discussed what should happen next. We planned for you to continue your athletic pursuits with minimum stress. But having a plan doesn't mean you don't worry about the plan. Losing a parent is hard. You're almost grown, though. You'll do okay with it and you'll help Leek through it. I feel good about that."

Well, that made one of us.

I asked, "Why are you saying all this now?"

"Saying all what? We've talked about this before."

"No," I said, after carefully searching my memory for even one time any of us had been so direct about *this*. "We haven't."

We talked around it. Pop was a fighter. There was a tough road ahead. We had to enjoy every day we had together. Let's get everyone over here for a game night. That's how my parents handled Pop's cancer. The loudest parts remained unspoken.

Did him and Ma get more bad news from his doctors? Was that the reason for such plain talk? I checked the rearview again. An uncomfortably strapped-in Leek was focused on her phone and gave no sign that she'd heard or was bothered. How could she not be, though?

Pop's head tilted, really considering what I said. "You're right. Your mother and I haven't been very direct with you. That's . . . strange. Isn't it?"

"I don't know."

He shook his head like something inside was loose. "Well, no more of that. When you get home tonight, we'll have to sit you and Leek down to go over my estate-planning documents. You hear that, Leek?"

"Yep," she chirped from the back seat without looking up from her phone.

99

What was going on here? For real, like—

"Cade!" Pop shouted.

I slammed the brakes to keep from rear-ending a car stopped at the light ahead of us, unsure we'd avoid the collision. We did. Inches to spare. Pop would lay into me for sure. Would probably need a hit off that oxygen he brought along.

All he said was "Good reflexes. You're going to be fine."

15

Pop, who'd been shorter than me since I turned thirteen but seemed to have shrunk a couple more inches during his illness, finished adjusting the driver's seat and steering wheel to the proportions of an average-sized person. Leek got settled in the passenger seat (with her seat belt on, I made sure). I said, "Take it easy getting home. Take a break if you need to."

"I'm fine," Pop assured. Then joked, "If things get dicey, maybe I'll give Malika her first driving lesson."

Leek perked. "Seriously?"

"Can you even reach the pedals?" I said, playing along.

"You can see how long my legs are when I come kick your butt!"

"Whoa!" I was amused and shocked. Where'd that come from?

"Malika," Pop said in a tone that made the word a whole watch-your-mouth lecture.

"What?" she said, genuinely confused. "He came for me."

I mock surrendered, palms to the sky. "Bye, you two!"

Punching my code into the keypad at the secure entrance, an angry buzzer sounded, and the lock unlatched on fifteen thousand square feet of athletic training heaven. Weights.

Therapy rooms. Saunas. Pilates machines. On and on. It was supposed to be for all the Neeson athletes, but every other sport only got seasonal codes that expired the minute they played their last game of the year. Football players had 24/7/365 access.

Crossing the workout area for the locker rooms, I heard the chatter from a few other early arrivals. The bus would've gotten me here with minutes to spare before we took the field; now I had a leisurely forty minutes to kill. It was nice.

Until I got to the lockers and saw who else was here early.

Nate. Geared up and sweating like he'd already gone through a private practice. He sat before his locker, legs wide, holding court with Brady and some of the second-string guys.

"—hip flexibility is important. Power comes from there. The rotation at your core aids the ball's lift and— Yo, Cade. What up?"

I tipped my chin and dug into my own locker, tuning out his keynote address on biomechanics. It wasn't hard. Pop's voice was loud in my head: *I was concerned about how heavy it'll be for you once I'm gone.*

Jesus, Pop.

When I closed my locker door, Nate was right there like the slasher in a horror movie.

I tried not to flinch. "Bro."

"What is that?" he said.

I didn't follow at first, so confused by how much in my personal space he was. "What is what?"

Brady solved the mystery when he slid up beside Nate. "Super Bowl LI. Patriots and Falcons. Classic."

He got so close to my ring its face reflected in the yellowish glint of his eyes.

"Where'd you get it?" Nate said.

"Pawnshop downtown. It's a pretty decent replica, right?"

"Can I hold it?" Brady asked with something rapturous in his voice, already reaching, like he knew I'd say yes. Shiny things probably caught Brady's eye the same way they did mine.

I retracted my hand. Not aggressively, not to embarrass him, but others had gathered around and they laughed.

A second-string guy shouted, "Come on, Brady. You gonna pick his pocket next?"

A different heckler chimed in. "He could probably get some better shoes if he did."

A third quoted a ridiculously old meme and shouted, "WHAT ARE THOSE?!" before pointing wildly at the dirty, beat-up New Balance sneakers Brady wore every day with every outfit.

Yeah, I'd noticed them, too.

His complexion flared like he'd just gotten a sunburn indoors. His jaw flexed under his pimple-covered skin. I didn't mean to trigger this; I felt horrible. Before I could apologize and check the guys who'd taken it there, Coach Gibson emerged from his office with a coffee thermos in hand. "Morning, gang."

"Morning, Coach," we barked in near unison.

A deflated Brady waved him over, happy for the distraction. "Cade's got a cool new ring."

Coach leaned in, whistled at the sight. "Now that's what I'm talking about. Nice to know I got players with such lofty aspirations. The ones they give out for a state championship won't be this nice, but I don't think any of y'all gonna care too much if we bring that title to Neeson."

"When." Nate was stone-faced.

"What's that, son?"

Nate repeated himself. "*When* we bring the title to Neeson. Not *if.*"

Coach Gibson grinned wide. "I like it. Hustle up then, get 'em on the field."

Nate bellowed, "You heard him! Hustle up!"

Everyone present scrambled. Nate got annoying sometimes, but that *when, not if* thing was bars. I suited up as other guys leaked onto the field. Nate hung back, waiting. He sat next to me while I laced up my cleats.

"What, Nate?"

"When we run that post-route play for you, I want you to get ten to fifteen yards farther downfield before I hit you."

My eyebrow arched as if snagged by a fishhook.

He said it again. "Ten to fifteen more yards."

"Why?" That play was already a deep throw—essentially a Hail Mary—and Nate's accuracy wasn't great at that distance. Something we ran on third downs when we'd already

104

lost yards and didn't see a realistic way to get a first down. Desperation before we punted. I said, "That's what Coach wants?"

Nate didn't reply.

"Seriously?" Nate had some autonomy on the field, but Coach was going to roast him and make us do laps for stupidity if he called that play and threw garbage. All that private coaching had him feeling brave, I guessed. "All right, man. If you say so. I'll get to the spot."

"I know you will." He left for the field.

I finished double-knotting my shoes, about to close my locker, when Brady rounded the corner looking sheepish. "Hey, Cade, I'm not trying to be a pest, but is it still cool if I check out your ring?"

"Uhhhh . . . sure?"

I'd set it on the top shelf of my locker but plucked it back out and let Brady have it. I didn't know why he was acting like that goblin-looking dude from *Lord of the Rings* over it, but whatever. Since I got him and his shoes roasted, it was the least I could do. "I'll get it after practice."

He slid it onto his ring finger and was so deep in concentration I don't think he heard me.

Practice was fun. Seriously fun. Completely different from what I expected once we got conditioning out of the way and started running plays.

I'm the best on the team. I got no ego about it, it's just facts.

Nate was my closest competition, and I *knew* I could smoke him in every conceivable way. Most days.

But that private coaching worked wonders because it felt like a different quarterback throwing the ball. Not only was he handling those longer post routes easily, but after a couple of receptions, I needed a break because the ball *stung*. His mechanics were improved, sure, but his confidence was on a thousand. His dropbacks, his reads on the plays that weren't for me, he orchestrated the offense like a god.

It wasn't all him either.

Everybody moved with almost unconscious efficiency. We were a good team, so the average spectator might not have noticed the change, but I saw something in my guys I'd never seen before. Fearlessness.

After yet another flawless set of downs, Coach cheered from the sidelines, his face red and veins popping from the sides of his neck. "One thousand percent beast mode, gang! This is the kind of effort I want to see against Forestbrook on Monday. Hit the showers! You've earned it."

Clean and not looking forward to "estate planning" with my parents, I took my time at my locker. Stretched out on the bench with my towel coiled around my waist, I squeezed my eyes shut. I sensed movement around me from the other guys, then felt a still, unnerving presence next to me. My skin crawled, and I opened my eyes. Brady stood over me, looking . . . angry?

"I did something stupid, Cade."

I sat up slowly. "What?"

"I lost your ring. It was on my finger, and I needed to refill the water coolers, and when I looked again, it wasn't there—"

"Hold up, B!" I held both palms out, trying to get him calm.

He punched himself in the thigh. Hard. "I'm stupid! I'm so stupid!"

"B. Chill. It's right here." I opened my locker door wide and pointed at my ring sitting on the top shelf. I'd clocked it the minute I'd come off the field. "You put it in my locker and must've forgotten. That's all. You all right, man?"

The rage in his eyes subsided as he stared at the ring, looking at it like some trick thing. A hologram that might blink out of existence.

He said, "That's not possible."

"It's gotta be, fam. How else would it be right there? You got a lot going on, is all." Considering what was happening in my life, it was a little wild I was calming *him* down. The burdens of leadership.

He nodded. Accepted what I was saying, I supposed. Kept staring at the ring. "Yeah. Yeah. I'mma let you get dressed."

Brady quick-stepped past teammates who'd been watching. He wasn't quick enough to escape their chuckling taunts. He never was.

Odd guy.

16

My stomach was a mess getting on the bus home because of what happened the night before. But it was a different driver and different weekend passengers. No one had a problem with me at all. That didn't help my stomach because then I was thinking about the stuff Pop wanted to discuss the whole ride.

Was it procrastination or cowardice? I don't know. When I arrived in the Court, I didn't go home. I went to Gabby's.

I knocked and heard immediate shuffling. "Who is it?" Gabby yelled at the same time the peephole darkened.

"Cade."

A beat passed. Then two. "I said it's Cade."

A chain rattled, the dead bolt clacked, the door swung inward. She frowned and leaned into the hall, scanning both directions. "Was anyone outside the building?"

"Naw."

She grabbed my jacket and pulled me inside, then checked the hall again.

"You good?" I asked.

She closed and locked the door. "Some One-Eights were hanging around the stoop earlier. Asking about Book."

That's when I noticed the bruise on her arm. Gabby's

complexion was light brown, the shading on her forearm to her wrist was like smeared mud. A big hand had squeezed her tight. I could guess whose.

"Treezy do that to you?"

She wore a loose sweater with the sleeves rolled up. She tugged the one on her bruised arm down as if that was going to erase what I'd seen. "Why are you here, Cade?"

"Didn't think I needed a reason to come through. Tell me what happened to your arm."

"It's not a big deal, so don't make it one."

We stood in the small living room, awkwardness reverberating like an echo.

She said, "What's on your hand?"

Man, this ring got a lot of attention. I slipped it off and handed it over mainly to have something to talk about.

Gabby examined it in the sunlight coming through her blinds. "It's heavy."

"I know. Only cost me five bucks. Crazy, right?"

She gave it back. "I appreciate you coming by, but I'm heading out."

"Where?"

"To see my brother."

Why she say it like that? What was with her?

"The One-Eights ran up on you and you think I'm letting you go by yourself?"

"I didn't say they *ran up on me*, and I'm fine. You know how it gets around here sometimes."

"I do. That's why I'm coming."

She grabbed a jacket off a chair. "You don't have to."

It sounded more like she didn't want me to.

If she was going to see Book, I was, too. Given the public nature of his spot, it wasn't like I needed an invite, or permission. I said, "Let's go."

Weather was good, not too hot, not too cold. People were out. Music flitted from open windows as playlists dueled. This was the best kind of day in the Court. I couldn't enjoy it. "You gonna tell Book about the One-Eights messing with you?" I asked.

"He knows," Gabby said, incredulous. Like I'd said, *You gonna tell Book that water is wet?*

She got a few steps ahead of me, but I had a long wingspan, so I snagged her elbow despite her efforts. "Yo, are we okay?"

"Why wouldn't we be?" She tugged free of my grip, gently, with the effort of someone being deliberately calm. "We are fine. This stuff with my brother is a lot."

"He's my brother, too," I said to be clear. "You're my sister. We're family. We gotta get through this. In a couple of years, when I go pro, we're gonna laugh about this."

We hadn't talked about it in a while. I mean, I hadn't been around to talk about it, I can admit, but *there was a plan*. I didn't have Book's and Gabby's pictures on my vision board exactly, but I'd never not seen them with me when I go to the next level. When Webster Game Night was a regular thing, and we were on something like Monopoly with all those fake dollars in loose stacks, we talked about what being rich and grown-up was going to be like. I ain't forgot.

I needed to do a better job at making sure Book and Gabby didn't either.

We walked.

The loudest music blasted from the barbershop, with equally loud conversation punctuated by roaring laughs. The usual, really. Except for the old-man crew on their chairs and stools outside. All four clutched brown bags concealing anonymous bottles, and there wasn't a single smile among them. I said, "Hey there, Mr. Stuart. Mr. Brown."

Gabby, as familiar with them as anyone on the block, rounded out the greetings. "Mr. Rapier. Mr. Epps."

Sharp nods and grunts of acknowledgment. Nothing more. The vibe was so off from how they usually were, I had to ask, "Is everything okay?"

Mr. Stuart, who I'd never seen drink—it seemed too much at odds with his church deacon/player persona that'd be on display for all the little church ladies tomorrow—took a long swig of something brown that I smelled from a yard away. He wiped the excess liquid from his lips with the back of his hand. "Joe dead."

Gabby leaned in like she misheard. My stomach sank.

I said, "Corner Joe?"

Before the words were fully past my lips, Mr. Brown shook his head, chastising me. "None of that today, son. The man's name was Joe Reeve. *You* might've known him from the corner because you too young to have known him like we did, so don't disrespect him."

Some knee-jerk defiance welled up in me because no one liked getting checked. I ate it, though. "My bad."

Mr. Rapier tapped an unopened card deck on his knee. "You're fine. Ain't your fault you don't know things that happened before you was born."

"Could you explain for us, please?" Gabby asked, real direct. Unusual for her.

Mr. Epps cocked an eyebrow and laughed like someone remembering the love of their life. "That man y'all call Corner Joe used to own the hottest nightclub in the city."

"The Hype Box!" Mr. Stuart hooted fondly.

"The Hype Box," Mr. Brown repeated with something like reverence.

Mr. Rapier said, "All good until it wasn't."

Gabby looked as surprised as I felt. This . . . was news.

How'd I never hear this before? Corner Joe was a business owner? Not just any business, but a cool business? I said, "How'd he end up on the— I mean, what changed?"

Mr. Rapier put the bottle down and shook his cards from the pack like his hands needed something to do to tell the story. "Wife and little girl got shot in front of him. He wasn't ever right after that."

Me and Gabby flinched like we heard the bullets.

Gabby asked, "Did somebody shoot in the club one night?"

Even as she said it, it didn't sound right to me. Why would a little girl be in a club at night?

Mr. Brown said, "Nope. Not like that. Broad daylight. A business meeting. Joe was never quiet about wanting to expand his empire. Even when he made money and left Jacobs Court, he couldn't stay away. Got his hair cut right here with that big ole chain dangling. Would tell anyone who'd listen his plans. Said he couldn't lose. Claimed he had one of them genies with the three wishes or something. How'd he used to say it?"

Mr. Stuart deepened his voice, mimicking: *"I'm a sexy chocolate Aladdin."*

Mr. Brown nodded. "Yep. That right there. He talked up this deal he was putting together. Talked about it too much. We all knew when it was happening. Even back then, there was always some goon looking for a come up. The idea of Joe—who seemed hood rich by our standards—gathering other rich folks in one place for the deal of a lifetime was a little too enticing for the stick-up boys. They crashed his meeting with some high-powered artillery."

Mr. Epps sipped and jumped in. "Wrong place, wrong time for his lady and his kid. Some folks said they happened to come by after doing some shopping, some say Joe *told* his woman to bring the child so she could see her daddy doing big things. However it went down, it was a bloodbath. Joe the only one made it out."

Gabby's breathing quickened. She hugged herself. A wave of anxiety hit me. From deal-of-a-lifetime to your family's gone just that fast. I heard Joe's voice in my head, his bad-day rantings hitting me with new weight, the weight of a wrecking ball. *A deal's a deal.*

I twisted my ring just so I didn't have to be still with his words in my head.

"The most messed-up part, according to the streets anyway," Mr. Rapier said, "was Joe had closed the deal before the shooting started. He'd gotten a couple of new clubs, was set to expand into other cities. Sexy Black Aladdin's wish came true and it was terrible. He never pulled himself together after the tragedy, and all of it went away. Y'all know the rest."

Mr. Stuart said, "He never let that chain go, though."

"That's something, ain't it?" Mr. Brown said. "I'm shocked none of these boys 'round here ever got him for it."

"Well . . ." said Mr. Rapier, ominous.

Everyone leaned in.

He went on, "Butterbean said it wasn't on him when they loaded him in the coroner's van. In the little time it took to grab a tablecloth out the diner to cover the man, somebody did Joe dirty and snatched it off his corpse. Butterbean said that chain gone."

All the old men shook their heads and made disappointed *Mmm-mmm-mmm* sounds.

That chain gone.

I didn't know why that made me more uneasy than all they'd already said.

But it did.

17

It was a ten-block walk to Book's spot, and we did it mostly in silence. People in Jacobs Court had died before, but they felt more distant. Joe felt like death was closing the gap between me and mine. Honestly, I'd felt that for a while.

With one block to go, I checked in with my too-quiet friend. "Are you having a hard time with the Joe thing, too?"

"No, I was thinking of a song. Got this melody in my head. Wanna hear it?"

She started belting before I answered, loud enough to surprise me and a woman pushing a baby stroller past us. The mother said, "Okay, sis! I see you!"

Others on the sidewalk slowed, or straight-up stopped, to hear Gabby freestyle some spontaneous lyrics interspersed with some impressive vocal riffs. It couldn't have been more than a minute, but it felt fast and slow. The kind of moment that changed everything after it.

My songstress friend cut the vocals and welcomed applause from strangers like she was used to it. "Thank you! I'm Gabby Payne, I'm on IG."

What . . . was . . . happening? Getting Gabby to sing was usually like pulling teeth.

"Gab!" I said. "That was *fire!*"

"I have to agree." She shrugged as the crowd dispersed.

Then we were walking like what she'd done was some fever dream fading in daylight.

We reached our destination and climbed the concrete stairs to Book's hideout—the public library.

Inside, foot traffic was mild, so the open building yawned before us, the pulpy smell of old paper thick. Several curated displays broke the open floor up like tiny islands, and the theme was horror. Expected, given the month. Stephen King. Tananarive Due. Ronald L. Smith. Tiffany D. Jackson. Other names I didn't know, though the covers you weren't supposed to judge their books by were chilling enough for the season.

Beyond the circulation desk, librarians coached some elderly patrons through the self-checkout lanes. We swung right for a staircase leading to the second level. Mounted along the ascending wall were monitors playing various broadcasts on mute. A nature show on the local NBC affiliate. CNN. ESPN, where I clocked Ohio freaking State playing and was impaled by a spike of envy. One day.

A set of cubicles by a railing overlooked the whole main floor. Good view of the entrance that offered plenty of time to react if someone you didn't like came in. Though Book swore that wasn't why he chose that particular spot. He'd been coming here for years, well before he'd had problems with Treezy and the One-Eights. He made up stories about the people who came and went. He liked imagining lives that weren't his.

His chair faced the first floor, his chin resting on the safety rail. He didn't look at us when he said, "See that dude in the coveralls? He works on luxury cars. Lamborghinis. Maseratis. Sometimes he gets to drive them, too."

Book's stories about the patrons were always spoken with certainty. Like he knew them. We never challenged him. Whatever got him through the day.

He faced us, and I was happy to see he looked mostly like his old self. The bruises were faded. There were some faint marks from a couple of cuts, but there probably wouldn't be scars. I grabbed two chairs from vacant cubicles so me and Gabby could sit.

She took her seat and said, "Mama's got an overnight trip. The offer stands."

Book squeezed her hand but didn't answer.

She scowled. "You're too stubborn. That's one thing Mama ain't never been wrong about."

Even I flinched. She was on one today.

"What's the word on your situation?" I asked, deflecting.

Book shook his head. "Still hot. Won't be that way forever, though."

You would hope. Treezy's rep for holding grudges was as well-known as his jump shot.

I said, "You haven't had any problems here?"

Book shook his head, but his eyes were low. On my ring.

Gabby said, "Funny how the One-Eights avoid this place like vampires avoid church."

Facts. Treezy was a grudge guy, but traditionally grudges in Jacobs Court were low effort. It wouldn't be hard to find Book hiding in the library, but why ride ten blocks and start a fight where someone would call the cops? Treezy was probably betting he'd catch Book slipping on the block eventually, while Book bet on something else drawing Treezy's attention and deprioritizing their beef. In the Court, you gambled with blood and bones.

I said, "You been able to get into the office at night?"

"Yes. That's been clutch, bro. Thank you."

As usual, a stack of books occupied the desktop in the cubicle Book had claimed. I checked the spines. Something by Teri Woods, two graphic novels, some manga, and a nonfiction book on the Mafia. Next to the stack were a couple of yellow legal pads and a bundle of pens held together by a rubber band. One pad was nudged to the side, its top page crammed with Book's handwriting. The other sat with half its sheets rolled over to expose a page with more notes.

Anything he read that seemed even a little bit interesting, he wrote down. It's why he knew stuff like how the original version of the Game of Life was way more twisted than the colorful plastic version we had now. Once when me and Gabby called him out on his school absences before he stopped going altogether, he'd said, *The library's the best school in the world. You can learn anything, not just what some-one tells you.*

Gabby reached for the nearest notepad. "Let me see."

He snatched it from her.

While she grabbed it again, starting a tug-of-war, a famil-iar face on a wall-mounted TV made me forget they were there.

It was the local news broadcast. A photo filled the display over a banner that took up the bottom fourth of the screen: *Police Standoff Continues.*

The picture was of Officer Boyd, one of the cops who gave me a ride home last night.

The black bars from the closed captions scrolled, but I was too far away to read them. The picture changed, and the sec-ond officer I'd ridden with—Warner—was on the screen.

Rising, I crossed the floor on weak legs. I wanted to pre-tend that was from that morning's practice, but it wasn't the case at all. Who were Boyd and Warner in a standoff with?

The image shifted again to an aerial view. A helicopter hovered over some plain gray building that was surrounded by dozens of cop cars. Many officers were out of their vehi-cles, taking cover behind tires and open doors. Most aimed weapons at the mystery building. I was so confused. If all those officers were also in a standoff, why did the news focus on Boyd's and Warner's pictures?

Close enough to read the captions, I tried to decipher what I'd missed.

—evidence lockup for the entire county. There would be significant amounts of seized goods. Perhaps cash, drugs, guns, and so on.

REPORTER: *Would the alleged assailants be unaware of the silent alarms?*

RETIRED DETECTIVE POWELL: *It's possible. There'd be no reason to broadcast every security measure to every single officer, so it's not inconceivable the two of them wouldn't have factored additional surveillance into this brazen robbery attempt—*

The *two* of them. Boyd and Warner. Were trying to . . . rob the county's evidence locker?

RETIRED DETECTIVE POWELL: *The world's changed quite a bit. To think that two men who put on the badge and the uniform every day, who've served something like eighteen years combined, would throw it all away on such an irrational—*

REPORTER: *I apologize, but we're cutting back to the scene. Something's happening.*

The aerial footage resumed. Several cops closest to the building began shouting and tensing the arms that held their weapons. Two figures exited the building in full body armor, black hockey masks, with *Call of Duty*-looking rifles pointing in a tragic direction. Then—

The footage cut back to the studio. No captions described whatever happened, but the news anchors flinched in a way that said it all. When the anchor spoke, it took a moment for the captions to catch up.

ANCHOR: *Um, here in the studio, we just heard a barrage of what I'm guessing is gunfire. Can our air team confirm?*

REPORTER (SHOUTING OVER HELICOPTER ROTORS): *We're circling and trying to get a better angle, but yes, it appears the assailants are down. They aren't moving. It is unclear if there are any other injuries. We pray that no one else was—*

I backed away from the TVs and rejoined Book and Gabby, who stared like I'd just done a series of back handsprings across the library floor.

"You all right?" Book said.

"Uh, listen, I, uh, I gotta go. I'll hit y'all later."

"Ohhhkkkayyy," Gabby said.

Then I left, needing the long walk back to Jacobs Court to process everything. The fresh air and slow strides weren't helping.

So I ran.

That didn't help either.

I only remembered the kind of conversation I was in for once I stepped inside the apartment, still shook over how the two cops who'd given me a ride home just last night tried an insane heist that likely got them killed. I didn't think I could handle any of Pop's end-of-life talk tonight and was prepared to tell him. Only he wasn't home.

Ma was on the couch, one of those Lifetime murder mystery marathons on, munching tortilla chips and salsa. "Hey, baby," she said.

"Hey. Where's Pop and Leek?"

"Williamsburg."

I thought I'd misheard her. "Where?"

"Williamsburg. That Great Wolf Lodge place with the indoor water park." She finished off a chip, then raised her hands to make air quotes. "'A daddy-daughter date.'"

Williamsburg was an hour's drive from here. On the highway. The kind of driving my father hadn't done in months.

"They took me to practice," I said, like that somehow contradicted her. "This morning."

"I'm aware."

"Did they come back here?" I moved toward Leek's room and shoved the door open, looking for evidence of . . . what, exactly?

Ma scooped up more salsa. "I don't think so. I slept late and saw a text from them when I woke up."

"Do they have clothes? Does Pop have his medicine?"

"He's due for refills and said he'll get them from a pharmacy by the resort."

Her calmness had the opposite effect on me. I stood in front of the TV, going for her full attention. "Aren't you worried about Pop driving that far given his issues?"

"Worried?" She said the word like it was something French she'd just learned. "Over what? They're already there."

I squeezed my eyes shut and dug my fingers into my temples. "What is going on today?" Then, "When are they coming back?"

"Tomorrow," she said through a snack-filled mouth. "I think."

"You think?"

"Oh, and your father says we're coming to your game Monday. Said it's been too long since he's seen you play."

That much was true but didn't make me feel better. *Williamsburg?*

"Ma, this is super weird. When has Pop ever done something like this?"

"Never," she admitted.

"That's all you're going to say?"

"Oh, no." She stood and left the room in a hurry. I figured to get dressed, then help me think of a way to get to Williamsburg and check on the terminally ill and adolescent members of our family. She returned quickly, still in her robe, holding an oblong box. "Your phone came. That was fast."

In my room, the door shut, I upended my wastebasket, spilling loose paper on the floor. I didn't have to look hard. The receipt was right there. I snatched it up, flipped it over.

When the strangeness begins, come back.

Say less, dude.

18

Skinner's Pawn & Loan wasn't on Maps.

I spent a lot of the night getting my new phone charged, then updated with all my apps. I checked in with Pop and Leek, who were ordering room service and watching movies in their hotel room. I hit up Gabby and Book to let them know I was back on comms. Then I looked for the store.

Simple search, right? Figured I'd check the business hours to make sure I wasn't wasting a trip. Nothing.

Then I tried to remember the street it was on, but the stress of dodging the cops that night made that impossible. I did remember one thing, though: the Knitmus Test.

I brought the yarn store up on Maps, then expanded the grid until I could see other nearby establishments.

Sure enough, I found *a* pawnshop. The name was different, though—*Wilson's* Pawn & Loan. Not *Skinner's*. Based on its proximity to the yarn store, though, it felt like the right spot.

Skinner was a real estate guy—he sure owned enough of Jacobs Court. Maybe he bought the store and no one bothered to update it on GPS. Whatever, the place was open seven days a week. I caught the nine thirty bus on Sunday morning.

• • •

The street was deserted, and the store felt that way, too. I
tried the door; the chimes tinkled immediately. Inside, the
place was gloomy, with only every third overhead bulb lit,
the morning sun providing most of the light. Eddie sat
behind the counter on the stool in what looked like the same
outfit from the other night. He locked eyes with me as I traversed the center aisle. When I got close to the counter, he
hopped off his perch and greeted me, eager, and said, "You
saw my note."

"I did."

He finger brushed his messy hair. "It's happening fast, then."

"Clarify." I unfolded the receipt from my pocket and slid
it across to him so he could read his own handwriting. "Why
did you write that? *What's* happening fast?"

"I'll explain. Before I do, tell me what's changed in your
life to make you come back here."

Now that I was in front of him and the light of a new day
had me second-guessing everything, I felt silly answering.

Eddie, intuitive, said, "Doesn't matter if you think you're
tripping. Doesn't matter if it sounds ridiculous or unbeliev-
able. Say it. It's okay. It won't be the wildest thing spoken
here. I can promise that."

Did he think that sounded comforting? I deflected, "You're
in a better mood today. Felt like you barely wanted me in
here the other night."

"I *didn't* want you in here. For your sake. The store fights.

125

It only lets me say so much until the transaction's completed. When I fight back, I'm punished. That's what you felt."

Silence stretched between us. Finally I said, "None of those words make sense."

"They will. Unfortunately. What's happened to you?"

"Nothing's happened to *me*," I began with what felt like honesty, "but people around me have been . . . *different*."

It all spilled. From the ride with Boyd and Warner and what they eventually did, to Pop and Leek running away for a quick vacation and Ma not caring. My football team playing better than I'd ever seen them. Gabby turning into SZA on the street. He said insignificant didn't matter, so I wondered if he regretted the encouragement when I didn't stop talking for a half hour.

I finished, and he nodded, his expression giving nothing away. Though he caressed the note he'd written on the back of my receipt.

"Well?" I said.

"You know, this note . . . I never tried that before. Most customers are terrible people who want selfish things, so why would I? Darkness draws them here. I felt like you were different. Not chasing but chased. It's why I tried to warn you. When you bought that ring and said what you said, I felt the change instantly. Tried to take advantage of it. That part worked, I guess. What now?" He stroked his chin.

I was no less confused. "Bro, you're still not making sense."

"I'm sorry. This is a lot. I'll say it plain." He pointed to the rafters. "You see the sign? 'Whatever you wish at a price you can't dismiss'? That ain't clever marketing. What you said the other night when you made your purchase, 'I wish everyone would stop acting so scared around me'—you *bought* that wish. It affected me immediately; it's affecting everyone you have and will have contact with. It will go catastrophically bad because the wishes always do. But maybe, maybe, what we do in the meantime might be worth the pain."

19

I shook my head, mumbling.

Eddie said, "What's that now?"

"Something my pop told me. Every smart man is a con man."

"I don't—"

Backing away from the counter, I felt like punching myself. I got out of bed for this. "You're like one of those psychic palm readers that gives somebody enough information to let them jump to conclusions so they can be easily scammed. Pop had a case once where his client sued one of y'all. Won it, too. You almost had me, bro."

Eddie rushed to the little flip-up shelf that let him come to my side of the counter and crossed the border between us. "The items in this store are talismans of a sort. Customers are drawn to them, they bond to you. When you wish—"

"I feel stupid, but the whole setup's pretty sweet. The note you 'never wrote before.' Even if it was a month, something would've seemed strange and I might've come back, right? What's the longest it ever took for someone to bite?"

"I'm not a con man. I'm trapped. We both are."

"Me? Trapped? Google me. Man, my future so bright I got

the whole state squinting. But please, give me the whole act. I gotta hear it."

Anger flashed on his face—of course; he was caught—but he kept it cool. What choice did he have? Dude was like five foot seven. If he stepped wrong, I was going to stomp him into this old, crunchy carpet.

He said, "A lot of bad over a lot of years has changed the very land this store sits on. Imagine a canker sore that never heals. Around it, everything's healthy, but there's the one spot you poke it with your tongue, and it stings. That's where you're standing right now."

"Nice analogy. You should write *that* down."

"Listen to me. People get drawn here. Mostly they're selfish, violent, or plain evil. So the store caters to them by granting them something desirable they'll use to be *more* selfish, *more* violent, and *more* evil for a time. Like a power boost before burning them out."

"Evil power-ups. Cool. Got it. Thanks." I backed down the aisle toward the exit, keeping an eye on Eddie. "If I have more trouble, I'll reach out, and I'm sure you'll tell me what I need to Cash App you."

He followed me but at a distance. Definitely a smart con man. "When things start to go bad, a person may approach you. He's old, scary old. He drives a—"

"You're talking about Skinner."

He recoiled. "How do you know that name? You've seen him already?"

"Everybody knows Skinner. His name's on the sign outside."

"It is?"

This was getting ridiculous now. "I'm gone. You're crazy."

He was still behind me, speeding up. When I nudged the door open and stepped outside, he stopped short of the threshold, examining the doorframe like it was rigged with booby traps. He did not come farther. "If what I'm saying to you begins to make sense, you can come back."

I started for the corner. Eddie did not come outside, but his voice got louder, faster, and more hysterical. "Don't talk to Skinner if he approaches you! Never talk to him, and don't take any new deals from him! Please! For your sake!"

"Only deals I'm taking are rookie, shoe, and beverage!" I yelled without looking back, though I twisted my "cursed" ring for luck to spite him.

THEN

The being Arvin still thought of as the Night Merchant had a preferred name, and a title, apparently. It took many years of service, and many depraved acts of self-preservation, for Arvin to learn them, but by the 1940s he knew he worked for Zazel. Not a demon—do NOT call him a demon—but a *broker* of sorts. A dealer in the outer limits of despair.

"*Demon* was fine during the ages when we could nudge your kind into warring over your preferred deities," Zazel mused on the night of the tobacco plant fire Arvin set to get another extension on the life he'd already overstayed. They'd watched from a rooftop across the James River while flames slashed through the city of Richmond, the gray smoke swirling through pockets of flickering orange making the skyline indistinguishable from hell itself. "The suffering from how you butchered each other in a centuries-long game of My God Is Better Than Your God filled our coffers just fine. As with all our ways, the more sadistically attuned among you inevitably sense our influence and co-opt our strategies for your own means, diluting the overall effectiveness. Diminishing returns and whatnot. Some of my brethren keep a few ideologues in their portfolios, but I see those kinds of fanatics as underperformers. I have no use for them. You, on the other hand, are quickly becoming one of my top earners. This factory fire is special. This begs for a bonus."

For the way the fire's destruction generated death and suffering that bolstered the Night Merchant's portfolio, Zazel doubled what Arvin originally negotiated for it: twenty more years of stolen life instead of the agreed-upon ten. And money. Lots of money. That was 1945, a banner year for Arvin. In the following years he'd yet to have another like it. That was a problem.

By the late 1950s, Zazel's opinion of Arvin's contributions to his portfolio, or lack thereof, became loud and degrading. Zazel, impatient, asked, "Are you not done yet?"

Arvin strained, tugged, until wet popping sounds peppered the air, followed by an abrupt release that sent him stumbling backward. He lost his grip on the organ—a gallbladder. It smacked wetly on the warehouse floor by Zazel's feet.

The still-living vagrant Arvin extracted the organ from shrieked agony through his gag. The man should've died a while ago, but Arvin had been studious and knew a myriad of ways to prolong the suffering. He said as much to Zazel: "I'm keeping him alive so that his torment might provide you additional dividends. Every little bit helps, right?"

Zazel nudged the loose organ with his pitch-black toe. "This is beneath you and me, Arvin."

"No," Arvin said, speaking with active hands, the motions

spattering blood droplets about. "The city will panic over another killing. The despair will spread. Can't you taste it?"

"I taste pennies!"

Arvin didn't know what to say, his frustration getting the best of him. He clamped his wet hand over the vagrant's mouth and nose until the frantic bucking man was still, his soul gone to whatever eternity he'd earned.

Zazel spoke as if explaining simple chores to a child. "Your warehouse fire was fresh, the sheer scale of suffering as profitable as a day of war. But how often can you repeat it? Plus, my brethren have caught on; they have their own earners manufacturing a variety of mass events. I predict a day where such large-scale casualties are so common your lot becomes numb to them. Me, I'm a forecaster. I don't want what *has worked*. I want what is *next*. I've seen some true innovation, Arvin. Sadly, not from you."

Disappointment and rage made Arvin want to lash out like a child. Now he wished he'd kept the vagrant alive a while longer.

Zazel offered a final, conciliatory note. "I'll give you two additional years for the effort. You have more than most in this world, just as you wanted. Enjoy it. Because there will be no pleasures when you finally, finally come home to me."

Zazel vanished, a rush of foul air filling the empty space he'd occupied.

An angry Arvin cleaned himself up, erased enough traces

of his crime to avoid any intrepid lawmen, and stepped onto an empty street. Frigid gusts coming off the water cut like knives, so Arvin was not surprised by this late-night solitude. Was grateful for it. He found no comfort in the additional years of life he'd deposited and wanted to sulk in peace.

Murders alone no longer satiated the Night Merchant. The despair of snatched life was not *innovative enough*? Arvin cursed.

Zazel's threats of what awaited Arvin after death held little sway because Arvin never planned to die, plain and simple. He'd banked decades of extra life, and Zazel showed he would pay a pittance of time for small acts if Arvin ever grew desperate. The horrors he courted in the afterlife didn't bother him as much as the implication he wasn't smart enough to keep ahead of whatever curve the demon—because that's very blasted well what Zazel was, whether he liked the word or not—valued.

The implication bothered him so because, in his heart of hearts, he feared it might be true. Tonight wasn't the first night Zazel had denigrated Arvin's lack of ingenuity. His plot to murder randomly and terrorize the city from the shadows was from his long, apparently useless, list of new ideas. Maybe it was time to accept that any new idea worthy of Zazel's praise might have to come from elsewhere.

He angled toward Broad Street, where he could flag a taxi.

The home he cabbed to was decadent, the many pitches and slopes resembled mountain ridges in silhouette. A servant granted Arvin access and ushered him to a cobblestone patio, where its owner peered through the brass-and-teak telescope he'd fixed to a post, admiring the constellations as he was known to do.

Arvin joined the man, who greeted him warmly. "Skinner! How'd the meeting go? Able to squeeze a few more dollars from those mysterious investors of yours?"

"My meeting was absolutely gangbusters." Arvin faked his widest smile for Winton Jacobs, the sharpest, most innovative, most unconsciously cruel businessman he knew. "And what are you working on these days?"

20

Leek and Pop were back from Great Wolf Lodge. With souvenirs. We each got a shirt that said *Wolf Pack* with a stylized paw print on it. Mom got an extra piece of seashell jewelry from one of the Colonial Williamsburg gift shops. Leek wouldn't shut up about the waterslides and how warm the pool was, even though it was chilly outside. She also LOVED crab cakes now and wanted Ma to make them next weekend. While she swiped through pics she and Pop took, he didn't say much. He sank into the couch cushions, a slight smile on his face, but he was gripping his oxygen tank hard and watching me watching him. He looked exhausted.

I made a show of casually focusing on Leek's photos. From the corner of my eye, I watched him take a long pull off his air mask, his eyes clamped shut from the effort. It didn't help the coughing fit that followed, one of the worst I'd heard from him.

We went into action like soldiers in a war movie manning battle stations. Leek ran for ice water. I went for the coffee table candy dish holding strong cough drops that Pop swore were magic. Ma wedged herself between him and the arm of the chair to pat his back and get him leaning forward. Between hacks, he sipped the water Leek provided. Got one of my unwrapped cough drops past his lips and squeezed Ma's hand. Pop locked eyes with Ma. Her brows were raised with a question he didn't need her to speak aloud. He shook his head like, *You don't have to call anyone. Not today. Not yet.*

The coughing did subside. It felt like a year passed, but when I checked the wall clock, it'd been three minutes, tops.

With Pop breathing steadily, as raspy as it was, he still looked like he was tired on a cellular level. It was only mid-afternoon, but I made the call. "Pop, you're going to lie down."

He managed a chuckle. "You're sending me to my room."

"I'm saying get some rest. You've had a busy weekend. I'm going to go down to the Wing Spot, get some dinner plates, and we'll chill the rest of the night. You're coming to my game tomorrow. I want you at a hundred to watch me do what I do."

He grinned and didn't fight me when I tucked my hand into his armpit and just about lifted him from the couch one-armed. Jesus, he felt as light as Leek.

Guiding him to his room, I glanced over my shoulder, wondering what I'd see on Ma's and Leek's faces. They had to be as concerned as I was.

Their expressions were flat.

Almost dazed.

I widened my eyes as a signal to Ma. Only then did she mouth a casual *thank you* as if I was lugging a basket of laundry instead of her husband. Leek was back on her phone.

Me and Pop made it to his bed. I knelt to get his shoes off. He said, "You know, a nap don't sound half bad."

"I figured. How'd you do with all that driving this weekend? Did you need to take any breaks?"

"Oh, no. Leek did most of the driving, so it was fine."

I'd placed his shoes neatly under the bed and was in the process of peeling off his second sock when that sank in. "No, seriously, Pop. I was worried because you haven't been behind the wheel that much."

He retracted his leg from my grasp and slid beneath his comforter, the oxygen tank next to him like a teddy bear. "Told you I was going to give her a driving lesson. Took to it faster than you. I said, 'You're doing good. Keep going.' And that's how we ended up at Great Wolf. Girl ain't scared of nothing, I swear."

The questions I had were alarming. But the old man was asleep before I fired off a single one.

There was someone else I could ask, though.

"Ma," I said, "Leek's coming with me to the Wing Spot."

Then I grabbed my sister's arm and got us out of the apartment before she could object.

"Heyyyy, let go of me!"

We were on the street when Leek finally shook loose, staring at me like we should fight now.

I said, "Did you drive to Williamsburg?"

She snaked her neck, full of attitude. "And *from* Williamsburg. Driving's easy."

"Not when you're eleven, Leek! When you're eleven, it's illegal!"

"If Daddy wasn't worried, why are you?"

That was a loaded question. I mean, I knew why *I* was worried, but the reason Pop let any of this happen was perplexing as long as I chose to remain logical. And I chose to remain logical. I refused to think about Eddie at the pawnshop for even one second.

I chewed my lip, then ordered her forward. "Walk!"

We crossed streets, waved to a few folks, and I watched my gangly, in-the-midst-of-a-growth-spurt sister move with strides that weren't quite skipping but not quite walking either. In school, we watched footage of gazelles bounding, and Leek put me back in that classroom. We got to the crosswalk by Lim's, let cars pass, then when we went over, Leek turned hard for the store's entrance.

"Where you going?" I said.

"I want gummy bears."

"You got gummy bear money?" If that didn't sound like Ma . . .

"Daddy gave me money yesterday. I got some left over."

I followed, pausing in the entry to let my eyes adjust from bright daylight to the dimness of the store. Mr. Lim was in his box, grinning wide at my sister. "Hey there, Malika! You got big!"

"Hey, Mr. Lim," I said, leaning on his counter.

He took a second to acknowledge me. In that second, his eyes darted to my ring. "Fancy," he said.

Feeling self-conscious, I tucked my ring hand in my pocket.

Leek returned to the counter not just with gummy bears but apple juice, Flamin' Hot Cheetos, and one of those clicky torch things like you use to light a grill. I grabbed it off the pile she'd dumped on the counter. "What's this for?"

"I don't know," she said, running the words together in a mushy mumble. *I-on-no!*

I shoved it into her hand. "Put it back."

She rolled her eyes but returned it to the shelf.

I waited to see if she actually had enough to pay for her snacks, already deciding to cover any gap because as frustrated and confused as the last couple of days were, it *was* impressive that she'd gotten her and Pop up and down the road safely. I hated that it happened but was glad she'd pulled it off.

Mr. Lim said, "$8.48."

Leek wiggled a thick fold of twenties from her hip pocket.

I snatched the money from her, able to tell by touch that if it was *all twenties*, I was holding over two hundred dollars. "Are you serious? From Pop?"

"Yes!" She swiped for it but missed. "Give it!"

My head whipped around, aware of the dangers that flashing this kind of cash could attract. It was just us in the store. Still.

140

It became a game of keep-away. Leek leaping and me darting my hand beyond her reach. It was embarrassing, so I was glad Mr. Lim was the only person in the store to see it. His eyes bounced with my hand, following the money.

Or the ring, I thought, distracting myself enough for Leek to retrieve the bills successfully.

"Mine," she said.

"Why did he give you all this?" I asked, leaning in like it was a private conversation.

Her face screwed up. Indignant. "He said there'll be plenty of money for us once he's gone so it's no big deal."

That hit me like a slap.

Leek peeled off a twenty, passed it through the money slot in Mr. Lim's window, and he provided change. Then she waited for me by the door. "You coming?"

We kept it moving to the Wing Spot, where we got our family's usual order.

She paid.

21

"Another dynamite day, huh, young man!" Headmaster Sterling said, sneaking up on my way to homeroom.

"Yes, sir!" I was on autopilot and barely listening to what he said. Pop didn't really eat the dinner I'd brought him last night, claiming his stomach was off. He never got out of bed, and dozed without seeing me backhanding tears away.

He said there'll be plenty of money for us once he's gone . . .

Headmaster Sterling was saying something about the game now, how he looked forward to seeing me work my magic against Forestbrook and how we needed to show those brutes what true mental and physical superiority looked like.

I shook my head, hearing more of that part because that part sounded weird. "What'd you say, sir?"

"I was saying how we're all looking forward to another virtuoso performance from—"

"Nah, I mean the brutes."

His grin tightened a bit. "Oh, you know."

"I don't."

What I did know was Forestbrook was a great team. Not our main rival—that would be Belmont Prep, last home game of the season—but for real competition. I'd be seeing a couple of Forestbrook guys at the college level. They'd been in the news lately, though. Not for their talent, unfortunately. Forestbrook was a mostly Black team. A coach (that would be Coach Roof from *Belmont Prep!*) recently had to walk back some comments about how they "played with *animal intensity* that you just gotta be born with, a sort of *gorilla* instinct."

When the comments blew up and the calls for his resignation/firing began, he apologized and swore he said *guerrilla*—G-U-E—as in soldiers, military precision, a compliment, so take that, Woke Mob!

Weird, given the "animal intensity" part of the statement—but selling a horribly mixed metaphor was preferable to admitting blatant racism, I guessed.

Following the controversy, Sterling's "brutes" comment felt poorly timed. So, clarify, sir. I'll wait.

"Those boys play rough," he said, no smile now and no further explanation. "Carry on, and don't be late."

He merged into the hallway traffic, nodding and greeting other students gleefully.

The threats we'd received had made Monday afternoon home games standard around here. That didn't do much for enthusiasm and attendance. I'd heard one classmate say Monday games felt like more homework and I had no good response. To counter this, the media club, whose faculty adviser was none other than my favorite communications director, Sheila, started running any local news stations' sports segments that mentioned us—me—on the corridor TVs between classes and during lunch. All day, I heard some variation of *"Cade Webster's explosive gameplay is sure to give the Sparks an edge . . ."* or *"Cade Webster's got hands like Scotch tape the way he makes catches . . ."* and so on.

No lie, it got me amped.

During the last class change, which had me heading to the gym for PE, allowing me to take my time because phys ed was essentially a free period for me on a game day, I caught a longer clip from the Channel Eight sports guy.

"Kincade Webster IV instilled a healthy dose of fear in his regional competition. His speed, length, and high IQ for the game have turned him into a sort of boogeyman for defenders—"

I entered the gym, where there were no monitors, but that snippet stuck with me.

. . . instilled a healthy dose of fear.

Past tense.

By final bell, when I spotted the Forestbrook team buses pulling into the lot, I wasn't so amped anymore.

22

We suited up; my clothes, phone, and Patriots ring stowed neatly in my locker. Coach gave the pep talk and went over the game plan. Nate got the guys going with a foundation-rattling "WE MUST PROTECT THIS HOUSE" chant. Everything was all good going into the coin toss.

My family was front row at the fifty-yard line. Leek wedged between Ma and Pop. Ma waved and hollered when she saw me looking. Pop, eager and alert, gave me the same do-your-thing nod he'd been giving me since I was a kid. It put a battery in my back, a straight dose of electric adrenaline.

Me and Nate met Forestbrook's team captains and the head referee. We gave good sportsmanship fist bumps, though they all seemed to hesitate a moment before grazing my gloved knuckles. I didn't think much of it when the coin went in the air, winking stadium light all the way up, then down. Forestbrook called it correctly and got the ball first. Here we go.

Forestbrook managed a thirty-five-yard return on the kickoff. I stood next to Nate, watching our defense collide with our opponents. Their quarterback called an audible, and in a blink, they'd moved the ball fifteen yards for a first down on a rushing play. The running back, a kid whose game was mid at best, weaved between our guys in a burst of speed and agility he'd never, ever displayed before.

Feeling confident, they reran that same play, but our defensive line smashed the runner. A crunching collision that made the cheerleaders flinch. He wouldn't be trying that again.

Except . . .

On the second down, that running back ran directly into one of our linemen *without the ball.* Literally threw himself at a guy who outweighed him by sixty pounds only to bounce back. There was a flag on the play because Forestbrook's center hadn't hiked the ball yet. What was that about?

Their running back scrambled to his feet and got in our lineman's face. Yelling spittle, cursing, shoving him in the pads. Some of the guys laughed. Not me. Forestbrook was playing weird, and I'd experienced too much weird since Friday.

Our guys on the field kept it cool because the refs weren't messing around. They tossed that player from the game and gave Forestbrook two penalties. An offsides, and another for unsportsmanlike conduct. That erased all their previous gains, and they didn't make any of it up on their next plays. They punted to our thirty-yard line, so it was time for me to go to work.

We executed Coach's plan, which boiled down to me cutting up the defense like a scalpel. We picked them apart methodically for short gains, but on a third down at their forty I saw a hole and I punched it. I shook their cornerback all the way out of bounds, hit a nasty spin move on his help, then caught a Nate pass in wide-open field. Twenty. Ten. Touchdown!

Score: 0–6, Neeson.

I decelerated, then dunked the ball over the goalpost, sending my teammates, my family, and the few fans who were in attendance into convulsions. Walking back to the sidelines so special teams could go for the extra point, I spotted a lone spectator high in the bleachers standing and slow-clapping with eyes on me.

Skinner.

He was dressed as he always was. A long black coat that looked too formal this close to a football field. That hat, with silky gray hair hanging like curtains. Even from the field I saw the deep wrinkles that cracked his face like dry clay. He stopped clapping and pointed one long, crooked finger at me.

"Cade!" Coach shouted.

I hadn't stepped fully off the field yet. Scrambling, I got with my guys, but couldn't help looking over my shoulder at Skinner, who remained standing and staring at me every time I glanced his way.

Forestbrook moved into field goal range and their kicker did his job. Score was 7 to 3, and I got back on the clock.

Nate called that long post-play he'd been obsessed with and threw like a sniper. I got thirty-five yards on the catch and ran the remaining twenty into the end zone. 13 to 3, we were crushing these dudes.

I spiked the ball and pumped my hands in the air to get the crowd even more hyped, making sure not to even look at rows above the bleachers' midpoint because I didn't want Skinner's improbable attendance to kill my vibe.

THUNK!

Something hit my helmet with enough force to make me stumble.

Regaining my balance, I saw the projectile resting near my feet. A Forestbrook helmet.

I pivoted in time to see the first defender I'd lost on the play rushing me without head protection.

Football is like a country where I'm a native. I know the provinces. Can peg the regional accents. Can tell when someone's pretending to be from somewhere they're not. This guy's aggression . . . wasn't from Forestbrook.

Nothing about this team was like any of my previous encounters with them. There was little time to analyze further because he scooped me by the waist, then slammed me to the turf before beating on my face guard with his fists.

For the record, football fights are dumb. I always thought so. Too much equipment for anyone to do any harm, like a couple of armored knights slap boxing. Normally.

I still had my helmet on. His hands were bare. Wild punches to my face mask erased skin from his knuckles. The subsequent cracking sounds could've been his knuckles breaking.

He snarled, "How you like that, boogeyman! Ain't nobody scared of you! Nobody!"

Clearly he'd caught the news, but that was beside the point.

Ain't nobody scared of you!

My teammates pulled him off me, and more Forestbrook guys came after them. The end zone became a mosh pit. Guys on both sides pushing, pulling, shouting, punching. The blending of several referee whistles became like shrill wind in a storm.

Even Coach Gibson jumped in, tending to his top priority. Me. He tugged me free of the melee and ordered me to the sidelines.

Unsnapping my helmet, I made the long walk backward, keeping my eye on what might morph into a real brawl until I couldn't stand it anymore. I turned to the spectators, expecting to see horror on Ma's face and stoic anger on Pop's. They were seated calmly, though. Confused, maybe, but very little concern. Leek hadn't even bothered to look up from her screen. As for the rest of the crowd, some yelled—at players, at the coaches, at the refs—but most cheered on the spectacle.

This was still the first quarter.

The end zone shoving match settled. The player who threw his helmet was ejected and the game continued. The on-field battle got more fierce. Tackles and blocks that had guys limping back to the huddle. One play ended with a Forestbrook tailback on a stretcher, his arm hanging in a way a shoulder shouldn't allow. His backup came in unbothered and scored a touchdown.

The game's intensity forced my gameplay to a new level. Because to play slack, even for a second, could mean an injury that ruined every plan I had. These guys were trying to hurt me.

One of Nate's passes was short, forcing me to slow down. I made the catch, but the defender got both arms coiled around my thighs. When we hit the turf hard, he planted his knee in my upper thigh, diverting all his weight through me to get to his feet. It felt like my hip would pop out of the socket. On another short play, two defenders caught me, one high, one low. I had the foresight to leap right before the initial impact, and that sent me cartwheeling out of bounds, breaking the fall with my forearm. That hurt but was better than if I had a foot planted when two wrecking balls hit me. I saved my body, but not the possession. I fumbled and Forestbrook ran it back for a touchdown.

It was like that all night.

By the start of the fourth, we were tied 27–27. Forestbrook's defense seemed to key on me exclusively, and Nate kept throwing to me because that's how we normally played. Single coverage, double coverage. Being the best could get me killed out there.

At every single snap someone on Forestbrook went for plays that only the dirtiest players would've condoned—aiming for my knees, swiping at my face mask. Thing was, we were doing it, too.

During a time-out with a little over two minutes left in the game, Coach barked strategy that I only half heard because a crazy ache running from my wrist all the way to my elbow distracted me. I'd landed awkwardly the last time I was tackled and was having trouble flexing the fingers on my right hand. There was a bulging, pulsing sensation inside my glove that made me wonder if I'd broken a finger but was being shielded from the real pain by adrenaline. Even through the glove I detected swelling, so I peeled it off to see what I was dealing with. The world went mute.

There was nothing wrong with my finger, not technically.

But there was something very wrong with my finger because my Patriots ring was on it. The ring I definitely left in my locker. The ring a man recently told me was going to bring great pain to my life.

All the sound rushed back into the world the way it does when you've been swimming underwater and you break the surface for air. My attention was snatched two ways, first to just beyond the huddle where Brady, gripping his team manager clipboard, stared a hole in me. Before I could get into that, I spotted another spectator past him, on the other side of the short fence that separated the crowd from the field.

Skinner.

His eyes wide and yellowed. His smile depraved and

stained. "Bravo! What a performance!" he shouted over the din of the crowd. "You are something special, aren't you? We should talk. Soon."

"On three!" Coach said, vying for my attention.

The team counted in unison. "One, two, three, SPARKS!"

I didn't join in because too much was happening. It was a level of sensory overload that I'd never experienced because I tracked movement in the bleachers along with everything else happening around me. My father, rushing forward with purpose, his oxygen tank bouncing on his hip. He pointed and shouted, and though he was too far away for me to make out what he was saying, he jabbed his index finger in an unmistakable direction. At Skinner.

Pop came down the bleacher walkway fast enough to make my stomach sink, faster than he'd moved in a long time. Ma chased him, and Leek finally broke from her phone's trance, curious.

As others noticed the spectacle, the crowd quieted enough for me to catch Pop's final rasping yell. "Get away from my son!"

Then he was on his knee, clutching at his chest, on the landing right before the final five steps. His eyes rolled to the top of his head, his clutching hand relaxed, and he pitched forward, taking a nasty, thumping tumble to the ground, where he lay too still.

I was in motion, moving like a superhuman. I hopped the

fence and covered the short yardage between me and my father. "Somebody help!" I screamed.

On the ground beside him, I propped up his head and chest and put his oxygen mask to his face in case it helped. Ma and Leek joined me at about the same time the EMTs, who'd been dealing with game injuries all night, reached my father and fell into their routine.

While they worked on him, I scanned the crowd for Skinner. He was gone.

Apparently he'd seen all he came to see.

An ambulance took my father away from Neeson Field. Ma rode in the back with Pop, and I drove me and Leek in the family car. I'd forgotten all about my team, Forestbrook, the game.

Not Skinner, though. Not the ring.

At a red light, while we sat with no radio, listening to engine noise, I rolled down my window, worked the ring off my finger, and when the light turned green, I dropped it on the asphalt and sped off.

23

The ICU allowed one visitor at a time and that was mostly Ma, though one nice nurse allowed Leek to go back with her once, and quickly, so my little sister didn't have to see our father hooked up to tubes, hoses, and wires all alone. Though, if I was being honest, neither she nor Ma displayed the signs of trauma I expected—and was feeling myself. The most logical part of me grasped for reasons and rationales for why my family was not behaving the way I thought they should when Pop was in trouble. Very little had been reasonable or rational since I'd done business at Skinner's Pawn & Loan.

Just before midnight, during that time when Leek and Ma went back to see Pop, Brady arrived in the waiting room. It was confusing; I half-expected him to toss me a squeeze bottle of Gatorade and order me back to the game.

He said, "Coach Gibson told me to tell you that your family's in our hearts and prayers. He also sent this."

Brady handed over a duffel bag containing my street clothes, phone, and other belongings from my locker. I nearly broke down in tears because I was prepared to sit in this hospital all night in game gear. Brady saved me from doing one more thing I didn't want to do, and I needed that so bad.

"Thanks, B," I said, trying not to break.

He smirked and nodded vigorously. "You don't have to thank me. It's us against them, know what I mean?"

I did *not* know what he meant. Seriously. I liked Brady fine and all, but when did me and him become an "us"? Gratitude overrode my confusion, though, so I said, "Yeah, man. How'd the game wrap up?"

Brady told me we won, no surprise, but the rest was mildly troubling.

He said, "People are talking about it all on the socials. Nine players out of the game from injuries or dangerous rule violations. I heard Coach get a call from the head of Virginia high school athletics about it before I came here. They're already calling it the Blood Bowl."

"Whoa," I said, torn between admiring what was, admittedly, a very cool title and the potential consequences of that kind of infamy.

I contemplated it briefly while I changed in the bathroom. The smell of a strenuous football game lingered, but this shift to streetwear was better than nothing. At the sink, I splashed water on my face and tried to will my eyes to something other than bloodshot. No luck.

Brady collected my pads and jersey, nodded a goodbye, then stopped short of exiting the waiting room. He faced me again, and asked, "Where's your ring?"

The question felt random and too personal, like he'd asked what color underwear I had on. "I threw it away."

"Why?" It came out quickly, with the snapping tone of an incomplete insult. *Why would you do something stupid like that?*

I said, "Because it's mine."

"Where—" He stopped whatever he was going to say, maybe realizing he was sounding way too intense. "Where did you say you got it?"

"I didn't."

"It was downtown, right? A pawnshop?"

"Ay, man." I motioned vaguely in the direction of the ICU, ending this uncomfortable conversation. "I need to focus on my dad . . ."

Brady sputtered, shrinking into the subordinate I was used to. "Yeah, sorry. Of course. Sorry. See you at school."

Then he was gone, and I gave myself the luxury of not considering his concern for the pawnshop too deeply. Brady loved football and that love extended to a Super Bowl ring. That's all. I'd point him at eBay or something if he asked again.

My turn visiting with Pop was short and far from sweet. He wasn't awake and looked part man, part machine with all the stuff they'd hooked him to. The only sounds were the sporadic beeping of monitors and the slow *THUMP-hisssss-THUMP* of the ventilator that breathed for him. It was like my father was deflating and the ventilator pumped him back up. He seemed fifteen pounds lighter than he'd looked in the bleachers a few hours ago. Staring at him through fresh tears didn't help.

I returned to the waiting room, where Ma had settled on a couch with a sleeping Leek's head in her lap.

I sat beside them and grabbed Ma's hand.

She squeezed mine and said, "This isn't right."

"I know. It's not fair."

"No." She tugged her hand free and swept it past her head, then chest. "I don't *feel* right. I've been with your father over half my life and what I'm feeling right now—or what I'm not feeling right now—I don't understand."

She shook her head as if she lacked the words to explain.

I thought of the ring I'd tossed. Maybe . . . maybe I could've shed some light on her confusing emotions.

I was too ashamed, though.

Instead, I swapped places with her so she could go in with Pop. Leek barely stirred during the exchange, and I didn't mind when my sister's drool soaked a dark spot in my jeans. Before long, I dozed, too. Slept sitting straight up, under those bright waiting room lights all night.

At 6:00 a.m. I jerked awake through a haze of throbbing pains throughout my body from the beating I'd taken on the field. That wasn't what woke me, though. It was the new, cold, dead weight on my right hand.

The ring I'd thrown away miles from the hospital was on my finger yet again.

24

Snatching it off, I assured myself there was absolutely no way that a wish-powered fear-canceling ring I'd thrown out on the street had magically reappeared on my finger. No way.

"Brady," I whispered while pinching the ring between my thumb and forefinger.

He'd been asking weird stuff about it. He must've found it on the road on his way here and decided to play some weird prank.

Yes!

No.

No, no, no.

That didn't make any sense because, first of all, *how*? He'd driven the same streets I had to get here? Maybe. Then what? He was supposed to have spotted the ring in the road, stopped to pick it up, then decided to play dumb like he wanted to know where I got it when he had it on him the whole time. Naw.

Brady was a little weird sometimes, but, like, normal weird. Not creepy weird.

"Stop shaking," Leek mumbled from my lap. "You're making my head hurt."

I didn't realize I'd been trembling. I tried to get it under control before she awoke fully, but it was too late. Leek sat up, stretched like a cat, and groaned. She kept one eye squeezed shut and stared at my ring with the other. "I dreamed about that," she said. Then, "I'mma go pee."

When she rounded the corner, I put the ring back on, afraid to see what happened if I tried to dispose of it again.

The good news: Pop woke up. He was tired and couldn't talk due to the ventilator tube down his throat, but he squeezed Ma's hand when she asked him yes/no questions. His vitals improved every time the nurses checked.

"If he continues on this trajectory," Ma said, "they'll move him out of intensive care later today."

"When can he come home?" I asked.

Ma's lips pinched into a thin line.

"I mean, if he continues to improve, what? Like a day or two?"

She said, "Take Leek home and sleep in your own beds for a bit. I'll call your schools and let them know what's happening. Be back here this evening so we can all sit and talk with him together."

Her tone suggested these were direct orders. I obeyed. Unquestioning.

Didn't think I'd like the answers to anything I could've asked anyway.

•   •   •

At home, first things first . . . a shower.

Leek had made it clear that my smell was gag-worthy by the way she rolled down her window and stuck her head out like a dog. Fresh and clean, I got into some sweats and recognized how little rest I'd actually gotten on that waiting room couch. Waves of fatigue pounded me, and when I saw Leek seated at the foot of her bed in pajamas, staring at the window, I asked if she wanted to be in the same room with me.

"We can take Ma and Pop's bed if you want more space."

She shook her head. Nothing more.

She'd find her way to me if it got to be too much, I decided. Ignoring that she hadn't done that, at all, for several nights now.

In my room, my gaze shot to the ring on the nightstand, where I'd left it while I showered.

I dreamed about that.

It hadn't moved.

I fell onto my bed, wary but way too exhausted to let my unease keep me up. I dozed into a heavy, restless sleep. I dreamed nonsense. Blurring images that didn't connect to anything. Strobing and colorful party lights became people I didn't recognize in old-timey clothes. A factory. Smoke. Fire. Screams. Screams. Screams. Screams and screams. A road at night or a road that *was* night. Then a voice I recognized. Corner Joe, distressed and sensible at the same time. "Get down from there, girl! It ain't your time. Not like this."

My eyes snapped wide. It was four hours later and not a

pleasant awakening. Every bump, bruise, and cut from the game sang like an off-key choir. I groaned, took shaky steps to the bathroom, and found the Tylenol bottle. I dry swallowed two and estimated the minutes until they kicked in. Maybe Leek would be kind enough to throw some ice in a Ziploc bag for her big bro.

"Leek!" Shifting my weight triggered aches in my right quadricep, left pectoral, and neck.

Maybe a few ice bags, then.

"Leek!" I called again. When she didn't answer, I figured she'd fallen asleep with her earbuds in, so I hobbled to her room.

I shoved the door open, sucking in a breath to say her name again. Her bed was empty.

Next, our parents' room because she loved that big queen-sized mattress. Nope.

"Leek!"

She wasn't in the living room watching TV or in the kitchen. Our apartment was decent-sized but not big enough for hiding. At our door, the dead bolt was turned to the right. Open.

The heater kicked on, blowing a warm breeze from a ceiling vent that set a loose sheet of paper on the coffee table into a lazy spin. I squinted, recognizing Leek's crooked scrawl immediately.

On the roof.

I sprinted out the door, no longer feeling any pain. I pistoned my legs into every third stair and was at the access door, where a brick was wedged between it and the frame. I burst onto the crunching gravel rooftop and looked in the direction of the street. My sister was there. Not just "on the roof."

On the ledge.

25

Leek walked the narrow brick lip like a gymnast on a balance beam. Casually. Almost mechanically.

I nearly screamed her name but held back. What if I startled her? What if I was the reason she . . .

No. Not what if. *I was the reason.* Me, and my ring, and my refusal to listen to Eddie the shopkeeper. He warned me, and if I thought he was some clever scam artist before, it was hard to see how he engineered my sister being a strong gust of wind away from a seven-story fall. Every smart man might be a con man, but no con was that smart.

That was something to contemplate later. Now, as quickly and carefully as I dared, I crept toward that ledge, having a heart attack every time the gravel crunched under my feet. Thankfully my approach remained stealthy because Leek had her earbuds in.

This was a red zone drive, I told myself, making it a football thing because the gridiron was where I handled pressure best. A situation where time and space compressed and things went very right or very, very wrong. Twenty yards from the roof access door to the ledge. I'd already cut the distance in half, and I had to keep pushing, had to envision the win before it happened. I saw myself reaching Leek without her even noticing. Saw my arm loop around her waist and snatch her to me. Imagined yelling at her all the way down to the apartment before pouring us two big cups of grape juice and trying not to cry.

At around five yards, she faced me and unscrewed one earbud, her little face scrunched. "Something's wrong, Cade."

It was like roots sprouted and anchored me in place. A breeze kicked up, rocking her, and she seemed unbothered. I nearly threw up. All I could think to say was "Come over here and tell me about it."

Instead, she turned away from me, and I fought not to hyperventilate. She said, "This should be scary, shouldn't it?"

"I'm very scared, Leek." Nothing but extreme honesty felt right. "The ledge isn't safe."

She pivoted to face me again. "Why aren't I scared of Daddy dying? I used to be."

I abandoned extreme honesty with shameful speed. "I don't know. Come down now, please."

"He's not going to last much longer, is he?"

"Don't say that. We don't know."

"Yeah, we do. We do."

Her maturity shocked me. Maybe this was another effect of the ring, or maybe I hadn't noticed she'd aged five years in the last six months.

She resumed her ledge pacing.

When she was a toddler, first learning to walk, she

wouldn't follow commands. Pop and Ma spent most of the day saying, *No, Leek* and *Don't open that cabinet, Leek* and *You better not be in that toilet, Leek.* On one especially hectic "No, Leek" day where it was just Ma and me because Pop was in court, I asked Ma if Leek made her mad.

She said, *Of course not. It's tiring chasing a baby, but everything is new to her. She's going to test the limits.*

Something new was happening with Leek now. And Gabby. My coaches and teammates. Everyone I'd been around. Limits were being tested. *Please don't fail this test, Leek.*

Somehow I regained the use of my legs, but could only manage an inch or two forward. Sudden movements were the enemy. "Come here. Give me your hand," I said; she'd have to come off the ledge to do it.

She stopped pacing again but faced outward, gazing at the rooftop across the street. Maybe the city lights beyond that. Three pigeons that were perched on an outcropping below her chose that moment to take flight. The rustling of wings and commotion distracted Leek. She lost her balance.

It happened like it did on the field. Time slowed. As she began tipping away from me, the adrenaline spiking my system felt like a drug that made it impossible not to move. I closed the gap between us, whipped my hand out, and snagged the waistband of her jeans. A good grip, but—I'd think about this for a long, long time after—it was difficult to reel her back because she wasn't fighting the fall. Most people

165

would've reached for me, too. Grabbed my arm because that was their anchor to the roof. Maybe screamed, *Don't let go! Don't let go!* while scrambling to correct their momentum.

Leek didn't make a sound.

Because she weighed less than a hundred pounds and I was very strong, one good yank snatched her back to safety. We fell to the gravel, side by side, me panting and trying to control the *ohmygod-ohmygod-ohmygod* anxiety screaming that my little sister almost died. Her . . . breathing calmly, staring up at the sky. "The stars are pretty tonight. I'm going to take a picture to show Daddy."

She wiggled her phone from her back pocket and did exactly that.

We didn't talk about what happened. We got dressed in decent clothes like we were going to church and returned to the hospital, where my father had a regular room we could all sit in at once.

Pop's breathing tube was out, and though he said his throat was sore, he was in good spirits. He talked about movies and music with Leek, asked me what got into the Forestbrook boys. Ma sat quietly in the corner, letting us have our time with him. She didn't give us any updates from the doctor, didn't tell us anything medical. That didn't sit well with me.

Pop was chatty and that was nice. Though him not bringing up Skinner at my game—his outburst—also didn't sit well. All of us were keeping quiet secrets. Me and him would need a private conversation. Soon.

After a while, I excused myself to grab snacks for everyone from the cafeteria while coming to a decision I didn't love.

I needed to go back to the pawnshop.

But not without a scouting report.

In a secluded corner of the hospital cafeteria, I facetimed Book.

He answered immediately, the familiar layout of the library his backdrop. He whispered, "I'mma hit you right back."

Moments later, the return call came from a bathroom stall, graffiti-strewn green tiles visible. Him still hiding out at the library all day was concerning for sure, but I had bigger problems.

"What's the deal?" he said.

I told him, "You know the library better than the librarians by now, right?"

He shrugged.

"I need you to look into something for me. That old dude that owns a bunch of the Court, drives the white Cadillac."

"Skinner," he said.

"Find out everything you can for me."

26

Pop remained in the hospital, his condition unchanged. I took that as good news. If he wasn't getting worse, he could get better. Nothing illogical there, right?

I'd had moments alone with him but didn't bring up Skinner yet, because of a thing Pop taught me. Whether it be school, talking to football recruiters, or anything . . . do your homework. Take the first step yourself, so the questions you asked later were about what you couldn't find on your own.

Yeah, I'd handed the task to Book, but he owed me for all those nights he'd been staying in Pop's office, so I was okay with it.

While Book researched, Gabby visited with balloons and a get-well-soon card from her and her mama. Pop was so excited to see her, even if his energy levels only allowed him to express it with a quick squeeze of her fingers. They talked, though. Talked like I wasn't in the room.

He told her, "When you get that first record deal, don't sign anything without the advice of a good lawyer. There's an old song by A Tribe Called Quest that talks about how shady that industry is, and I believe them. Promise me."

"I promise," she said, a little hitch in her voice.

He muted the television and said, "Let me hear something, Gabrielle. I'm tired of HGTV."

"Any requests?"

Pop pressed his head back into the pillow and squeezed his eyes shut, thinking. "I was always partial to Anita Baker. I think you sound like her. Do you know 'Just Because'?"

Gabby swiped a hand across her eyes, and it came away moist. "Mama likes Anita Baker, too. I know it."

"Could you do that one, please?"

She did. Oh, she did.

I'd heard the song before, but not really. The lyrics from Gabby in that moment made it something more than a profession of unconditional love. I couldn't imagine ever hearing that song again without openly weeping because that's what I was doing by the time she hit the second verse. I had to step into the hall, let her and Pop have the rest of the performance for themselves.

When they were done, she came to me, her face as sloppy wet as mine. We hugged, and I said, "Thank you."

She said, "Thank you for sharing him. He's a wonderful man with a wonderful family I'm glad to be part of."

Facts, Gab.

All that sadness. All that emotion. Annnnd . . . I still had homework.

Because of Pop's condition and, this being a bye week for the team, there was no game that weekend, Headmaster Sterling and Coach Gibson let me do my assignments at home. Coach gave me a clear message to "rest up and come back ready!" for the following week's away game against Leesburg High, a bottom-tier district team that we barely needed to practice for. A relief.

Ma spent most of her time at the hospital with Pop, leaving me the car. Leek wanted to go back to school, so I made sure she got there; after that, I kept my movements limited, tried not to get too close to new people for fear of what I might do to them and/or what they might do to me in return. It felt like a smart do-no-harm strategy. It wasn't a strategy everyone in my world shared.

Got some clarity on that front through a text from a teammate, Neal Boucher.

Neal
Bro, sorry to bother you while you're
with your family. Hope your dad's
doing okay.

Me
Thanks, man. Appreciate
you. What's up?

Neal
I felt weird hitting you up about this,
but a few of us on the team thought
you should know.

Neal

It's trash, for real, but we didn't
want you surprised. Here's the link.

It was an IG account called NeesonFriedChicken. I
immediately recognized a clip of me getting slammed by
a Forestbrook player during the Blood Bowl. There was a
"sound on" badge flashing across the bottom corner of the
reel. I tapped it and some kiddie music I didn't recognize
played. There were a lot of comments with laughing emojis
beneath it.

One commenter proclaimed: Deep cut! LMAO.

I swiped to my browser and keyed in some of the lyrics.
The results almost made me crush my phone again.

It was the theme song from an old '80s cartoon. The
Monchhichis. A bunch of little playful monkey people.

There were a dozen more posts on the account, all from
this week.

One was a duet where half the screen was a disheveled
white woman on a racist rant in a McDonald's, going on
about how lazy and ungrateful Black people are. The other
half of the screen was the scrolling yearbook photos of every
Black person at Neeson, me included.

As messed up as this was, it wasn't the first time something

171

like this had popped off at Neeson. This sort of thing was part of my parents' concerns about coming to the school because a bunch of students got in trouble for posting racist stuff years ago. It was in the news and everything. Some kids got expelled. Some lost college and scholarship offers. Every year at orientation vague warnings about this sort of behavior were hinted at when Sterling read the cyberbullying section from the code of conduct. It was supposed to scare the wannabe edgelords.

Not anymore.

In the last post I bothered checking that Thursday, it was more of the same. I felt numbed to the repetitive racist content. It was the comments that got me.

No lies detected.
You know how they are.

A bunch of cosigns from people using their fake accounts. Problem was, I knew who most of them were anyway. My classmates. Even if I wouldn't have gone as far as to call them friends, I thought they were at least friendly.

Then there was the one comment from ResearchDom79: **About time someone was brave enough to put the truth out there.**

That wasn't a Finsta. It was his real account.

Mr. Dominick was my history teacher.

I was on the couch by the window in Pop's room, the

day overcast and gloomy. I closed IG and sat the phone on the windowsill, attempting, but failing, to focus on math homework.

About time someone was brave enough to put the truth out there.

With Pop sleeping, and what felt like all the time in the world, I didn't finish a single assignment.

On Friday afternoon, when my long-quiet phone buzzed in my pocket, I was tempted to ignore it. I didn't. Good thing, too. It was the text I'd been waiting on.

Book
Cade, come to the spot.
I got something.

Since Book sent that message to the group chat instead of me privately, Gabby responded first.

Gabby
Got what? What are you talking about?

I heavy-sighed, then responded.

Me
Gab, I'm picking you up.
Book, see you soon.

173

27

Book caught us coming through the main entrance and waved us past the stairs toward the private study rooms where we could talk without making the librarians mad. Inside there was a conference table with seating for six. With the door closed, Book offered me nearly the same comforting words Gabby had when I picked her up. "Tell your dad I'm thinking of him, and I appreciate him trying to put a word in with Romeo. If there's anything I can do for y'all, just say it."

Briefly I wondered where he was with his One-Eight problem, but couldn't get into that now. I thanked him, moved on.

We only needed three chairs, of course, but all the table space was occupied with book stacks, notepads, and print-outs. Anxiety welled up in me. "You found all this on Skinner?"

"No." He pointed to a short stack and a few paper-clipped pages clearly separated from the rest of the stacks. "That's your guy right there."

Gabby nudged some of the other stacks around so she could read the spines better. She keyed on one immediately. "*The Art of War*?"

Book shrugged. "I read a little bit of everything. You know that."

We did. But I eyed the stack Gabby called out. *The Prince* by Niccolo Machiavelli. *The Book of Five Rings* by Miyamoto Musashi. *The 48 Laws of Power* by Robert Greene.

I didn't know what was in any of those books, but I'd heard every one of the titles for years while getting my hair cut or in between b-ball runs at the park. Older guys around the Court—particularly those rocking One-Eight ink, and/or who had done time—swore by them. I mentioned Machiavelli to Pop once.

He'd said, *I'm never going to discourage you from reading anything, but people often misinterpret those writings. If you feel you gotta go there, talk to me if anything confuses you. Deal?*

My reading remained limited to school assignments and athlete biographies, so we never needed the conversation.

I was going to ask Book what he thought about them, but he spoke first. "Bro, why you want to know about that creepy old dude anyway?"

I figured this question was coming, and I'd debated how much I'd say when it did. I punted. "You find something weird?"

He winced the way he did when he wasn't satisfied with his performance. A missed jump shot or a misplayed card. "A little, but—it's easier if I show you."

Me and Gab sat while Book stood at the head of the table like a teacher ready to lecture. He started with the printouts.

"First of all, my guy's name is Arvin Skinner. *Arvin.* You know he caught some beatdowns over that."

Gab snickered, but nothing about this could get a laugh from me.

Book went on. "I couldn't find his birthday or anything, but what makes the most sense is he's in his eighties. I'm basing that on the earliest mention I could find of his business deals in Virginia, starting around the 1960s." He passed me a photocopied newspaper clipping mentioning a groundbreaking ceremony for the new Winton Jacobs apartment complex.

I cursed under my breath and passed the paper to Gabby. She skimmed it, then went bug-eyed. "This was the start of Jacobs Court."

"Yep," Book said.

I asked, "Who is Winton Jacobs, though?"

"*Was,*" Book corrected me. "He *was* a real estate developer. A rags-to-riches type of dude. Found all sorts of stuff on him being an immigrant and a sharecropper. But he didn't live to see the building finished. He fell into the foundation before they poured the concrete."

"Stop playing," Gabby said, leaning forward.

But Book had already slid the photocopied headline to her. "Real Estate Mogul Dies Tragically."

He said, "This is the part where I can't really make the connection. Jacobs buys the land that becomes Jacobs Court. He dies while the first buildings are going up. I can't figure how it ends up with Skinner owning it. It's weird because there's, like, no information about land being for sale, Skinner buying it, nothing like that. It's Jacobs's dead, boom, Skinner scoops up the Monopoly card."

Gabby offered as reasonable of an explanation as any. "Maybe the land sale wasn't big enough news to make the paper. Or maybe there's a gap in the papers the library has."

Book nodded, but I could tell he wasn't satisfied. "True. There are missing editions. And I did find other Skinner real estate deals later. He's got some stake in that fake Disney World with the big walls up in the mountains. You know what I'm talking about?"

Pop watched a documentary on that place once, mumbling about, *Rich folks don't mind spending money to get away from us.*

I couldn't remember the name of the resort, was too occupied with Winton Jacobs's untimely demise to think too hard about it. I motioned for Book to keep going.

Book said, "I guess city hall might have records, but we don't need all that for your purposes. Do we?"

There were only a few more sheets in the pile of papers Book had been referencing, but he abandoned those for the books he'd stacked next to them. The bindings were cracked with age. The pages they held together were yellow-gray. The titles seemed the kind of dull I couldn't even explain. *Virginia During Reconstruction. Cash Crops of the South. Economic Wellsprings of the Twentieth Century.* Putting Book on the case was the right move because I wouldn't even have pulled those things off the shelf.

Book picked up the one on Reconstruction. "There's a huge gap between what I could find on Skinner and the Jacobs building and anything more modern, so I went backward looking for where Skinner came from. Found some references to cotton farming in the early 1900s. I'm thinking that's Skinner's father or grandfather. The family eventually got into tobacco, though. So, we're talking *old* Virginia money."

Every schoolkid in the state knew the importance of two crops: cotton and tobacco. If Skinner's people were on that early and didn't mess up the money, yeah, he was very rich.

But what else was he?

Book slid the Reconstruction book aside for the one on cash crops. "The Skinner name pops up a lot after the Depression. Not growing the tobacco but processing it and manufacturing cigarettes."

Gabby laughed. "More money."

"More money," Book confirmed. "Until it wasn't. Their warehouse and factory burned down in 1945. It was a big deal because over thirty workers got trapped in the building when it went up. All of them died. The story goes the Skinner operation was located in the city, what's considered downtown now, and the fire jumped to some residences and other businesses, too. Killing fifty more people and leveling a bunch of buildings." He opened the book and read a passage:

178

"The slogan for Skinner's Tobacco Company was 'A Smoke for All!'—it was never more true than when those flames licked the sky and a sulfurous white cloud hovered over the region. The entire city smoked that night."

Book stopped to let that sink in. He asked, again, "Why you wanna know this?"

I kept it simple. "Dude showed up at my game the other day. Cheering me on or whatever. It was weird."

Gabby's face scrunched. "Hello. That's way more than weird. I've never seen him outside of his Cadillac. I thought he was glued to that car."

Book focused on his final printout, hesitant. "I saved this for last because I didn't know how much of the other stuff you'd want to hear once I showed you."

That sounded ominous.

"Go on," I said.

"Not much on Skinner between the stuff in the 1960s and now. Then like ten years ago there were wild stories in the local papers. A bunch of his tenants filed a lawsuit against him over their horrible living conditions." Book slid one of those stories to me. It had a picture, but not of Skinner.

My father—younger and healthier than I could remember—stared at me from the grainy photo.

"Your dad fought Skinner in court. And won."

Book had been right to show me this last, because I barely heard another word he said.

179

28

There was more about the case and outcome that Book went over, but it was the stuff already in the article. I didn't want that version. I wanted Pop's.

I gathered the printouts, preparing to exit. "Gab, I'll drop you by your place, then—"

"Hold up," Book said, arms crossed and pressed back in his chair. "What's all this about?"

"All what?"

Book exposed my poor deflection. "Question with a question. The last time you were here you got all weird and bounced on some To-the-Batcave type stuff. Nope."

"Blade's better," I said, attempting to dodge the question again.

"Don't do that," Gabby said, serious.

How much should I say? Rather, how much should I say if I didn't want them to think I was suffering from delusions? Guess I took too long deciding, because Gabby shoved me hard in the chest. I'm a foot taller than her and outweigh her by a hundred pounds, so it felt like getting bopped by a lightly tossed dodgeball. Still. Her aggression was off the charts today, and I thought I knew why.

Instead of copping to my part in it, I said, "Keep that same energy for those One-Eights who put hands on you."

Book was out of his seat. "What?"

He pinned her with a stare. My head whipped between them, regretting putting that part out there. I thought he already knew. Clearly I was wrong.

Book said, "Who?"

"It wasn't anything," Gabby said. "Don't get mad."

He got loud. "Treezy touched you?"

The gap between them was closing, and if the verbal tension devolved into one sibling putting the other into a headlock, it wouldn't be the first time. Our private study room was glass on one side, and while we could have animated conversations, the librarians would probably frown on a wrestling match. I wedged myself between Book and Gabby.

While she tried sidestepping me, he backed off, retreated to one of the book stacks, tapping his finger on the top volume. Not the Machiavelli pile, or anything related to Virginia cash crops. This was a stack I hadn't paid attention to because I'd been on the other side of the table, the spines facing away. Now the bold-font titles were clear. *Pulleys, Weights, and Measures. 507 Mechanical Movements. How Things Work. How to Fix Everything for Dummies.*

How to fix everything . . . it'd be nice if there was a chapter in there for me.

Book stayed down a rabbit hole, particularly in the library. What got him digging into mechanical engineering stuff?

181

Gabby's attention was back to me, so I didn't think on it long. "Cade! Since you're telling my business, how about we get back to what you're hiding? Why do you care about that old slumlord Skinner?"

Book refocused, too. "Yeah, man. Talk."

I threw up my hands. "Fine. It's weird, and you're not going to believe me."

"You'd be surprised what I'm willing to believe after looking into that guy. You got up so fast, you didn't let me finish breaking down what I found."

I said, "What's that mean?"

"You first."

It took an hour. From how the game got rescheduled to my busted phone to the pawnshop where I made my wish, and on and on and on. They didn't interrupt me. Didn't laugh or scowl or accuse me of lying. "So Skinner owns the shop, and I want to know more about him before I go back there."

Gabby crossed herself, then whispered a quick prayer. When she looked at me again, she said, "Nothing you said is of God. You know I don't mess with magic and stuff."

Before I could respond, she said, "Let me see that ring, though?"

I handed it over. "Do what you will, Deaconess Payne."

She stood, held it up to the light, squinted as she rotated it. "It looks and feels real. I'm not a jewelry expert, but we've all seen the cheap stuff. This ain't it."

Book said, "Toss it here."

Gabby flung it sidearm across the room and my adrenaline spiked like she'd thrown a grenade. Book caught it easy and performed his own examination. "Real gold, platinum, whatever don't mean it's got magic powers."

"Not powers, plural," I said. "Just the one. Anyone who gets around it isn't afraid of stuff anymore."

"Not you, though. You *sound* scared."

"Not me." I tried not to sound jealous.

Gabby said, "You can't throw it away. It comes back. Like those Australian Frisbees."

"Boomerangs," Book corrected, still inspecting the ring. "That's the hardest part for me to believe. That means this thing can teleport, and nothing can teleport."

Indignant, I opened a video on my phone. I had tried throwing the ring away twice more. Once in the back of a passing trash truck, and another time down the sewer. The last time I set up my phone to record myself sleeping, see if I could catch the moment it returned. Had clear footage of my hand, no ring. I tossed in my sleep, turned away from the camera, my hand out of frame for a second, then my hand flopped back in frame, and the ring was there. The video ended in a freeze frame and I already knew what Book would say. "That looks like an edit, Cade."

"I know it looks like an edit. Why would I edit it, though?"

He didn't have an answer for that.

I retrieved my ring. "If you don't buy the video, then tell me this . . . do you two feel different? You acting different."

183

"Different how?" Gabby snarled, defensive.

I motioned to her Wolverine-like posture. "I gotta say more?"

Book was quiet. One hand absently grazing the engineering books. Finally he said, "Let's game it out. You gave us examples of why you think wishing on that ring is doing the thing you said. They're significant examples but not concrete evidence, and it'd be hard to run any kind of controlled test."

"Why?"

"Everyone's afraid of different things, so for most of your interactions you wouldn't have a baseline to judge from. In the absence of fear, behavior could be as varied as people already are.

"Let's say you're one of those people who are afraid of crowds but deals with them anyway because you gotta go to work, get groceries on payday, or whatever. That person runs into you; now all of a sudden crowds are comfortable. It might not read as odd to them because they've had to face that fear anyway. It could come off as, like, growth. Either way, you wouldn't be able to tell."

"I know y'all, though."

Book nodded. "Right, so Gab sings and writes songs. We know she's good, but she's been scared to show any of that to the world."

Gabby said, "Stop talking like I'm not in the room. I wasn't scared. I was just . . ."

We waited.

She sank in her seat, contemplating.

Book stood and pointed at the wall. "That's brick. If I punch it, I could break my hand, so I'm not going to punch it. Is that fear of the pain or me being smart?"

"I'm not sure," I said.

"Gab," Book said, "sing us the last song you wrote."

"No."

"So is Gabby still afraid, or is she being stubborn because I called her out?"

I looked to Gabby. "*Could* you sing right now? With no worries?"

Reluctantly she nodded. Then she gave us a few bars of something new. Easy. Her voice like velvet with this room's acoustics.

Book said, "If I walked you to the second-floor landing so the whole library could hear, could you still do it?"

She considered it, glancing over the busy main floor, then nodded again.

Book said, "That's a check in the Magic Ring column. Still not enough to say for sure. Gab could just be tired of . . ."

When he trailed off, I said, "Tired of what?"

She gave him a pointed look. "Tired of *having so much material and not doing anything with it*. Go on, Book."

He said, "The only way it's obvious is if fear was keeping someone from doing something they desperately want to do, and now that roadblock's gone. Again, how would you know?"

"If they suddenly rob an evidence lockup and get killed doing it. If they nearly fall off the ledge of my building because they're acting like Simone Biles."

Book chewed his lip. "That's a problem, then. That means the biggest, most noticeable fallout from your wish is always going to be when fear was blocking the path to something truly scary."

"That . . . makes sense. What am I supposed to do about that?"

"Stay away from scary people," he offered, then grabbed *How Things Work* off the top of his engineering pile. "But how would you even know who they are?"

What an incredible closing thought. "Y'all believe me, then?"

Gab said, "I don't know, Cade. That's still a lot. If anything it's a little too unholy for me to get comfortable with. God's in control, so I don't know if He'd let something like that happen. I think you believe it, though. If that means something."

"Fair. I guess. Now that you know, what was the other thing you wanted to show me?"

Book grabbed some additional printouts. He handed them to me, and I keyed on the header on the top page. Obituaries.

"The people your dad represented in that case against Skinner," Book said. "They're all dead. Lung cancer."

29

I shoved my way into Skinner's Pawn & Loan and stomped to the counter. Eddie was in the same spot, in the same shirt, staring into the distance. I was about to snap my fingers in front of his nose to break the trance. He blinked on his own, finally noticing me.

"How bad has it gotten?" he asked, his voice flat like he'd asked me about the weather.

"I need information."

"Pretty bad, then. Go on."

I spread Book's printouts on the counter. My body went statue-still when I noticed a piece of jewelry beneath the glass that hadn't been there on my last visit. A gold rope chain with a jewel-studded medallion that said *Big Joe*.

That chain gone.

Didn't go far, though.

"What's wrong?" Eddie asked.

I shook my head. "You ever hear of a big tobacco ware-house fire that happened right around this area?"

He skimmed the printout. "No. This is news to me."

"Would you consider it good news or bad news if I told you Skinner's family owned the warehouse?"

Eddie's mouth opened like he might say something, closed, then opened again. "His *family*?"

"This was in the 1940s. Maybe his grandfather or father."

Eddie shook his head before I finished my sentence. "I don't think so."

"Bro, it was definitely his family." I jabbed my index finger at the page. "Look farther down in the article."

"I get that's his name, but that's not his ancestor. It's him."

I shook my head. "No. Look at the dates. There's no way. He'd have to be—"

The door chimes jingled.

Eddie peered past me, and I turned to see who'd come in. No one was there. The scent of sweet smoke tickled the back of my throat.

When I faced Eddie behind his counter again, he wasn't alone.

Skinner stood beside him.

THEN

The wealth Arvin accumulated—the dollars, not the years of extended life—put him in circles with other wealthy men who talked. Braggart fools thinking themselves masters of the universe because they didn't understand what mastery of such forces meant or cost. As Zazel said, intuitive entrepreneurs mimicking the power behind the power.

The ways of Winton Jacobs—a manufacturing and real estate magnate born from humble beginnings—were different, though. His was more than intuition of commerce. Most wealthy men were oblivious to the despair their pursuits caused. If they noticed at all, they convinced themselves it was simply an unavoidable side effect of doing business and bought more outlandish toys. Jacobs's form of mimicry *gravitated* toward suffering. Arvin didn't think Jacobs even realized it.

That was part of what attracted Arvin to the man several years back. To observe how someone naturally swayed to cruelty for profit, to maybe co-opt a bit of his vision for some plan that would put Arvin back in Zazel's favor. It was a long play, which was fine; one thing Skinner was not short on was time.

One evening in the early 1960s, as they dined at a supper club south of the city, Jacobs spoke on a particularly nasty piece of work.

"My patent for this machine part was a boon. Every steel shop in the country uses it now. The bumper on my new Cadillac was pressed with it. I'm telling you, it's the small things that accumulate the biggest rewards. You know what I'd rather own than a company? A part that every company needs."

"That include body parts?" another inconsequential rich twit joked, to hearty laughs around the table.

Jacobs said, "I am aware that several machine shops have installed my innovative upgrade incorrectly and that has resulted in injuries, some more serious than others. But, as my lawyers would tell you, misuse of my products isn't my fault."

That was a lie. Jacobs's engineers had warned him of potential injury due to a faulty design. Instead of correcting the issue, he checked with his lawyers, determined his liability would be minimal, and sold his "upgrade" to the tune of two million dollars profit.

After dessert and brandy, Arvin and Jacobs left together in the showroom-fresh white Cadillac Winton had been flaunting. It was a gorgeous vehicle, like the chariot of an American king. It would've looked better in black.

"Do you ever have strange dreams?" Winton asked, interrupting Arvin's admiration of the automobile's interior.

"Strange how?" Arvin turned the question back on Winton instead of admitting a secret he kept. He didn't have strange dreams because he didn't dream, not since the night he first met Zazel so many years ago. No huge loss, he told himself, and mostly believed.

Winton took them through the heart of the city. "Dreams like this. Like a drive through a city but there are no buildings. Only shadows and road."

Arvin shook his head, already bored with the topic.

Winton said, "I have that sort of dream a lot. Only, sometimes, in the shadows, I see glimpses of things. Occasionally faces, but only in the loosest sense. Too many mouths and eyes. Sometimes I see ideas."

Arvin didn't like that bit about too many mouths and eyes. That imagery filled him with much despair, and it was not his place to feel despair. "Lay off the whiskey before bed, Jacobs."

"Ha! I figured you'd say such. Never mind my odd dreams, then. Let's take a gander at our dream, made real. What do you say?"

Before Arvin could agree, Jacobs made a turn, taking them deeper into the city, away from the penthouse Arvin occupied downtown.

They didn't speak for the rest of the ride. Arvin knew where they were headed and tried to summon some enthusiasm. It wasn't long before they arrived at a huge, cleared plot of land surrounded by tall fencing. The tobacco factory he once ran, and eventually destroyed, was but a couple of miles from here.

Arvin gazed in the general direction of his last great conquest and murmured, "You love visiting your mudholes, don't you?"

"*Our* mudhole, partner. If you want to do more in construction, you'll learn to love every phase, too."

"As you've said." Arvin choked back a yawn.

In truth, this joint undertaking they'd agreed to—housing units subsidized by the government—was of little interest to Skinner. His fortune was massive, and he invested in all manner of things. The motivation for getting in bed with Jacobs on this venture was to maintain proximity to the man. Nothing endeared a rich man to another rich man more than feeling their fortunes were aligned. Arvin was investing in access.

Jacobs turned off the car, leapt nimbly from the vehicle, unlocked the padlock on the fenced construction site, and waved Arvin deeper inside. "Have you ever put much thought to the race issue?"

Arvin joined him. "What race issue?"

"The Negroes harping about equality. We know they're not going to get it. Shoot, just a couple of hours west in Prince Edward County they shut the entire school system down because they didn't want the Negroes learning arithmetic in the same classroom as the white children. Those people suffer so much."

Arvin heard glee in Jacobs's voice. Where was he going with this?

He never saw what was supposed to be the logical next step in whatever vision Jacobs teased. Despite several years attempting to absorb observations and conclusions that had earned the man his fortune, Arvin still couldn't guess the machinations that fed his unconscious sadism. He wondered if he constructed his ventures instinctually, as a spider did a web?

Regardless, Arvin believed that's one of the things Jacobs liked most about their "friendship"—being a step ahead.

"Just tell me what you're getting at," Arvin snipped.

"I'm not just telling you." Jacobs grinned. "I'm showing you."

They walked. Arvin observed heavy excavation equipment and the stockpiled materials of future construction. They stopped at a deep pit that would serve as the building's foundation, the potbellied cement cylinders on the edge like sleeping beasts.

Jacobs said, "That sort of slow hope Negroes excel in will be very profitable across the various lots we've secured. They've been conditioned to have low expectations of the world around them. Positive change for them comes in decades, not days."

"So?"

Jacobs slipped an arm over Arvin's shoulder. "The materials we're using to build here cost sixty percent of what I'd use in higher-quality buildings. I've had our architect reduce unit sizes by a barely noticeable five percent so we can squeeze more families in. We'll provide nominal maintenance on a fiscally opportune schedule. Our gains will be enormous while they suffer the indignities that, frankly, they're already accustomed to." He chuckled. "At least they'll all be together under one roof."

Arvin didn't catch the last bit of the monologue. His mind snagged on *our gains will be enormous while they suffer . . .* Lightning cracked behind Arvin's eyes!

Inspiration!

Finally, after enduring this boor's company for so long, true, true innovation. Sudden, but not fully realized. He talked it out. "Their suffering wouldn't have to be simply consequential. It could be instigated. Farmed. In one convenient location."

Jacobs released Arvin, taken aback. "Now what are you on about?"

Arvin was not talking to Jacobs but walking himself through the broad strokes in his own way. "You could be a puppet master of sorts. If Zazel can be convinced to grant a small bit of eldritch power, the opportunities to exploit generations could be at our fingertips. Their housing. Retail. Crime! The anguish you could wring out of them through generations . . . like breeding livestock."

"Zazel . . ." Jacobs's eyes bulged. He grabbed Arvin by the sleeve, his expression rapturous. "What does that mean? It feels like something from my dreams."

"Oh. I probably shouldn't have said that aloud. Apologies, partner." Arvin's hand pistoned into Jacobs's chest and shoved him over the edge of the pit, screaming. His body struck bottom and the night went abruptly silent.

Kneeling in the soft earth, Arvin drew the proper sigils, recited an incantation, and waited for Zazel to answer the call. The Night Merchant appeared, radiating impatience.

"I've got some new ideas," Arvin said, "and I think you're going to like them."

30

"The man himself! Cade Webster! C-4!" Skinner said, his voice boisterous, like a fan. That energy went cold when he addressed his shopkeeper. "Eddie."

Eddie stared Skinner down.

Skinner seemed surprised. "You are truly unafraid of me. A first. That wish of yours is a potent one, Cade. Yes, indeed."

He hunched over the counter, scanning the stories I'd brought to Eddie. Stories about him. My heart tapped the inside of my rib cage with aerobic speed.

"I can explain all of this," Skinner said, as if I'd asked him to. "It's a big misunderstanding." Skinner glided to the countertop hatchway. He lifted the gate and stepped to my side. He wasn't even Eddie's height, and frail. He smelled like an ashtray.

He said, "I respect you doing your due diligence. It's important to know who you're dealing with. I've always thought so. These articles you've compiled simply do not tell the whole story. My—our—predicament is nobody's fault."

"Don't believe a word he says," Eddie nearly growled.

Skinner's gaze landed on him. "I liked you better afraid. Don't interrupt again."

Eddie's angry stare didn't waver; Skinner's words hadn't frightened him because I'd made him incapable of fright. I was plenty afraid for both of us.

He the devil.

I still didn't believe that, but what was the point of being shy now?

"What are you?" I asked.

"A businessman. A dealmaker. *An innovator.* That is a skill set that I bring to my investor. Has your father spoken to you about economics and finance? He doesn't have much time left at all, so I do hope so."

"Don't talk about my pop." Anger was a good antidote for terror. I held on to it.

"Oh, I didn't mean to offend. He is a formidable man who forced me to adjust my practices. The right words off the right tongue are something like magic, and your father's arguments are close to sorcery. Anyhow, I'm only curious how much of those smarts are going to live on through you. Your potential can help us all. We're in this together."

I had more questions than I could count, but I wouldn't ask any of them. Yet. Skinner was a fast talker, trying to twist me up. A Nugget of Wisdom™ dropped: While they talk fast, you think slow. Don't let anybody rush sound thinking.

"Okay, I see. I'm getting ahead of myself." Skinner wrung his hands. "A long time ago, I was tricked into an unfair arrangement. Over the years, I've partnered with highly motivated, like-minded people such as yourself in an attempt

197

to rectify the situation. What we have here is an opportunity to—"

Eddie laughed. "Lie."

The congenial smile fell off Skinner's face.

The old man looked the same, small and frail as always, but *felt* bigger. Bigger than Eddie, me, and the store. Like something barely contained, a balloon stretched to its limit by poison gas. I backed up a step.

Skinner told Eddie, "Your newfound bravery has made you insolent. You don't get to tell my story for me."

The store grew dim. Not the lights above, or the sun shining through the windows. The actual store, like it was becoming less substantial, the illusion of something fading to reveal something frightening underneath. Something very bad was about to happen.

Eddie lurched forward, his hands clamping to his mouth as if to catch a sneeze. Nothing came out, though. Instead, his hands stuck to his lips, cheeks, and jaw. The skin at the edges of his palm seared into the flesh of his face with the hiss of a steak slapping a hot skillet. Muffled screams worked through slightly parted fingers that quickly fused, cutting off even that sound. Eddie was in a wrestling match with his own body, trying to pull his hands free, but seemed stuck in a speak-no-evil pose, undoubtedly willed by Skinner.

I wanted to scream for Eddie. And me. I managed not to lose it, though, and said, "Please stop whatever you're doing to him."

"No," Skinner said. "Eddie needs this time-out."

Eddie tipped over, his skin going rapidly gray. Could he even breathe?

"I want to talk with you," I said, forcing my voice not to tremble, "but I need you to stop hurting him. Okay?" The next word felt like gargling glass. "Please."

"Fine. But Eddie better remember who's strongest here. In *my* store." Skinner waved his hand as if wiping grime from a window, and Eddie's hands tore free of his face. Charred black handprints scarred the skin around his mouth, and his hands looked worse, with raw red flesh exposed, but the wounds began healing as I watched. Within a few seconds a gasping, enraged Eddie looked as he had when I entered.

Skinner resumed talking like nothing had happened. "As I was saying, you and I are in a pickle. You want out of the predicament you wished yourself into, but that very predicament helps pay a debt I owe to a powerful individual. I know, I know. I don't like it any more than you."

While Eddie struggled to his feet, I asked my first question. "What does my wish have to do with any debt you have?"

"That's why I was curious about your knowledge of finance. Dividends?"

"That's got something to do with the stock market."

Skinner snapped his fingers, enthusiastic. "Very good! There are certain companies you can invest in, and if those companies do well, they'll share some of their profits with you. That incremental payout is what's called a dividend. The larger the profit, the larger the dividend."

"Okay."

"I'm the company. Quite a bit has been invested into me. My various ventures produce a certain kind of profit that my investor desires. When things go very well—as in, someone like you makes a wayward wish in my shop—the results produce a dividend my investor loves."

Eddie, finally finding his raspy voice, interrupted again. "Suffering is the dividend. You gonna tell it, tell it all!"

Skinner's eyes narrowed, annoyed, but he didn't let the outburst slow him down. "Eddie. I wish you didn't make me take such actions. Despite how you tried to disparage my character, you served as an example of the malevolent power that targets us all. It's good Cade now knows what we're up against."

I didn't know, though. I was more confused than before. I didn't *want* to know more, not after what I'd just seen. I shouldn't have come here.

I snatched the Super Bowl ring off. "I don't want it."

Skinner said, "I'm sorry."

He didn't seem sorry.

"I want a refund. Take it back."

"That sale is final. I can give you back the currency, but that's not really what you paid when you bought that ring and uttered the words 'I wish.' You offered up a piece of yourself that I can't give back."

"Not even if you wanted to, huh?" Eddie said.

I threw the ring. It rebounded off Skinner's chest and then clinked on the floor.

Skinner said, "You know that's not going to work."

Pat the Patriot looked up at me, transmitting a silent promise that we would never be apart for long.

"So pick it up," Skinner said, sounding sympathetic. "Save yourself some trouble."

Weren't we beyond that?

I knelt and retrieved my ring. I stood quickly, because it felt too close to kneeling before Skinner like he was my king.

He said, "Can I answer any more questions for you?"

The newspaper printouts I'd brought to Eddie remained on the counter. "The people in these stories fought you in court and won. Most of them are dead from lung cancer. My father's going to die from lung cancer." My voice cracked because I really, truly knew the answer to what I was going to ask. I needed to hear him say it! "Did you do that?"

Skinner dropped all that aw-shucks-we're-in-this-together stuff. "Your father was a very good opponent. He bested me. Admittedly, I'm a bit of a sore loser. I asked my investor for some assistance and was granted a mode of recompense. Apologies."

Despite what I'd seen, knowing there would be consequences, I almost went at him. A full-speed, shoulder-down tackle that had sent guys twice his size limping off the field in tears. He for sure sensed what I wanted because he grinned a silent dare. "Remember who the strongest in the store is, Cade. I'd hate to have to give *you* a time-out."

With that admonishment, the room dimmed again, power crackling in the air unseen like static electricity. Self-preservation prevailed. I backed off. "What now?"

The room brightened. Skinner beamed. "Whatever plans you already had for the evening, I suppose. Since you'd returned to my establishment, I only wanted to introduce myself properly."

"That's it? I can leave."

"Of course. You're an earner now. I won't ever stand in the way of that. Enjoy your weekend."

It had to be a trick, right? Yet I couldn't stand still, couldn't be close to this man—or whatever he was—one second longer. So I took a step, then another, then three more, and I was outside, sprinting for my car, certain I wouldn't make it, that I was maybe already dead and in a place where Skinner was the strongest, forever and always.

The drive home, the miles I put between me and that store, still felt far from safe.

31

I needed to talk to Pop, needed to better understand the history between him and Skinner, all while containing the rage over what Skinner had admitted: that he was the reason my father was dying. What could I even do with all the anger? How could I not burn the world with it?

Pop. I'd focus on him. I'd box that anger up and make everything about him.

We'd have a necessary conversation when we could, but the hospital made it hard. Friday night was a bust because of Ma and Leek and the nurses who kept floating in and out of the room, and while I had to sit on my hands to hide the tremor I had since I'd left Skinner's store, I kept my mouth shut.

Saturday became my window. My intent was to get up early, catch the bus to beat Ma and Leek. After all that had happened, I didn't expect I'd get too much sleep, but maybe learning about some of the unseen monsters of the universe was something like a game day, where your energy and emotions are so wound up you think you might never come down. Then you do, hard. Full-body crash. I slipped under my covers late Friday, awoke to the sounds of the Court's Saturday-afternoon hustle and a note on my nightstand.

Don't think I haven't noticed you aren't sleeping well. You need your rest. Leek and I will be at the hospital. Love, Mom

While I'd awoken to find the note, I hadn't come out of sleep naturally. Aside from the sounds of the block, someone was pounding on the apartment door.

Swinging my legs to the floor, I wondered, not for the first time, if it would've been a better wish for all fear to be taken from me instead of from those around me. Because the fear I felt lately was crushing. What if it was Skinner outside?

At the peephole, squinting at the warped sight on the other side of the fish-eye lens, I was like, *What?*

Snatching the door open, I said, "Nate?"

He was turned sideways, neck craning like a building inspector looking for evidence of foundation problems. "Is this a project?"

"Huh?"

Our eyes locked, and he said, "Is this a *project*? *The* projects? It's nicer than I expected."

I debated if one of the worst effects of the ring was people's sudden willingness to say the quiet parts out loud.

Suffering is the dividend.

I yanked Nate inside by the front of his letterman jacket.

"We're a neighborhood. Not *a project*. We're all Jacobs Court. You got a problem with that?"

"Do you?" He sounded genuinely curious.

"How do you know where I live?"

"Got your address from Brady. This is a long way from school."

"What are you doing here?" Even as I asked, I noticed the gear under his jacket: a Neeson Football hoodie and shorts over thermal leggings.

"You haven't been practicing."

"My dad's in the hospital. Coach knows."

"That doesn't change that me and you need to stay sharp." He motioned toward the stairs. "Is there a park or something around here? Let's get some reps in."

He couldn't be serious.

"Don't tell me you're too busy."

I stepped an inch deeper into his personal space. "I'll tell you whatever I want. You're in my house. You're not my boss."

He remained unfazed. "Ohio State's coming to our next home game."

"How do you—"

"*My* dad made a call. He let their staff know they really want to pay attention to the certified one-two punch of Donaldson and Webster. So, we probably wanna make sure they don't waste a trip. Though I could be making a poor assumption." He let it hang, leaning on the same great negotiating tactics I'd learned from my father.

Not wanting to make it too easy for him, I said, "What did you drive here?"

"Porsche 911."

"You might want to check it's still where you left it. I'll meet you outside." Then I shoved him into the hall, locked the door, and got dressed.

It took a moment to get loose, but once I was, me and Nate were money. We ran every route several times. Go. Slant. Curl. Nate's passes were laser accurate. He'd improved even more since the Blood Bowl. Playing without conscience.

I'd scoffed at the one-two-punch thing he'd said in the apartment, but he was throwing as good as five-star quarterbacks I'd played with at camps I went to last summer. I didn't think Ohio State had a shortage in great quarterbacks they could recruit. Still . . .

Kids and adults gathered to watch the display of speed and precision, cheering every pass I caught, though I began fumbling a few catches that should've been easy. Nate wasn't having it.

"Hey! Get your head right. Your hands are trash right now! What's with you?"

It was the audience. Off to the side, a good twenty yards between me and them, but what was the range on my ring? Would them stopping to see a future pro mean when they got home all of a sudden they'd want to try skydiving, parkour, lion taming? Or worse?

What if someone scary was too close to me right now?

Hands on hips, chest heaving while I checked the crowd, Book's words chilled me more than the autumn wind.

How would you even know who they are?

"Cade!" Nate barked. "Line up!"

I shook off the discomfort.

Our next home game was in three weeks. Senior Night.

Your football and your education, that's what YOU control.

Stay sharp, then.

It's what Pop would want.

Hours later, me and Nate looked like we'd stepped out of a pool. It's hard to sweat through a hoodie, but we did that and it felt good to move my body. When he packed up his gear in the Porsche, the trunk being in the front of the sports car, a bunch of Court kids gathered to gawk and I backed up several steps, despite the distance I put between me and them likely being futile. Nobody noticed how skittish I got because PORSCHE.

"Man, you rich?" one little boy asked.

Nate said, "Sure am."

"How much that car cost?" asked another.

"Hundred grand, but the more custom you go, it's going to get pricier."

The kids cheered like he'd spit a fire freestyle.

A little girl said, "You should get a green one. Green's my favorite color."

"Naw, shorty," Nate said. "Red or black. Those are the only acceptable colors for a Porsche."

"For real?"

"If you understand Porsches, yeah. You'll see one day."

It always bothered me how Nate spoke so casually about money. In front of these kids, I got a different sense of it, because he wasn't talking down to them. Nate didn't think his wealth was exceptional. He was wrong, but something about that *You'll see one day* was, I don't know, charming. I wasn't the only one noticing, unfortunately.

A couple of One-Eights had entered the park, eyes in our direction. I got close again, clapped Nate on the shoulder. "Let's go."

It was getting dark. He needed to be gone. Or someone in the Court might get a better understanding of a Porsche sooner than either of us liked.

On the short drive back to my building, he wanted to talk football, but we'd done enough of that. There was something else I wanted cleared up before I stepped foot on Neeson grounds Monday.

"You seen that NeesonFriedChicken account?" I asked.

"Yeah."

"You know who started it?"

Nate shook his head.

"Would you really tell me if you did know?"

"Depends on if I thought you'd go MMA on them and

get yourself suspended, messing up our season. I *don't* know, though, so it's not a call I gotta make."

"What's the vibe at school? Are people, I don't know, protesting it or something?"

He pulled to the curb in front of my building, chuckling.

Anger bubbled in me. "You think that garbage is funny?"

"No," he said plain, "I don't. But, my guy, the dude who founded our school was, like, in the Ku Klux Klan. Half our classmates' families come from plantation money. The whole school doesn't buy into NeesonFriedChicken, but enough do. I thought you were smart enough to know where you were."

I pressed back in my seat and considered how accurate everything he'd said was. I knew, just ignored it. Or confused the praise that came from my gameplay as progress. There were a few—very few—other Black kids at Neeson. Some walked the halls with their heads down and books tucked tight to their chest like armor, skirting around our white classmates like mice dodging traps. I'd gotten good at not noticing that part. *My* football and *my* education. That's what I controlled. I'd barely thought about how their week had been since that racist account dropped.

Aggravated, I asked, "Is your family different, then?"

"Yeah. We're from California."

"Is that a real answer?" Okay, scratch all that Nate's-kind-of-charming stuff from earlier.

"What do you want me to say? I'm about football and thought you were, too. Let's do what we do on the field, win a chip, get gone. Don't let some anonymous online coward get in the way."

Well, if Nate didn't sound like a leader right then . . .

I nodded, begrudgingly accepted the direction of my quarterback, and climbed from the car. He gave me some decent advice, so I returned the favor. "Drive right to the highway. Don't stop at any red lights if you don't have to."

"Why?"

"Just trust me. Hopefully I'll see you Monday."

BOOK

The word around the Court was Booker "Book" Payne was too smart to be a gangbanger. It was a sentiment shared by his mother, which was her primary reason for kicking him out when she assumed he'd gone down a path like his father.

"I ain't burying two men!" she'd screamed the last night they'd been under the same roof and she'd found the shoebox full of cash and fake credit cards he'd hid sloppily.

Gabby had curled up in the corner crying, begging him and their mom to stop fighting, while he'd crammed things in a duffel bag with no real destination, though he ended up sleeping at Romeo's awhile. The thing about it was, Book understood where his mother was coming from. He always had the ability to see a problem from multiple sides. So at the same time his mother's position infuriated him because he wasn't doing anything that would get him "buried." That's why Romeo, the former One-Eight leader, loved having Book around. He also thought Book was too smart to gangbang.

Book put Romeo and the rest of the gang on to nonviolent ways to get money. It started with stolen identities from the dark web rolled into fake credit cards. Those fake credit cards purchased real goods—TVs, jewelry, sneakers—that the gang resold at irresistible prices for one hundred percent profit. It always worked, it always earned, and while Book couldn't control everything the gang did with the proceeds (like buying drugs with the intent to distribute, the crime that eventually sent Romeo and other One-Eight leaders to jail), he'd been pitching Romeo on a scheme to invest the money in brokerage accounts under fake names instead of slinging dope.

Then the inevitable happened. Things changed. Treezy moved up, and he was completely committed to the style of gang life that would get a lot of people buried, eventually sending Book into hiding at the library during the day and climbing the rickety fire escape into Mr. Webster's old office at night.

Book, patient, with an ability to see the long game, could've kept that up for quite some time. Happily. Until Treezy went after Gabby.

She never confirmed it was him; she didn't have to. Now that she was in the equation, Book identified the variables and potential outcomes near instantly.

Variables included everything: weather, time of day, Treezy's mood in any given moment, the performance of the One-Eights in whatever schemes Treezy had initiated since the home invasions went south, so on and so on.

Potential worst outcome: In an effort to draw Book out, Treezy might kill Gabby. It was possible. Maybe not *probable*, but odds didn't matter when it came to Book's sister.

What he felt about the possibility was not fear but resolve, so he made his decision almost as fast as he'd considered Gabby's demise.

And that's what led to the change of heart that Book never planned on telling Cade about. He now believed Blade *was* better than Batman.

Nine p.m. on Saturday and full dark, Book left the library with no plan to return. Things would go either very right or very wrong tonight. Whatever happened, he was okay with it. Machiavelli said, "There are no perfectly safe courses; prudence consists in choosing the least dangerous ones."

The man was spitting bars with that one. You can't avoid danger, you gotta calculate the risk and *act*.

Just a ten-block walk back to the Court, and One-Eight territory. Saturdays, Treezy shot pool at the Cue It Up billiards joint, a spot Book passed unnoticed, with the brim of a baseball cap tugged low. A sideways glance confirmed Treezy was in the building, at his usual table with Rah-Rah Moore, another One-Eight, loud talking with money stacked by the corner pocket. Good.

Book moved on for the moment.

"Few are born bold" was something Robert Greene wrote in *The 48 Laws of Power*. Book had contemplated that the last few nights he slinked from the library to Mr. Webster's office to do quiet sweaty work he prayed no passersby noticed.

He realized now that his sudden shift to a man of action

was the biggest evidence that Cade's ring really did what he thought. Being fearless didn't mean getting sloppy, though. Book was way too smart for that.

The plan didn't come to him right away. Shreds of it were there from the beginning. Some questions needed answering first. Like, how do counterweight pulley systems work?

The library was still the best school in the world, so he'd put together a crash course on some basic engineering principles. Then it was a matter of prep, and the hardest part there was learning how to work the blowtorch.

By 10:30 p.m. things were as ready as they were going to get. Book approached the pool hall more excited than nervous. He imagined it was the feeling a rocket scientist had the minute before a liftoff. All would go as planned, or there'd be a catastrophic failure. It wasn't necessarily a coin toss, but it got the adrenaline pumping. Book flung his baseball cap in a trash bin on the curb, took a few deep breaths in front of the Cue It Up neon sign, then pounded on the window with his fist. Treezy finished pocketing the six ball before Rah-Rah dared tap his shoulder. His body language was all *WHAT? CAN'T YOU SEE I'M BUSY?* Until he followed Rah-Rah's pointed stare.

Book tipped his chin to Treezy, almost friendly, then slowly mouthed some obscenities. Treezy dropped his stick. The chase began.

This was the second-riskiest part of the plan. Book was

slim and swift, but he was more suited for desk work than long sprints. If the distance between Cue It Up and Lim's was much farther, Treezy, long limbed and athletic, might overtake him. Book had bet on two things: One, he could maintain a sprint without slowing or tripping—that adrenaline was mighty useful. Two, Treezy and Rah-Rah had been drinking at the pool hall.

Book maintained a gap between him and his pursuers all the way past Lim's—with Mr. Lim clocking the commotion through the window—and into the alley. Now, the riskiest part.

There'd been no real way to test the final element of the trap. In theory it should work, but the timing had to be precise, and Book was relying on his gut to pull it off.

So, Batman and Blade. For a long time Book overlooked Batman's literally fatal flaw, the rule he wouldn't break. His unwillingness to take permanent steps toward ridding Gotham of villains meant the bad guys always came back to do more harm. The Joker had paralyzed Batgirl and beaten Robin to death with a crowbar. Both tragedies preventable. If only . . .

Book ran beneath the raised fire escape stairs, slowing only to grab the steel ring he'd placed on the alley floor. A threaded wire ran from the ring through a series of eyelets he'd affixed to the wall. There was enough slack on the cable for him to run another dozen yards before the wire went taut, right when Treezy rounded the corner, gasping, just ahead of Rah-Rah.

"You trying to die tonight?" Treezy said, slow walking like the predator he was, ready to pounce. Too cocky to be mindful of his surroundings. Too reckless to be the leader of the local gang. Book had known it from the moment Treezy took power. Thanks to Cade's ring, and his insistence on Blade's superiority, he was in a great headspace to do something about it.

Blade was a vampire hunter. A monster slayer. His foes did not come back.

Now, Book had no illusions about defeating Treezy in whirling martial arts combat and driving a silver stake through his heart. He knew this was the real world. Physics would do.

The thing about pulleys and counterbalance systems is if the weights are disconnected, there's no more balance. Something heavy will fall hard and fast unless something impedes the motion—like the slim steel rod on the far end of Book's cable, the one holding the fire escape stairs in place since Book used an acetylene torch to sever the cables connecting its counterweight the night before.

Treezy stepped in the right spot, still talking. "I'mma take your head off, Book."

Book said, "Me first."

He yanked the cable.

The stairs fell. A few hundred pounds of rusted iron swinging with such force the bottom riser hitting the alley floor sounded like a bomb. The eighth tread up was the one that did the trick, the one that hit Treezy. The eggshell crack of the straight edge colliding with his forehead, triggering an explosion of fine red mist that swirled in the air as he collapsed, still, was horrifying. And satisfying.

It took a moment for the trailing One-Eight to understand. Rah-Rah spoke meekly, like a lost child calling for a parent. "Treezy?"

He was never going to answer.

"Hey!" a new voice shouted. Mr. Lim, outside his bulletproof cage with his shotgun leveled at Rah-Rah. "What you doing back here? What's wrong with him?"

The shotgun barrel swung toward the prone Treezy, then reacquired its original target. Though Rah-Rah would have a hard time answering questions when the authorities showed up.

The mastermind—a Blade convert with Batman's flair for exits—was gone.

32

The Do Not Disturb status on my phone was preset. Went on at midnight, went off at 6:00 a.m. automatically. At 6:01 on Sunday morning, my phone spasmed with all kinds of missed messages, vibrating itself off my nightstand, clattering to the floor. I pawed for it, not quite ready to open my eyes and break the spell of peaceful sleep.

A bunch of notifications. Maybe two dozen texts from Gabby. A few texts from other folks in the neighborhood who had my number. A news station alert because I wanted to know when the sportscasters discussed me, but I also got other stories around the area, and local news was breaking.

I read Gabby's stuff first. Was up and pulling on my sweats before I'd gotten through half her messages. More news alerts popped. All of them about Mr. Lim's store.

I must've been stumbling around the house like a bull, because Ma left her room cinching the belt of her robe. "What's wrong?"

"Something happened at Lim's last night."

"Is he okay?"

"I don't know. I'm going to see."

"Be careful," she said through a yawn.

Outside, Gabby was on the sidewalk, waiting. It was chilly out, enough to see breath. My always-cold-even-in-summer friend seemed unbothered. The events she'd detailed in her text must have taken her mind off the temperature. The message that had me most distracted was the four-word bubble.

Gabby
They saying Treezy dead

In Jacobs Court there was always a mysterious "they" who had CIA-level intel on everything that ever happened. Whether the information was accurate was always the question. Something as monumental as the most troublesome gang leader in the neighborhood getting bodied tended to be less ambiguous.

We started the walk together, and she relayed what was too much to text. "Maisha Morris lives across the street from Lim's and said she heard a big boom last night. Twenty minutes later the cops were there, then an ambulance, then a fire truck, though the firefighters only stood around. The whole street got blocked off and they wouldn't even let people who'd parked on the block get their cars. She said there was a body bag."

I only half listened, remembering my last run-in with Treezy. *Where Book at?*

When we got to Lim's, the scene Maisha described was over. The street wasn't blocked. No first responders were present. The store was dark and locked. It looked like it did any other morning because things snap back to normal like rubber bands around here.

Gabby had her phone out, typing. A moment later my phone vibrated. Our group text.

Gabby
Me and Cade are at Lim's.
Where are you?

After a few heartbeats, I said, "Come on."

We rounded the building and it was in the shadows of the alley that the cops had stretched their *Caution: Crime Scene* tape, blocking the way forward.

"What happened here?" Gabby asked.

The fire escape stairs were down. Maybe we should bypass the tape, go up, and see if Book was in Pop's office, but me and Gabby's phones pinged at the same time.

Book
I'm downtown got a room

Me and Gabby were very confused.

Me
Where? Details fool

Book
Doesn't matter

220

Book
I'll hit you up later

Book
Long night

                                            Me
You know about Treezy?

My phone shook. Not with a response from Book—he never answered that question. On the screen a photo of me, Leek, Ma, and Pop. Incoming call from my mother.

I accepted and said, "Hey."

"Come home. We're going to the hospital."

My heart slammed the back of my sternum. "Is he okay?"

"He's asking for us. We should go."

I hung up and started to explain to Gabby, but she waved me off. "I heard. Do you want me to come with?"

I kind of did, but I knew she wanted to catch up with Book. "Thank you, but I'll be okay. Find him."

Something in my gut repulsed at the idea of Gabby being too close to Book right now, same as if she was going to find a walking, talking lightning rod. But I couldn't dwell. My fast walk became a jog became a sprint. Though I didn't know if I was running toward something or away.

33

When we arrived, the flat stares exchanged between Ma and Pop felt like watching TV on mute. Something important transmitted between them that I had no hope of making out. Pop eyed Leek and said, "Hey there, Muppet!"

"Hey, Daddy," she said back, her phone stowed in her pocket for once.

Another silent communiqué passed between Ma and Pop before he directed his attention to me. "Missed you yesterday."

A twinge of guilt shot through me like electricity. He eased my mind almost immediately. "I'm glad you took a break from this place. Your mom said you were working out with Nate."

I nodded.

"Good. That's good. Hey, Cade, let me holler at you for a minute."

Ma had already grasped Leek's shoulder and was ushering her away. "Text when you two want company."

Alone, finally, I took the chair next to his bed. A hard thing, like walking at the bottom of the pool. That's how much I'd been terrified of this moment. "Hey, Pop."

"Hey."

"How you feeling?"

"Decent." He scooted up in bed. "I'm coming home."

I leaned in, gripping my armrests and resisting the urge to pump my fist like an end zone celebration after a touchdown. "The doctors said you're good. That's what I'm talking about!"

His smile was small. "I *asked* them to send me home. That's where I want to be, son."

My joy deflated. This was what I'd been most scared of. Not getting into the whole thing with Skinner, but the thing I'd felt creeping toward me in the dark for the last couple of years. I said the words: "There's nothing else they can do."

He shook his head. "There are things I can try. Experimental and expensive and probably ineffective."

"We should try them anyway," I insisted, trying not to let anger leak into my voice. Anger for Skinner. The monster who did this to him.

"The doctors have a plan to keep me comfortable. A way to let me do this part in my own space."

Let me do this part.

I swallowed a lump.

"It's okay, son. I'm not afraid."

"You should be! You're not feeling what you're supposed to feel. If you were afraid, you'd try harder. That's on me and it's not right."

Then I was hunched over, head in hands, sobbing.

"None of this is on you." He stretched beyond what could

223

be comfortable in that bed, his ribs pressing into the safety rail to rest his hand on my shoulder.

Lifting my chin felt like curling eighty-pound dumbbells. My tears were shame pouring out of me, but I wanted him back in a position that wouldn't strain him more. Every exertion deducted from whatever time he had left in my simple estimation. I got him settled and stated the fact. "You're not scared."

"I'm not," he said.

"You don't understand." I lifted my ring hand to show him.

He cut me off. "No, *you* don't. From the time I was diagnosed I haven't been afraid of *the dying*."

That . . . confused me.

He said, "You don't remember your grandma, do you?"

I shook my head. Ma's parents died when she was a teenager. Never met them. Pop's pop—Kincade Webster II—passed before my father finished college. But Pop's mom didn't die until I was three years old, so the clearest memories of her typically required some hazy photo of baby me sitting on her lap as a trigger—even those recollections could've been fabrications. Me *imagining* I remembered her. I feel like she was nice, though. Pop and Ma loved her. I'm sure I did, too.

"When my dad died," Pop said, "I was devastated. The universe robbed us of time we should've had. God got it wrong. All the stuff anyone thinks when they lose a parent, probably. I went through a dark, dark time. You may feel some of that because you don't know the rest."

"The rest of what?"

"The rest of the game."

I flashed on Book's Checkered Game of Life.

"When your grandma died, I was so very sad. But it was nothing like how I felt losing Pop because by that time I had you."

Leaning in, I wanted more. I wasn't seeing the connection.

"After you were born I was absolutely terrified every day. Once when you had just started walking, you fell and whacked your head on the stairs leading up to the apartment. You were woozy and kept wanting to doze off. I drove me, you, and your mom to the hospital like I was in one of those *Fast and Furious* movies." He did a weird, throaty Vin Diesel impression: *"It's about family."*

I laughed. This was not a place I'd ever thought I'd do that.

"You were fine, of course. But I thought you weren't. The pain of that—it made my father's funeral seem like a birthday party. There can't be anything more horrible than losing a child. That's the worst fear. You see what I'm getting at?"

Maybe. "When Grandma died, *you* were there. Her worst fear never came true. She never lost you."

"Yes. I was alive. Healthy. Doing okay. She won the game in the best way. You and Leek are alive and well and incredible. Do I wish I'd be around to see what you do with the next few years? See if you decide to get married, or have children of your own . . . yeah, who wouldn't? I don't get that choice, so I'm going to take this *W* and be okay with it. One request, and it's one you can completely ignore if you want. I don't own you, and I'm not going to try and control you from the other side. But I'm at least going to ask."

I was crying again, but not hysterically. What he said had gotten through a little. "What is it?"

"If you have a child, will you keep the name going? Kincade Webster V."

"Why?" I asked, but backpedaled, thinking it sounded harsh. "I mean, I'm not against it, I just want to know the reason."

"As you should! Keep that curious mind, son. Always ask your questions. My dad told me his dad, the first of us, said there's power in names. Each generation—each iteration—of Websters has done better than the last. From factory worker to small business owner to lawyer"—he patted his chest—"to whatever you end up doing, whether that's pro ball or something else great. Life has a lot of different games, and I'm betting the Kincade Websters of the world can keep this particular win streak going."

I nodded. Yeah. I could do that.

"I don't expect you to not feel sad," he said. "You will grieve. What I'm trying to get across is that's going to pass, and the good stuff will remain."

The good stuff. Maybe. I said, "I need to ask you something important. What's your deal with Skinner?"

The entire vibe changed. The air became charged. He shook his head, almost angry. "No."

226

"Pop. Don't do that. You just talked to me about the hardest thing ever; this shouldn't be what you shut down on. You said I should always ask my questions. This question is important."

He sat up, animated. "Did you not hear what I said? Having a kid was terrifying. Thinking about that kid anywhere near Arvin Skinner is—" His confusion was plain.

"You said 'having a kid *was* terrifying.' Not anymore, though." It wasn't a question.

Pop struggled for a response, and that wasn't him at all. "What's going on with me, Cade? You sound like you know."

I showed him my ring. "Skinner has a store, and it's not like any store you've ever been in."

I told him almost everything.

34

The story wasn't getting easier to tell. We sat quietly awhile after. Too long for my comfort. "You don't believe me."

"I don't know," Pop said, honest.

"Cursed rings and wishes and all. I know it sounds ridiculous."

Pop shook his head. "Not as much as you think. The thing that's selling me most on your story is that hearing you even utter Skinner's name should terrify me. I never, ever wanted him close to you, Leek, or your mom. You're telling me you're tied up with him and all I feel is anger. Like I could tear him apart. That's wrong."

"I found a newspaper article about you representing some of his tenants in a lawsuit. What happened?"

The muscles in his face flexed, showing the fine contours of his skull because he'd gotten so thin. "The most bizarre case I ever took. The daughter of one of his elderly tenants came to me first. Her mother's apartment was in extreme disrepair. Leaky pipes. Splintering wood floors. A dangerous radiator that'd burned her grandbaby during a family visit. The daughter wanted to sue Skinner for not performing fixes he was responsible for as the building's owner. She brought me a copy of the lease, and it was insane.

"Among standard property rental clauses were sentences in Latin, or other languages I didn't recognize. There were paragraphs printed backward. Watermark symbols that made your eyes hurt when you looked at them. The first night I spent reviewing that lease line by line, I started to feel like a bunch of people were in the room with me looking over my shoulder even though I was alone. It was so weird. But also actionable. I put together a case to help the woman. And not just her."

I knew how important a solid, correct contract was because Pop wanted me ready if I ever got the opportunity to play in the pros. A prepared person left nothing open to interpretation when signing away chunks of their life. Every promise, every demand, even the signature itself needed to be above reproach, or you left yourself open to trouble later. With my father on the case, Skinner had a problem.

Pop went to Skinner's buildings and left business cards for others to call if they were having repair issues—those who did brought him their leases, too.

"Every lease was different but equally strange. There were faint, gruesome drawings under some of the text. Inverted Bible passages. Stuff like, 'If there are children on the premises, they must not pray to benign deities after sunset.' I'll never forget that one."

Even I was caught off guard after all I'd seen. "Seriously?"

"One lease was on paper that didn't feel right, and I didn't bother reading it because it was leathery and warm to the touch."

I said, "Why were people signing them?"

"People in need of housing get desperate. They believe if they make too much fuss, someone less discerning will come along and snatch the apartment. They're not wrong. I began to believe Skinner's buildings were filled with the most desperate people in the city. The more I looked into him, the more I believed those were the tenants he sought. I never understood why." He stared at my ring. "I'm starting to."

Suffering is the dividend.

"You took him to court."

"Oh yes. I went ready to fight. I'm talking war! But on the day of, Skinner wasn't in the courtroom. His lawyer showed, a high-priced downtown guy, and rolled over immediately. They agreed to every one of our terms. Whole thing took maybe ten minutes. It was strange."

"Why was it like that?"

"I've thought about it a lot over the years. I think maybe Skinner didn't want me exposing the details of his insane contracts in a public forum. What I was doing was limited to my clients, it wasn't going to keep him from doing business with other people. Other victims. Anyway, we won compensation for my group, and they got free of those bogus leases. If only that'd been the end of it."

Pop coughed and didn't stop. It was a bad fit, one that had the heavy hospital bed rocking with each heaving wretch. I stood, ready to call a nurse, but he shook his head, indicated with his hands that he'd be fine. I poured him a cup of water from a pitcher on his bed's tray. He got a few sips down, then squeezed his eyes shut, willing his body into compliance.

Wheezy, he said, "My plaintiffs and I were gathered in the courthouse hall discussing next steps when Skinner emerged from the street. I smelled him before he pushed through the double doors, like ten people on a smoke break. He was full of purpose and rage, leveling his gaze on my clients, each heavy exhale seemed to pump more of that cigarette stench into the air. His lawyer tried advising him to walk away, but Skinner knocked the man's hand from his shoulder and got close. He told my clients, 'You think we're done,' then told me, 'You think you helped them.'"

Pop was slow telling the next part. I felt his shame.

He said, "I tried to respond. I tried to be the legal protector those people needed. I couldn't get a word out. I was choking on smoke. I couldn't see it, there was nothing visible in the air, but I couldn't breathe. We all began hacking. Tears in eyes, barely able to stand. Skinner walked away smiling. Only once he was gone could we breathe again."

Pop stopped talking. I offered him another glass of water. He declined. I thought about offering him the part of the story I'd held back, that Skinner did something to him and the others that day. Couldn't decide if that was right or cruel.

Instead, I asked, "Do you know where the plaintiffs are now?"

"Dead. Every one of them."

"How—how long have you known?"

"Since the first of them passed."

I asked my next question carefully. "Don't you think that's weird?"

"Of course. I thought maybe it had something to do with Skinner's buildings. Asbestos or something. I spoke to inspectors who'd been through the dwellings, and they found no problems like that. There was little to be done, especially once I started declining. The strangeness wasn't changing the inevitable."

He stared beyond me. Beyond the hospital walls.

"Pop?"

"Thank you, son."

"For what?"

"I believe your wish was real and in this case a blessing. I'd be a mess considering my fate and yours if fear was a factor right now. I'd be advocating for you to take your mother and sister somewhere far away. Instead, I feel levelheaded. I can advise you as I would anyone else who was in trouble. It's an odd disconnect. Useful."

"It . . . is?"

He stroked his chin. "Eddie's your play. You gotta talk to him again."

My stomach sank into the floor beneath us. "I don't want to go back to that store."

Pop rolled his eyes. "Does the store have a phone number?"

"Oh, um, wait." I pulled up the listing for Wilson's Pawn & Loan. "Yes, phone number."

"Let's start there."

I did start there. Where I finished was much more disturbing than I could've anticipated.

35

We were discussing strategy—what to say if I got Eddie on the phone, *how* to say it—when Ma and Leek returned. We'd been talking an hour by then, and I guess they got tired of waiting. Fair. Ma asked, "Mind if we join you?"

"Come on in," Pop said with exaggerated enthusiasm. He squeezed my knee, so I knew we weren't done.

Nurses roamed in, tapping things on their tablets. Pop's doctor came after lunch and didn't tell us anything new. A person I'd never seen before came in the early afternoon. Pop introduced us. Her name was Janice.

When she shook my hand, she said, "You're a stellar football player, I'm told."

"I do okay."

"Good, good. Has Mr. Webster explained my role to you all?"

I exchanged glances with Ma. She was as clueless as I was.

Janice smiled tightly, spoke plain. She would've been affected by my ring now, but I didn't get the impression her directness was new or confusing to her. She'd said these things many times. "I'm a palliative specialist here to discuss Mr. Webster's comfort plan."

A palliative specialist. I'd come across the term a few times when reading up on Pop's condition. They told you how to make death easier for the dying person. They also offered advice on how to make things easier for those left behind, but that felt like a job no one could ever get good at.

The hospital released Pop around four that afternoon. Ma sent me and Leek to bring the car around.

"You should let me drive," Leek said like she thought that would ever happen on my watch.

"I'd have to be real desperate."

"How about real *lucky*?"

I pulled her into a gentle headlock. "Come on."

On the way home Pop sat in the back with Ma, creating a bizarro effect of Leek and me looking like parents navigating a road trip. Pop asked me to turn on the old-school station. Ma, whose taste swayed toward podcasts and audiobooks, seemed appalled. "50 Cent is old-school now?"

Pop said, "I know, right."

I couldn't hold in my laugh.

By the time we reached the Court, wasn't much funny. We passed Lim's. Pop pressed his face to the window, observing the police tape crisscrossing the alleyway like neon webs. I thought he might comment since I'd told him what I suspected of Book's—and my—involvement in last night's incident, but he didn't. We had other concerns.

Getting him up the stairs was a challenge because, despite

235

his good attitude, he was weak. It occurred to me I should carry him—it'd be easy. I nearly broke down sobbing again when he made the request before I offered.

"Just this time," he said, apologetic. "I won't make you do it again."

It was hard not to read too much into that.

The sun was almost down. It was gloomy in the apartment. Ma and Leek turned on most of the lights and that's when I knew the gloom I felt had nothing to do with light or dark. I needed to make a call I didn't want to make. Needed to do it fast. Because now that Pop knew, I wanted all the advice I could get from him for as long as I could get it.

No need to pretend the time we had left was long, though.

In my room, I brought up the number I'd saved in contacts and had a hard time believing I could simply call a place like the pawnshop.

Eddie answered on the second ring. "Wilson's" was all he said.

"Skinner's," I corrected.

"Yeah. Skinner's. Hey, Cade. You wanna swing by and get me tortured again? I got no plans tonight."

Him joking like that . . . was it a good or bad sign? Didn't know. So, I told the truth. "I don't want to ever come back to that place."

"You're a little smart, then. Not a lot. Not that it matters. You're on the road now."

"What road?"

He chuckled.

Before Ma and Leek interrupted us, Pop had explained, very rationally and robotically, the significance of another Eddie convo.

When I was putting together my case against Skinner, he'd said, *there was no greater asset than the people he'd done wrong. The worse he'd treated them, the more eager they were to take him down. Eddie sounds aggrieved. You need him.*

Eddie wasn't sounding like an asset, just bitter. Maybe that was on me. Maybe I wasn't saying the right things. "Is there something I can do for you? I'll help you, if you help me."

"Help you do what?" His voice was borderline vicious.

"Reverse my wish. I felt like we were getting into that last time. Before he showed up."

"Brother, I don't want to get your hopes up. I've never seen a wish reversed by anyone but the old man. When he does it, it's not to improve your situation. Believe me. So, if that's all you called for . . ."

I dug my nails into my thigh, frustrated by hearing the exact thing I didn't want to hear. "How powerful is he?"

"Are you crazy, kid?"

"I don't understand any of this. Don't you think I should? All the warnings you're giving me about staying away from him and don't take any more deals, like, I can't make sense of that without, I don't know, a scouting report."

"A scouting report?" he scoffed. "Athletes, I swear."

The line was quiet. Maybe dead. I said, "Hello?"

"I'm not talking about him," he said.

I flopped onto my bed, defeated. I'd tell Pop this was no-go and hope he had a new play. That's what I was going to do.

Then Eddie said, "Not here."

I sat straight up. "Where?"

The line went quiet again. So quiet I thought he changed his mind.

Eddie finally said, "Go to sleep. Dream of the store. I'll be there."

He hung up.

I stared at my phone.

"What?"

36

Pop didn't need to know about the dream stuff. He was tired by the time we got him settled, and his evening meds knocked him out for the night. Ma and Leek got to bed while I stared at the ceiling wondering how I'd *make myself dream of the pawnshop.*

Eyes squeezed shut, I tried repeating the word in a low whisper. "Pawnshop. Pawnshop. Pawnshop."

That kept me awake more than anything.

My ring was on the nightstand. Maybe slipping it on would help? So I did that, halfway expecting some portal to open beneath me and send me tumbling into the dreamworld. No, that didn't happen either.

Eventually I settled on a white noise app. Slipped into that middle space where you know you're dozing and that urge to rock yourself out of it is fading, then—

I was on a road.

Every road I'd ever seen had stuff beside it. Houses. Trees. Landmarks. This road bordered nothing. The shoulders were swirling gray mist I didn't want to touch, so I walked the center line in a direction I didn't choose. It's like I was being towed by a heavy chain and hook buried in my chest.

The farther I went, the faster I went, that strange mist blurring past. At this speed, I could almost see shapes in the vapor. Faces. Big as my apartment building. The Neeson comms director, Sheila. Coach. Nate. Brady. Leek.

My sister's appearance struck me as wrong. Like those number puzzles where you're supposed to predict the next in a series, but one of the clues was a typo.

Then I was still, and the road ended. Right at the entrance to the pawnshop.

I pushed through the door to the familiar shelves and stock behaving in unfamiliar ways. Some items were levitating, frozen in the air. I ducked under an old-timey pressure cooker and sidestepped a floating wheelbarrow. The counter was farther away than made sense, like standing on the ocean shore and spotting a ship near the horizon. I took a step, and the counter was right there. I rested my hands on it, my ring clinking against the glass.

"Eddie," I called, the name feeling thick in my mouth. Was I using my mouth? This was the way of dreams.

Eddie was here. He didn't come from a back room and didn't appear. He was just here.

"You made it," he said, amused. "I didn't know if you could."

"What is this? How did I get here?"

"Ruin Road got you here." Eddie's face scrunched. "When you're asleep and dreaming, you're on the road between realms. Souls travel this path, temporarily or permanently.

Your best dreams are you skirting against a paradise. Heaven, for lack of a better term. Your nightmares—that's brushing against a worse place. Then there's all sorts of stuff in between—that's when you get into your super weird dreams. The pawnshop is located at an intersection. You and me are taking advantage of a rest stop right now."

"Why Ruin Road?"

Eddie shrugged. "Most folks only going one way."

"Oh." I felt wobbly-weak. "Wild."

Eddie grabbed my hand; I felt stronger. "Steady. It's easy to slip back to wakefulness. If that happens, the conversation's over."

"Can't happen. I need information."

"I'll go ahead and give you the bad news, then. You won't remember much of this. The benefit of communicating this way is Skinner can't surprise us. This is the secure line, so to speak. The *problem* with communicating like this is when you wake up, you'll only recall snippets, so write down what you can fast. Everything else will resolve into vague feelings. Déjà vu and whatnot. That can be useful, too, but maybe not in the way you're hoping."

That woozy-wobbly feeling was overwhelming. The dream rotated around me. I had questions, but it was like the one time I hung with my teammates while they were drinking and Brett, barely able to stand, started asking all kinds of overly emotional stuff like would we all be brothers forever, and what did it feel like to fall in love?

Instead of asking something important, I said, "Why are you mad at me, Eddie?"

"I'm not."

"You act like it."

He huffs. "I'm not mad at *you*, just *mad*. Mad I'm stuck in the store. Mad Skinner can do what he wants to me."

"Did you make a wish, too?"

"No. It's worse than that. The whole wish system . . . my father invented it."

Now we were going down a path I couldn't control. In that way this was still very dreamlike. I wanted to change direction, but I couldn't. I uttered another question I hadn't intended to ask. "Why'd he do something like that?"

"Big Eddie wasn't a great guy, and the longer I'm forced to sit and ponder and suffer, I wonder if anyone who opens a pawnshop is. The whole nature of the business is predatory. Someone comes in with some prized possession in a time of need, you lowball them for it. If they come back for their stuff, they gotta give up more than they started with. If you're coming off the street to make a straight-up purchase, you don't really know what you're getting until it's too late, you know."

That part hit like a truck. I did know.

"The cutthroat nature is what attracted Skinner to him," Eddie said.

"I don't understand."

"My father, when he knew he was almost out of time, told

242

me a lot of things I didn't believe because your mind looks for the rational. So him saying he once explained the business model to this rich old man as 'selling wishes to fools' and that old man took it literally, then became a partner . . . what do I say to that? I shrugged it off and kept the cash register ringing. I saw the numbers and knew the money wasn't making sense. The cars me and my dad drove. The house he bought for my mom. We shouldn't have been able to afford that stuff. Yet it never seemed like a struggle. I didn't question what we were selling, who we sold it to, and what happened to them a second beyond them handing over their dough and carrying newly purchased trouble into the world. As long as my family was doing okay, I remained willfully, gleefully ignorant.

"When my dad keeled over in the shop, right in front of me, I *saw* his soul standing over his body. Saw the confusion and horror as Skinner rolled up in a wicked black Cadillac. All of this was happening in the space between living and dead. No one who's alive is supposed to see the calculus behind the universe, but I got a big glimpse for being too close to Skinner's corruption. Skinner took my dad's soul, and since fathers and sons are bound by blood, he shackled me to his wayward wish of a store to keep the business running. Been here ever since."

"How long?"

"Since 2006. I think. Time's funny here."

Jesus. "Is . . . is Skinner going to collect me when I die?"

"You didn't make that kind of deal. Selling your soul is

more difficult than you can imagine because eager sellers are made worthless by their own misguided desire. Wringing suffering from you, a good kid from what I can tell, and those around you pays immediate dividends in Skinner's twisted economy. That wish of yours keeps him profiting off your pain, and his only incentive to undo the wish is a bigger payday. Your soul is the bigger payday because you *don't* want to sell it, but he'll look for a way to make you think you *have* to. You ever look around at the state of the world? How bad things seem everywhere?"

"I focus on my football and my education. That's what I control." It was more honest than I wanted to be. I was ashamed.

Eddie said, "Think about what fossil fuels have done to the planet. What drugs—I'm talking the prescription stuff as much as the streets—have done to people. Institutions that sacrifice the innocence of children to protect their religious standing in the world. How every day someone's going to die on one side of an imaginary line in the dirt because someone on the other side says they need to know their place. On and on. Everyone trying to squeeze more and more gains by breaking bodies and spirits. Even if they say it's about money, they mean power. If you look back far enough, dig deep enough, you'll find they all started with some kind of wish, too."

My knees felt weak and I couldn't tell if that was the dream or the ramifications of what he was saying sinking in. "All that is Skinner's doing?"

Eddie shook his head. "No. I think his dominion's relatively small. Parts of this city, maybe a little beyond. Those huge institutions are what he reveres. He speaks of them with envy, calls them brilliant. There are worse Skinners out there."

To think that monster, with his claws sunk into so many in my neighborhood, who collects wayward souls and was holding me captive with my own ill-spoken words, was a *small-timer*!

Eddie let go of my hand. The dream tilted like a capsizing boat about to dump me overboard.

I said, "Why'd you let go?"

"I didn't. You did?"

"I— What?" Dreams, man. This sucked. The shop tilted more and I rushed to ask what I could before time was up. "How do you know so much?"

Eddie spoke fast, surely sensing the short time as I did. "He gets chatty sometimes, especially when things are going well for him, which usually means they're going very bad for someone else. He's told me things that don't always make sense, though I've figured out some of it. Skinner has a boss. Maybe that boss has a boss. These beings are powerful, malicious, and not of our world. Their influence seeps into our realm, into us. We mimic them."

Eddie seemed far away. I repeated what he'd said. "We mimic them."

"That's what used to scare me most. Until you came along. Now I'm somewhat liberated. I can make moves I would've been terrified to consider before. Thank you for that."

"Why," I asked, "is people being unafraid around me a bad thing? I didn't mean it that way. It shouldn't be."

"It may not be a bad thing for everyone. That doesn't matter for Skinner's purposes. If an investor gets an asset that's worth a dollar and it makes them an extra dollar, it doesn't matter that it's *only a dollar*. It's one hundred percent profit to them. Double what they put in."

It's like he was shouting and I could barely hear him. I yelled, "I don't understand."

"Suffering is the dividend. Pain is the point. It doesn't have to harm *everyone*, as long as it harms *someone*. It's all profit to him."

There was a sound like wind whooshing past me, a sensation of fast travel. I could barely see Eddie in the distance as I was yanked back to the waking world, though I still heard him over the noise. I screamed the most important question. "Is there any way to help me?"

The last thing he shouted was "No."

I snapped awake. Sat upright in my bed, dripping sweat.

Quickly, I navigated to Notes in my phone and tried to type things that were rapidly fading.

Ruin Road

Make me think I have to sell

Suffering = dividend, Pain . . . point. No help.

What? What else?

Most of it was gone. Except one thing that lingered the way nightmares do.

We mimic them.

I closed the app.

37

My return to Neeson was rough from the moment I rolled out of bed later that morning. I hadn't gotten much sleep after the dream, and I couldn't help myself, so I watched new NeesonFriedChicken videos on the bus over. Not my best idea.

The account started on some weird "history" lessons about all the good past Neeson scholars have done for the country—the world!—and how all they got in return was hate from the people they helped who couldn't help themselves. Again paired with the photos of select Black Neeson kids. I didn't make the cut this time, but that seemed the same level of insult as being prominently featured at that point. NeesonFriedChicken was talking about all of us.

A few of my teammates greeted me in the hall, said the things you're supposed to say about hoping my pop was doing better, and if I needed anything let them know. I barely heard them because I kept silently interrogating every white face, familiar or unfamiliar, that passed. *Was it you? Did you make the account?* Even if the judge in my head felt it couldn't be him, or her, or them, I had to wonder if whoever was in my line of sight cosigned that racist trash through their Finsta.

Nate joined us, his words from Saturday ringing in my head. *I thought you were smart enough to know where you were.*

The hall was too loud and full. What once felt luxurious and spacious was more like a constricting tunnel. I wanted away from everyone.

"I'm headed to homeroom," I told my teammates.

When I broke away from them, a stocky redheaded boy I didn't know stepped in my path like a basketball player taking a charge. I stopped short of running him over. Arched an eyebrow. "What?"

The redhead, parroting sentiments featured prominently on the NeesonFriedChicken account, said, "I'm tired of you walking around like you don't know how good you have it."

"Excuse me?"

He poked his index finger into my sternum like he was trying to touch my spine. It hurt. "From the moment you got here you've thought you're better than us. Because you're big, and fast, and can catch a ball."

"I don't even know who you are." I envisioned wrapping my fist around his finger and yanking down until I heard the bone snap. The mood I was in, it might've gone that way. Until I looked around. Other classmates flanked him. All of them white, all their faces blank. Matter-of-fact. It registered that I'd interpreted the redhead's words as rage filled, but they weren't.

His voice was flat, like someone reading a book report aloud halfheartedly. Casually fearless when he said, "We

249

gotta listen to how all white people are bad, and how we didn't earn anything, and how we're racists."

"You're delusional. No one's said that to you." *My* words . . . definitely full of rage. I smacked his finger away but granted him the mercy of leaving the bone intact. When I attempted to sidestep him, he moved with me.

He crossed his arms, stood his ground. A larger crowd formed, backing him.

Inside me, a war. The flight and fight battling. The crowd backing him had surrounded me.

Black guys are supposed to be the terrifying ones. I always hated that notion, passed down from generation to generation to justify any and everything that's ever cost us a beating, a maiming, or our lives. It's why I'd made that stupid wish, even if I didn't know that's what I was really doing at the time. I never anticipated *not* being terrifying might be more dangerous.

That old notion might've given me some leverage. A way to bluff my way out of this with some loud talk and flexed muscle. This quiet mob wouldn't fall for it because I'd made them immune.

"You got something you want to say?" the boy asked, leaning in. I could smell his sour breath.

The others stepped in, too, giving the crowd the feel of a giant fist clenching around me.

Hands by my sides. Loose. No quick movements.

The warning bell sounded.

Cautiously I said, "I need to get to homeroom."

His cheeks and forehead flared with real anger. "We *all* do. See how it works when *no one* gets special treatment!"

There was light, slow applause from somewhere and a bunch of my classmates joined in.

Apparently satisfied with a perceived victory, the red-head boy whose name I'd never learned smirked and strolled away. Mission complete, I guess. Other witnesses surged around me while I spun in a slow circle, as paranoid as the new guy in the prison yard worried about getting shivved in the back. I no longer had a desire to unmask the creator of NeesonFriedChicken. That account was everyone, unleashed.

Through a break in the crowd, I spotted a smiling face and hated myself a little for how much it comforted me.

"Cade. Come here." Brady waved me over.

A few folks kept ogling me but most dispersed to their destinations. Me and Brady weren't in the same homeroom, so he better say what he needed to quick. "Yeah?"

He turned his phone so I could see. "Since we last talked I've been checking pawnshops in the city. It's wild because there are so many. But I'm wondering if this might be the place?"

It was the Maps app on his display. He'd found Wilson's—now Skinner's—Pawn & Loan.

I smacked the phone from his hand, and it hit the wall, then the floor, where it landed face down with the sharp crack of glass. Cursed at him. "What's wrong with you?"

Of course he was shocked, maybe hurt, because I'd never talked to him like that before. Something else flashed across his face that was neither of those things. I already knew it wasn't fear—I excluded that from every interaction now. It triggered something in me, though, something unsettling, like the moment between the lightning and thunder of a close storm.

Then it was gone and he was on his knees, retrieving his phone.

Only a few people saw what happened. All snickered. It sucked, I knew it did. My concerns were bigger than Brady's bruised pride. I said, "That's not the store. Don't go there."

I went to class and didn't think about him again until he was delivering a clean practice jersey to my locker later that day. As it should be.

38

Routine set in, as wild as that sounded. Ma worked from home to keep an eye on Pop. He slept a lot, so when I got in late after practice, she was often in bed with him and Leek, each of them holding one of his hands. I'd sit at the foot of the bed, gripping his knobby knee through the blanket. He'd force his eyes open and grin and wheeze something like, "The Webster gang all together." Then slip away again.

Whenever he dozed that way, my strange dream from the other night tugged at me. Something about being close to the border of something. I couldn't piece it together.

Football practice became useful in a way it hadn't in a long time. Knowing the effect I had on everyone around me, and how that translated to bolder, more dangerous play on the field, got me better at reading ill intent and ending a play faster, whether that meant running out of bounds to avoid a tackle or shifting into another gear to dust defenders and score the ball quickly. We had a mostly easy schedule except for the last home game, our rivals, Belmont Prep. Still, the players I'd face weren't as talented as us, or even Forestbrook, so I'd be able to keep myself safe through the end of the regular season.

What that meant for the playoffs, when we'd be facing better competition—what it meant for me in college, where every player was among the best of the best—I pushed to the back of my mind.

Toward the end of that first week, Ma took Leek to pick up dinner—maybe at Pop's request—giving us the first bit of alone time since the hospital. I got some pillows wedged behind his back to prop him up, making breathing easier for him, and he asked, "You talk to Eddie?"

"I did," I said. "He's not ready to help."

The lie was simpler than getting into the dream stuff.

"Yet. Persistence is—" He coughed, cleared his throat, then went into the most violent coughing fit I'd ever seen from him. I don't know if I hopped off his bed or the convulsions threw me off, but I was on my feet, grabbing the water bottle, and he waved it away, somehow managing to get one word out. "Ice."

I rushed to the kitchen and scooped ice chips into a cup. When I returned, he was grinding his fist into his sternum like something inside him needed to be tightened. He saw me and didn't bother hiding the deep concern that darkened his brow. He was so exhausted he could barely keep his eyes open when he said, "Could you put some in my mouth, Kincade?"

Of course I did. He crunched a few chips and fell asleep with my fingers hovering halfway between his lips and the cup.

I tucked him in. Reported what happened to Ma when she got back. Then I went to sleep. Rough and dreamless.

Like I said, routine.

By Friday—game day—things felt as close to normal as they ever did. I trudged through my classes (with my head down, avoiding eye contact with most of the Neeson students because I now knew the seething resentment many of them felt for me, and I wasn't looking for additional enemies), I gathered with my teammates in the field house, got ready for war. The thirty-minute ride to the competition's school had the whole bus rocking in a way that might've gotten us yelled at before, but now the driver had been exposed to my ring, so he let it be, unfazed.

The game itself was what I expected, and I managed it well. I'd begun noticing how the most dangerous fearless opponents were the repressed-anger guys. I didn't need to know anything else about the defenders who were willing to sacrifice life and limb to hit me. They were the ones who'd been wanting to hurt people for a long time and suddenly felt unleashed. They were wild cards that messed up my stats because I let them push me out of bounds so easily. Safer that way.

Coach was irritated at me for not gutting out the contact on those plays, but ultimately we did our thing, winning 32 to 12.

Changing in the visitors' locker room, I'd handed over my jersey and pads to Brady, who hadn't said two words to me since I snapped on him in the hall. I thanked him for taking care of the gear; he grumble-nodded, then trudged along. When we got back to Neeson, I was going to pull him aside to apologize. It was the right thing to do. While I considered exactly what to say, Coach's shadow fell over me.

"We need to talk," he said, motioning for me to follow.

We walked into a corridor leading to the parking lot. I braced myself for the verbal beatdown. My yards were below my average. I only scored one of our touchdowns. I'd probably be running laps on Monday.

He placed both hands on my shoulders. "Listen, do you have all your things? Whatever you brought with you."

"Huh? Sure. I think."

"Me and you are going to take an Uber back to your place. Okay?"

"Is something wrong with the bus?" As I said it, I understood nothing was wrong with the bus. He didn't say *we*—as in the entire team—were taking Ubers. Me and him. He was making sure I got home okay. There was only one reason I could imagine for that.

"Did I miss him?"

"Let's get the car."

"Coach"—my voice quavered—"did my pop die while I was playing?"

He nudged me along the corridor. "Let's get the car."

• • •

When I imagined Pop's death, and I could admit I imagined it a lot now, I thought I'd be at his side, holding his hand, and he'd say something like, *Remember, every smart man is a con man*, then, right before it was over, *I love you*. But I'd spoken to him last night, sitting on the edge of his bed. We'd watched some *Family Feud* because he thought Steve Harvey was funny. He'd nodded off right around the Fast Money portion of the show. That's all I could remember. Not the questions Steve Harvey asked the contestants, not the answers they gave or the ones my father guessed. I tried so hard to recall the last words I'd heard my father say and came up blank.

Never imagined that.

39

Fear and grief can look the same, but they aren't. I learned that in the days leading up to Pop's funeral.

The night of, when Coach got me home in time to see men from Porter-Rand Mortuary Services take my father away on a gurney, a respectful white sheet tugged to his neck but not over his face, I sat on Leek's bed, and she wrapped her arms and legs around me with her head pressed to my chest like she was little-little. I rocked her while she cried—while we cried—her sobs reverberating through my ribs. She looked up at me and said a thing that I forced myself not to think about later.

She said, "Where Daddy's going, do you think it's a long trip?"

"I—I don't know what you mean."

"In my dream, the road looked long. But I don't think it's the same as our roads."

I gripped her shoulders and leaned her back so I could look her in the eye. "Malika, what did you say?"

She shook her head and got back to crying again. I didn't press. Couldn't have even if I wanted to, because of the rage. If fear and grief look the same, rage doesn't look like either

258

because it doesn't have a look. It has a temperature. A boiling point I was dangerously close to. I wanted to go back to the pawnshop and drive a stake through Skinner's rotten heart even knowing that was stupid and I'd fail and maybe die. None of that mattered while I was tucking my exhausted sister in and listening to my mom's wretched sobs in the next room. Thankfully Pop's voice was louder than ever when a Kincade Webster III Nugget of Wisdom™ screamed in my head: Anger can be a good thing when aimed at problems instead of people.

I didn't think it was right referring to Skinner as a person, but the point stood.

Pop was gone, but his wise words might've saved my life. Perhaps not for the first time. I focused on the problem of burying family.

The numbness Ma complained about before, the wrong feelings Leek questioned with her whole little heart, were replaced by what must've felt natural to them. When Ma broke down crying in front of the funeral director, that was the grief of missing him, not the fear of being without him. When Leek didn't want to get out of bed the first couple of days, same thing, I reasoned. Grief convinced them they were feeling normal things again.

I went on autopilot to help with any tasks I could, keeping the image of my father's cold, hollow body in the basement of the funeral home as compartmentalized as a tough defense in an upcoming game. That was grief, too. I welcomed it.

It was better than being afraid. Better than letting those images of Pop's body drift into foggy thoughts of some long and frightening road. Better than wanting to kill a monster I couldn't.

At night, Ma sat down with piles of paper on the kitchen table, explaining the documents to me. Life insurance, Pop's will, the official death certificate from the state that activated all his plans like some kind of switch he flipped from the afterlife. He'd thought of everything, as a good lawyer does. It was supposed to make things easy.

Neeson allowed me another week off, of course. Something I appreciated for more than bereavement purposes. I'd come to hate stepping on the school grounds. We were studying Shakespeare's *The Tragedy of Julius Caesar* in language arts and I wondered if Caesar felt what I now did walking through his Senate in the days preceding the Ides of March.

The Sparks won the next away game without me on the back of a stellar Nate performance, and nobody talked trash about me on IG. Even NeesonFriedChicken must've known that wouldn't have played when I was about to bury my father.

Pop's funeral was on the Saturday after that away game.

My black suit hung on my closet door all night. That felt about how long I stared at it, too. If I got any sleep at all, it was only a few minutes, so I was bone-tired by the time I rolled out of bed. A quick shower and I was dressed, examining myself in the mirror. My ring was still on.

I twisted it off, sat it on my nightstand, and said, "Not

today. If you try to get to me, someone might see, and I don't think you'd like that, would you?"

I didn't know if the ring, or the power flowing through it, had any kind of sentience, but I had to try. I wasn't taking something from Skinner to my father's final ceremony willingly.

Ma knocked on my door, spoke through it. "Cade, baby, the car's here."

Maybe it was futile, but I spoke to the ring again. "Just let me have today. Okay?"

It was time.

40

We didn't speak much during the ride to First Baptist Church, a venue granted to us not because we were members—my family wasn't very religious—but because Pastor Eubanks, like so many, had my father to thank for getting him out of some legal thing during Pop's healthy days. The weather was nice. Fall warm. We passed some laughing kids dribbling a basketball up the sidewalk and it struck me how most people will never know that we're here, or when we're gone. No matter how your Checkered Game of Life ends, someone else is always playing on a different board.

Leek's hand fell on my knee and squeezed.

"What's up?" I asked, touched and confused by the gesture.

She used the heel of her hand to wipe away tears I didn't know I'd spilled, then slid into the crook of my armpit. Ma did the same thing on my other side, like they were holding me up even though we were sitting down. Maybe they were.

The car let us out at a reserved spot at the curb. A different car was parked ahead of us with black-suited funeral workers flanking it like the Secret Service. It was long enough for the coffin. Pop's ride, then.

My arms stayed around my mother and sister as we entered

the packed church. Every pew filled, with the overflow seats in the balcony taken, too. There were a few people ahead of us on that long center aisle, so I didn't have an unobstructed view of the coffin, something I was grateful for. I focused on the people who'd come to see Pop off as we made the long walk, the organ player doing a serviceable rendition of "His Eye Is on the Sparrow."

The first folks I noticed were my teammates and coaches. They must've come early, because they were forty deep in the back three pews, with Nate right on the aisle, tight-jawed and staring pointedly. I could read the look as clearly as I could in a huddle. *We got you, bro.*

So many people from the Court came; I recognized everyone. The old-man barbershop crew sat together in their finest suits. Some restaurant owners like Mr. Butterbean, who might've had to close his diner for the day to be here. Mr. Lim. At some funerals, there's a designated side for family and a side for friends. None of that worked today because Pop considered most of these folks family regardless of blood ties.

Like Book, who I was surprised to see. He sat mid-church in the only pew that wasn't packed because the people seated closest to him gave him a wide berth. He was dressed fine, a simple gray suit, white shirt, and a tie with the knot only loosely cinched. His face, though. It was marred by fresh bruising he tried to disguise with sunglasses. Unsuccessfully.

He gave me a condolence nod. I had questions, but this wasn't the time.

Only one person separated us from my father. As they angled away, I braced the way I would for a tackle. I'd have preferred the tackle.

Ma hiccuped a sob. I felt numb, like I'd taken a full-body shot of Novocain. Leek gripped the cushioned edge of the coffin like she planned to climb in.

I'd heard people say that when the job was done right, the dead looked like they were asleep in their coffin. It was a lie. They just looked dead.

We stayed until we couldn't, then trudged to our reserved seats on the front pew. We were the last to view my father. They sealed the coffin to no shortage of wails, including those from me and mine.

Gabby stepped out of the choir stand with a cordless mic in hand. She nodded an okay to the organist and began a jaw-dropping version of "The Battle Is Not Yours" by Yolanda Adams. The choir backed her like she was an angel because she for real sounded like one. While I recognized the forced fearlessness in her performance had freed her to blow the roof off the place, I was most struck by the song's lyrics. It was about a benevolent higher power—God—fighting the toughest battle for you.

Like I said, my family wasn't religious. I glanced at my bare ring finger, then squeezed my eyes shut, praying, praying, praying. Because I'd met some not-so-benevolent higher powers, and I could sure use the backup.

41

The day had three scheduled stops. The church, done. The burial ground—I'd zoned out during that whole thing. The coffin was a box. Nothing to see there. Then the repast—held on the sinking, water-warped auditorium floor at the Jacobs Court Community Center.

Folding tables with plastic cloths were set side by side to hold aluminum serving trays of all the staples: ham, fried chicken, green beans, mac and cheese, etc. All served by volunteer church ladies armed with tongs and slotted spoons, each committed to stress testing everyone's flimsy paper plates.

The repast flip from naked grief to It's a Party never sat well with me. I don't know where the DJ who couldn't read the room came from, but I seriously didn't appreciate him playing "The Cha-Cha Slide." Thankfully no one took the dance floor bait.

Ma did what I couldn't bring myself to do. She made the rounds, shaking hands with everyone from the pastor who eulogized my father to the young intern-looking guy from the funeral home responsible for transporting all the colorful wreaths. Leek got with the other little kids, phones out.

I sat at a back corner table, wanting space. Gabby shuffled over balancing a plate heavy with meats, sides, and sweet potato pie, caring very little for my desired solitude.

"Hey," she said, before stuffing her mouth with mac and cheese.

"Hey."

Book was close behind her, taking his seat, no food. I bet that swollen jaw of his was the cause of his sudden diet. I supposed we'd get to that.

"He was like a dad to us, too, you know," Book said.

Gabby nodded. "Yeah."

Of course I knew. No need to dwell.

Book motioned to my hand. "No ring."

I shook my head.

"You think it's gonna stay that way?"

I shook my head again. "I asked for a day off."

Gabby spoke through her food. "That's a weird way to put it."

"I don't know any other way. Weird is a given these days."

"Tell me about it," Book said, removing his sunglasses.

Gabby gasped and dropped her fork. "Booker! What—"

He looked like he'd been beaten with a hammer. Well, maybe not that bad, but hammers were the first thing I thought of so it was bad enough. One eye was purple and swollen nearly shut. Grotesque. It had me reevaluating his other injuries just to have something else to look at. The opposite cheek was raw with scabbed flesh, like he'd been dragged face-first over asphalt. His lip was busted, his chin bruised, there was a goose egg on the side of his head. Also, Book's hands were scraped, the knuckles exposed to the white meat. Whatever happened, he'd dished some punishment, too.

What *had* happened?

Book spoke before I could ask. "Gotta say, bro, this funeral went way better than the last one I attended."

Me and Gabby stiffened. We'd heard about him showing at Treezy's funeral. The "they" network let everyone know.

Treezy's service was a couple of days ago, midweek. They said that's the cheapest way to do it, and Treezy didn't have enough love in the community for anyone to subsidize something fancy. The T-shirt shop next to the Wing Spot had been running a special on airbrushed *Rest in Power Treezy* shirts featuring a not-so-great rendering of the dead One-Eight leader flashing his fanged grill and fanning hundred-dollar bills. A bunch of One-Eights got them. When they said Book came to the service wearing one, I hoped it was a joke.

I would've asked if he'd lost his mind, but I knew that wasn't what he'd lost at all. So I settled on, "Why did you go to Treezy's service? That was too reckless, bro."

"I got tired of running from . . . *the rumors*. I'm not hiding in the library anymore, so me and the One-Eights had to have it out sooner than later."

"About those rumors," I said. Carefully. "Are the cops looking into them?"

"Treezy died in a tragic accident. Even Rah-Rah said so. Why would he lie about such a great leader that the gang clearly loved?"

I willed my face not to react while I decoded the story. When I glanced at Gabby, her expression was as still as a photo; like minds. Book *did* set Treezy up. This was a performance meant to fix the lie in place. Rah-Rah would've told the police it was an accident because he probably hated Treezy anyway and that kind of lie didn't violate the no-snitching rule.

"So what happened to your face?" Gabby asked.

"Big Rick said I still owed for missing the home invasion. We handled it."

Big Rick was a Big Homie. A boss. Maybe *the* boss since some of the other higher-ups landed in jail last year.

Silence hung between us.

I said, "And?"

Adjacent tables started filling with attendees. The DJ went for some Afrobeats that would've forced the conversation into a shouting match.

Book motioned over his shoulder. "Let's talk outside."

It was evening hours and getting dark fast. We walked the block, away from the entrance and potential eavesdroppers. Gabby asked the question on both our minds.

"Is it done now? Because if you look like that and it's not . . ."

"It's done," Book said. "No one seems sad that Treezy's gone, so that helps. A lot of guys like doing things smart. They know I'm good at that. They respect it."

268

I stopped walking. Eventually he did, too. Gabby remained a few steps ahead of him. We all felt miles apart. I said, "You can't keep doing this gang stuff, Book. It ain't you."

"It's not?" He seemed genuinely intrigued by his own question. "I'm really good at it."

Gabby cursed. "What's that even mean?"

"Let's say the rumors about me being involved in dropping Treezy were true. Isn't that impressive? The planning. The logistics. Did you know there are government agencies that pay incredible money for people who can plan and execute missions that eliminate threats? Why is it okay to take down Uncle Sam's enemies but not Jacobs Court's?"

I said, "I don't know if that's okay either, Book."

"Nothing's impressive about killing," said Gabby. "It's a sin."

"Better him than me, right? Or you." Book smirked. "If the rumors were true, I mean."

Gabby looked all the way flustered. I squeegeed a hand down my face, trying to feel less . . . *dirty.*

"What wrong with y'all?" he asked. "I'm here. I survived. I'll keep surviving."

On the heaviest day of my life, I didn't want to obsess over what this could mean for us—my plan for us—but I had to get real a second. "Promise me you'll try to keep your name as clean as possible. At least for a few years. Once I'm in the NFL, you won't have to worry about One-Eight stuff, but it'll be hard to put you on if you got a bunch of gangbanger baggage with you."

The silence hanging between us made me question if I'd actually spoken aloud.

Then Book said, "Because if your corporate sponsors get a whiff of hood stench, you won't be able to sell Sprite and Subway sandwiches? I won't be able to be your business manager if I catch too many bodies? Gotta keep my nose clean so we can make the Jacobs Court movie, right? Gabby gonna write all the music, and sing all the songs, and we'll all win MVPs and Oscars and Grammys. That's the big picture."

I snapped, "It could be if you don't be out here acting like a—"

Gabby slid closer to her brother. "Like what, Cade?"

"Like we don't have an out."

Book closed the gap between us fast, angry, clapping his hands between each shouted word. "*We* do not, my guy!"

I knew he wasn't afraid of me. I wasn't afraid of him either. I didn't care what he'd done. Or who he killed. "Back up."

He didn't. "You're prep school now. You're D1 college next year. When you get drafted, you gonna be thinking about me and Gab in the Court, or all that training you gotta do so you can stay in the league? Just be honest about it, Cade. We ain't mad at you for it."

My gaze bounced between him and Gabby. "We?"

She lifted one hand and touched my cheek. "It really is okay. We get it."

"Get what? I'm trying to make it work for all of us."

She shook her head. "You're trying to be a good person

by lying to yourself. What does 'making it work' look like? You're getting us apartments in whatever city you go to. We get allowances."

"Yeah. Sure. Why not?"

Book said, "You're not around much, so maybe you don't feel how different things are, but something's changing in the Court."

Gab spoke like she was delivering bad news. "We've changed. I think we've got a little of what you've always had. I feel confident in the way you two have always encouraged. You know GeneBeatz, the producer on the Southside, I went to his studio the other day. Just showed up and started singing like y'all always telling me to do. He loved me, and we're working on music together."

"That's good, Gab," I said, resisting the urge to say *because of my wish*. I knew how crappy that'd sound. Instead, I said, "It doesn't change how helpful I can be when I make it."

"*If,*" Book said. "Anything can happen in three years, and we're not pausing our lives for a chance to ride your coattails. Sorry. I know y'all don't like it, but I'm good at schemes, and the One-Eights need me. I *hope* I get to cheer you on in a Super Bowl or whatever someday. Ain't nobody got time to wait on hope."

"I can keep us together," I said weakly.

They didn't believe me. Why should they believe me? Because my biggest hurdle loomed: college and the pros weren't going to work with my ring still erasing fear in

271

everyone I met. The best athletes on the planet coming for me with *less* caution was going to get me—and others—murdered on the field. Book said it himself, I needed to avoid scary people. The only way to avoid the expertly trained human wrecking balls intent on taking my head off was not stepping on a football field ever again.

What did that mean if the future I'd always planned on wouldn't be? How could I waste all the potential I had because of one mumble-mouthed wish? How could I let my friends and family suffer more?

What if there was a way out of my situation? Off this road?

What if . . .

BRADY

Brady did not attend the funeral for Cade Webster's dad with the Sparks football team. He kinda hated those guys. Which was probably why he'd gotten so good at threatening to kill them and their elitist fans.

He'd taken the painstaking precautions he'd read about in the online groups he frequented. He followed the recipe, as his mother would say. Don't do it from home. Use a different burner phone, email, and VPN *every* time. Sit back and watch rich jerks like Nate and Brett and Neal and even Coach Gibson squirm at the minor inconvenience of not getting their way. It's what they got for treating him like something they found on the bottom of their shoes.

Still, after he sent that first email threatening harm at a preseason scrimmage resulting in a rescheduling, he'd spent days expecting the cops or the FBI or whoever to burst into his house and drag him away. At the same time, he sat back and listened to the Moneybags—that's how he'd come to think of them with their cars and clothes that could pay him and his mom's rent for years—pound their chests over what they'd do to whoever tarnished a few moments in their perfect Moneybag lives. Brady felt like Clark Kent navigating a room of villains whining about Superman. That was its own kind of rush that faded too soon. Ultimately nothing happened.

So Brady did it again.

Getting a game pushed from Friday to Monday was low stakes and scratched an itch. Enough thrills and fears to last awhile.

Until they didn't.

The last threat he sent, the one that got the Forestbrook game moved, did absolutely nothing for him. He would've said the lack of a rush was startling, but that wasn't true. He wasn't startled even a little bit.

He was empty.

The new hollowness left too much room for Brady to contemplate hard truths that he'd pushed aside when his new hobby was really doing it for him. He was self-aware enough to know because he wasn't tall and jacked and rich he'd have a harder path through life, like a game where the default difficulty was set to high. Going to Neeson would help, he knew, but getting through Neeson was its own gauntlet when you didn't come from family money. It's why Brady liked Cade Webster better than anyone else on the team. He was a legit baller. One of the best players Brady had ever seen. And he wasn't one of *them*.

He'd been different since he started strutting around with that fake Super Bowl ring, though. Everyone was. It was like something in the air changed, became more pure. While it seemed silly to assign any shift in Neeson's atmosphere to Cade's ring, Brady couldn't shake the feeling. He'd even dreamed about that ring.

He narrowed down the locations the ring might've come from through minor deductions. When he tried to confirm with Cade in the hall, he reacted violently, knocking Brady's phone from his hand in a humiliating fashion.

This disrespect triggered rage. Turned out Cade was more like the Moneybags than Brady thought.

That was fine. Perfectly fine. When the Neeson Sparks disrespected Brady, it came at a price. Cade Webster just opened a tab.

But first . . .

Brady tugged the door handle and chimes sounded overhead. He began exploring Skinner's Pawn & Loan.

Right away, Brady was turned off by the smell. It was moist and moldy, and maybe something had died in the wall. The customer service wasn't better. The Black guy behind the counter seemed annoyed, like Brady was bothering him.

"You need something?" the clerk asked, his tone suggesting he wanted Brady to leave so he could get back to his nap.

"I'll let you know," Brady said, firing that attitude right back.

He browsed, unimpressed by the mishmash of junk on display. They could at least clean some of this stuff before trying to wring money from people for it. A horror movie–style machete caught Brady's eye, but the rust stains were unappealing. Still, he picked it up, held it extended like a thrusting sword, brought it back liking the heft. He ran his thumb down the cutting edge.

"Ow." Brady yanked his thumb back, blood already beading where he'd nicked himself. The machete looked dull but was plenty sharp. Bringing it closer for a better view in the dim light, he scratched a nail across the broad side of the blade. What he'd thought was rust flaked off easily, like—

"Well, hello, young man!" This new, high, chipper voice was full of warmth and welcome.

Brady turned to the counter and the Black guy was no longer alone. An old white man in a long coat and hat was with him.

Leaving the machete where he'd found it, Brady approached the counter. "Hey."

"Can I help you find anything?" the old man asked.

"I'm wondering if your store sells any replica Super Bowl rings?"

The Black guy sucked in a sharp breath and backed up a step. The old man smiled wider. "Oh my goodness. Are you a friend of Cade Webster?"

Fireworks burst in Brady's inner void. He knew this was the place! "Yes. I know Cade."

"You like his ring?"

"I do. Do you have any more of them?"

The old man's smile fell off his face. "No. I do not. Unfortunately."

"Oh. Well, I guess I can understand that. Can I ask you some questions about the ring? It's . . ." He didn't know how to say this part without sounding nuts. "It's strange."

The old man nodded as if he understood completely. "Yes, yes. You could ask me questions about Cade's ring, though I don't believe that's the best use of our time. That ring is specific to him and his desires. I want to speak to what I see in *you*. I see someone whose worth is not recognized. I see someone who's been forced to suffer fools. I see someone who has been trod upon by people sucking on silver spoons. Those aren't the sort we cotton to here. Those aren't our people, are they, Brady?"

"How'd you know my—"

But the old man was on a roll and couldn't be stopped. "Here, I provide a more bespoke experience for my clientele. The discerning types like you and me. How can I help *you* find what you're looking for?"

Bespoke? It was like something out of the *Kingsman* movies. Brady . . . loved that. The idea that something in this funky store was meant for him and only him. How the old dude sold the idea was hypnotic, almost. Not in a forced way. In the way Brady would *want* to be hypnotized. "I mean, I don't know, I came in here looking for the ring, but now . . ." He wasn't sure where to start.

"What do you want deep down in your heart of hearts?" the man asked. "What is it that you wish for most?"

The questions were like a song. Lilting, rising, falling.

Nearly bringing Brady to tears. Had anyone shown such compassion for his needs in . . . ever? His heart's desire. His deepest wish. Sometimes he'd been afraid to think it.

Not lately. Lately, he hadn't been afraid of anything.

Brady said, "I wish I could take a big ole dump on their perfect Moneybag lives. All of them. Make them pay for ever getting it in their heads that they're better than me."

The old man clapped. "Excellent! I know exactly what you need. Be right back."

He skittered through a curtain into a back room, barely gone a second, then returned with an old, heavy-looking crate in his arms.

"In my experience," he said, "people are the best explosives." He turned on his heel so they all saw the words stenciled on the wooden slats. "But in the absence of man's volatile nature, some good old American-made dynamite will do."

The crate said: *Neeson Power Company, Highly Combustible, 50 Count, Dangerous.*

"Now," the old man said, "how will you be paying?"

42

At home, after Pop's service, I put the ring back on voluntarily, almost grateful it'd stayed away as long as it had, knowing how toxic that kind of thinking was. I couldn't keep going like this.

The next morning had me feeling like a zombie walking. I hadn't slept, hadn't eaten much. Made it to the bus stop, though.

Got off where I needed. Walked fast before I had a chance to back out. Then I pushed through the door, triggering the chimes. "Is he here?"

Eddie moved with urgency I hadn't seen. Off his stool, around the counter, his hands on my shoulders, shaking. "What are you doing, Cade?"

"Skinner!" I yelled at the ceiling and into the darkened corners like that made sense. "Skinner, are you here?"

He didn't appear in a cloud of fire and smoke. He pulled up to the curb outside the display window, the white Caddy's engine low growling like he'd been waiting around the corner.

Eddie released me and backed away, disgusted as if he'd gone wrist-deep into a gigantic booger.

Door chimes welcomed the old man. He strolled the center aisle, rubbing his hands eagerly. "Cade Webster! I'm so excited to see you again."

This was a dangerous moment. The tension crackled around me as I balanced between rage and reason—even I didn't know how this was going to go. I came to talk, but what if I couldn't keep this anger toward Skinner coiled inside me and was torn apart by the store's magic?

We'd know soon enough.

I took a steadying breath and said, "I have questions for you. About your deals."

"Of course you do."

"Will you answer them honestly?" This was almost a futile question. If he lied, how would I know? Yet my gut said to put it on the table.

He said, "I don't deal in untruth."

A nonanswer. He was tricky and maybe knew that I knew it. Okay. I asked, "What would it take to break my wish?"

"Cade!" Eddie snapped.

Skinner didn't bother with a warning. He waved a hand and Eddie was struck suddenly mute, as if Skinner had pushed the button on a remote control. Eddie continued to mime his shouts, but another gesture from Skinner had Eddie retreating to the back room. Eddie fought the motion, leaning toward me like a man walking into a strong wind, but the invisible forces deployed against him were too strong and soon he was gone, leaving me and Skinner free to talk.

"What would it take?" I repeated, chilled by how quickly I'd adjusted to Skinner's sudden displays of supernatural power. "I'm only asking for terms, not agreeing to anything."

He nodded enthusiastically. "Understood."

Skinner strolled past me and rounded the counter, a negotiating position. I leaned on the display case so my forearm blocked my view of Corner Joe's medallion under the glass.

He said, "For the store to reclaim that ring on your finger, effectively nullifying your wish, I'd require a long-term agreement from you."

"How long-term?"

"Eternity."

Nothing ambiguous in the word, but I needed to say the rest. Claiming ignorance wouldn't do me any good later. "My soul."

Skinner tapped the counter. "There is an upside. You'd set the deadline. Ten years, twenty, fifty. I can't offer you much more than that—natural life spans being what they are— but that time would be gloriously decadent. I'd imagine, for you, that would mean a Hall of Fame football career, riches, and all the rest. I could broker a deal to make it happen."

Pop once told me that in a negotiation, the person with the most information wins. I asked, "How old are you?"

One side of his mouth curled up. "A bit over a century, give or take."

What did he give and what did he take to accomplish that, I wondered. "That's not a natural life span."

"It isn't. It is a life span that requires more than you'd be willing to offer, I imagine. We can discuss that at another time, if you so choose."

"My soul to break the wish, that's a deal you'd accept?"

He shrugged, looked truly distressed. "If I could do it differently, I would."

"You said I could pick my deadline. Ten, twenty, fifty years. Why wouldn't I pick the longest amount of time?"

"The shorter the time, the more intense the experience. Some crave that. I've crossed paths with a lot of rock stars." He motioned to a wall display crowded with guitars. "I'm giving it to you straight, Cade. Will you owe a debt? Sure. But it is your choice. You're more than welcome to keep walking around the world with that ring. My investor loves the results you've been getting."

I stared at Pat the Patriot, thought of the ripples me and him might still cause, and shuddered. "Why do people do it? Why take your deal when they know how it'll end?"

"For some the life they have, the life they *didn't* ask for, is already a hell of sorts. They see it as trading one form of doom for another of their choosing. The devil you know, I suppose."

"One more thing. How bad is it when it's time to pay?"

Skinner stopped smiling. "I don't know."

The unspoken part of his answer rang as clear in my head as a bell: *And I don't plan to find out.*

I almost thanked him. Habit. Nothing about him deserved politeness or gratitude. I backed toward the exit in silence.

Before I crossed the threshold, Skinner said, "You know where to find me."

It wasn't worth it. Eternity's a long time.

I said it over and over until I fell asleep that night. I dreamed. I don't recall the details, but I woke up screaming into my pillow.

43

Grief is weird and it lingers.

Monday, I got up for school and nearly told Pop, "See you later." My day didn't get better from there. I caught the bus to Neeson. In the hall someone laughed at something. Things were still funny for other people. If I'd heard the joke, would it have been funny to me? I didn't know.

I blinked. It was midday. Another blink, and it was practice time. My team went out of their way to make sure I was all right. The appeal of doing something physically difficult, running and catching and feeling the sting of a solid tackle, was high. But first . . .

"Hey, can I holler at you a sec?" I asked.

Brady braked his rolling basket of assorted team laundry by my locker.

"I've been dealing with a lot lately—"

"I know, Cade," he said.

His affirmation made me hesitate; the back of my neck itched.

Or I was projecting. It's hard to apologize and, you know, the grief. I forced the words past my lips. "I know I was out of pocket with how I've treated you. My bad. For real. I was wrong. You're a good guy."

I extended my hand. He dapped me up and said, "You looking forward to Senior Night?"

I pulled away, startled. I'd forgotten the next game against Belmont Prep was Senior Night, where all of us who were graduating took the field pregame with our families. What was left of them.

"I sure am," he said when I didn't answer. He pushed his basket toward the laundry room.

He turned the corner and left me pondering. Of all I considered, it only occurred to me briefly to wonder why Brady, a junior, cared so much about Senior Night.

I flopped onto the couch between Ma and Leek and became mesmerized by the big, gleaming white teeth of Steve Harvey addressing *Family Feud* contestants in a black-on-black suit.

"Pancakes!" Ma shouted at the TV, a guess at the top answer to whatever Steve's survey question was.

"I'm sorry to interrupt," I began, "but if Friday's game stays on schedule, it's—"

"Your Senior Night," Ma said, then she shouted at the TV. "Croissants!"

"Yeah, about that. I can tell Coach that I'm not going to do the family walk part so you don't have to worry about it."

Steve Harvey froze mid-belly-laugh. Ma had paused the broadcast to burn a hole in me with her stare.

Leek, head down in her phone, spoke absently. "You're really stupid sometimes."

"Hey!" I said, and knocked her phone to the carpet.

She poked her tongue at me, then dived onto the floor to retrieve it.

Ma said, "I've had my outfit picked out for weeks."

"I know. I'm just saying—"

"*I'm* saying we all knew the circumstance we'd be in at some point this year. Before Senior Night. After Senior Night. Your father and I talked about all of it. One thing he told me was not to let you take any undue burden on, thinking you had to fill some man-of-the-house role. No one's putting that on you. This is still your senior year, and we're going to enjoy it as we would've if your father were still with us. It's what we both wanted."

She tapped the remote. Steve resumed his hosting duties, roasting one of the contestants for a bad answer with his signature country drawl.

That was that, then.

The week rolled on. School was school. Practice, practice. The NeesonFriedChicken account was running new racist stuff, but I don't think I could've cared less at that point. Life at Neeson was its new normal. With one huge change.

Nate pulled me aside that Wednesday to play a voice mail. It went: *"This is Terry McKainey from the Ohio State University. I've had some enlightening conversations with your father and I've seen film. Big talent on your squad. Maybe Buckeye big! See you soon."*

When the message ended, Nate didn't say a word. He didn't have to. We got to work.

After practice Thursday I sent a message to the group chat I'd been avoiding. I wasn't the only one. I attempted to resurrect the dead chat with something simple.

> **Me**
>
> Hey Idk if y'all would be interested but we're supposed to have our last home game on Friday. It's Senior Night. If you want to come . . .

There was more I wanted to say. Like, *Would y'all walk with me because you're family, too?* That was too big of an ask when no one else was talking.

Dancing dots appeared. They stopped. Started. Stopped again. The message popped.

> **Gabby**
>
> I would, but I got studio time scheduled with Gene.
>
> That rapper from the beach,

Bop Boi, want me to sing on
a track. I'd get out of it if I
could.

Me
Hey, it's cool. I get it.
Kill em, Gab.

Gabby
You know it 😉

I nearly typed *be careful* but recognized that was weird.
Book never responded to any of it.

Friday. Game Day. Belmont Prep. Senior Night. If . . . nothing went wrong. If no one tried to sabotage it.

All day we waited for the inevitable threat that would ruin everything. They'd been as predictable as sunrise for every home game this season, so why expect something different this time. Morning. To midday. To final bell. Nothing.

By the time we were suiting up in the field house, not a single word from whoever had destroyed our nights so many times.

Guess they finally found something better to do.

44

The stadium lights popped on as the sun set. The marching band hefted gleaming brass instruments into the stands, and the concession vendors swapped empty carbonation tanks for the fresh ones in preparation for the gates opening. Spectators pulled into the lot and exited their cars with their seat cushions, blankets for the chill, toy pom-poms. Kids, maybe future Sparks themselves, hurled a mini-football on a sidewalk that wasn't crowded but would be soon. I couldn't see any of that from the field house, of course. But I knew what the vibes of a real Friday night home game felt like. It was as predictable as the seasons. Yet, in the locker room, minor chaos brewed.

"Where is Brady?" an assistant coach yelled while texting, presumably, a message to the absent team manager.

Brady was MIA? I'd have been less concerned if one of the second-string guys didn't show since some of them were openly bitter about how little playing time they got. Brady seemed like he was into his duties more than actual school. For him to be missing felt very wrong. That sense of wrongness permeated the locker room.

"Did anyone see him at school today?" I asked the room.

Noncommittal grunts were mostly what I got.

Brett said bluntly, "I don't know if I ever see him in school."

That got some lukewarm laughs. No answers, though.

Worry turned to irritation as we were forced to—GASP—gather our own gear and jerseys. A minor inconvenience made major by people who thought their tuition covered such troubles.

Coach gathered us for the pregame briefing and pep talk but sped through to address Senior Night business. "All of you guys graduating, we'll do the ceremonial stuff before the game. If you have family and friends present, they'll be gathered near the team entrance on the field. Sheila's going to arrange you however it is she wants. You'll do your walk, then I want everyone but Nate and Cade on the sidelines. You two know your places."

"Fifty-yard line," Nate said, indicating the coin toss protocols.

I nodded, confirming.

The underclassmen on the team took the field to cheering spectators filling in the bleachers. I spotted the glossy red-and-black Ohio State jacket on Mr. McKainey. He saw me and Nate stepping into the stadium light, greeted us with a tip of his hat.

Nate extended his fist to me, I bumped his knuckles with mine, and we split to meet our families. His mother and father greeted him with exotic-looking flowers. Ma and Leek met me with Mylar balloons that bopped in the breeze. The biggest balloon read: *You're Our #1!*

I hugged my mother, who did not disappoint in the outfit she'd been talking about. A navy-blue pantsuit with a shimmering cream top beneath. Some of the single and not-so-single dads did a double take when they passed her. Leek wore an old Sparks jersey over jeans and some fresh Nikes. Her Afro puffs had her looking like Mickey Mouse's silhouette.

"Gather round," Sheila shouted, herding everyone together. "We're going to line up alphabetically and . . ."

The instructions were simple enough. We'd slow walk when our names got called, do the pageant wave thing, pause for a photo op, then angle toward the sideline. One of Sheila's assistants rolled over a wagon full of props: decorative footballs featuring the date, our names, and jersey numbers we were meant to hold while the photographer did their thing. On the scoreboard a countdown ticked.

The band wrapped up some jazzy tune and the Sparks' announcer came through the speakers. "Everyone who is able, please rise for our national anthem. Performing our country's hallowed song is Neeson junior Taylor Maye!"

We faced the flag that flapped beyond the far end zone, while Taylor—who had one of the Finstas I recognized on the NeesonFriedChicken account—belted the song to the best of her unimpressive and unseasoned abilities. Gabby would've washed her.

Then I was thinking of Gabby in the studio with a real producer, and a real rapper.

We've *changed. I think we've got a little of what you've always had.*

God, I hoped she got everything she wanted.

Taylor wrapped to weak applause, then Sheila took her mic to begin the Senior Walk announcements.

There was a preamble, all the pleasantries about how we'd made Neeson proud, how we were going to go on to do great things, how much we were loved. No one would remember much of that.

She called the first name. "Alexander Astor."

There were nine seniors on the team, so the procession went fast. My last name put me at the end of the line, and sure enough, when Sheila introduced me, she went with, "Kincade Webster IV . . . better known as C-4!"

Over the thunderous applause, Ma leaned into me and said, "She knows you don't like that name, doesn't she?"

I nodded.

"Mm-hmm. I'mma have a word with her when we're done."

"Ma!" I said, nervous.

"I won't be mean," she promised. "No one gets to call my son out his name to my face."

Me and my family stepped forward together. I took a showman-like bow, boosting the applause slightly. When I straightened, Mr. McKainey of the Ohio State University thrust a thumbs-up at me, big grin, enthusiastic, ready for a show. I beamed back, ready to put in work and check another item off my vision board. For Pop.

I was so dialed in on the Ohio State recruiter, so focused

on what he might do for me, I barely comprehended the first explosion.

The boom, which wasn't as loud as the movies, seemed out of sync with the debris flying onto the far end of the field like too-big confetti. A column of black smoke coiled from a ragged hole in the bleachers where people had been sitting. It felt like an hour before someone screamed.

Even then it just . . . it didn't seem real.

The next explosion did, though.

Mr. McKainey's expression shifted from his excitement at seeing me to confusion as he tracked the commotion of the first explosion. Then a *POP* and a metallic shriek were the score to him vanishing—disintegrated. Dust and blood misted in the stadium's lights.

By the time we understood the danger we were in, there was nothing left to do but flee.

In a true display of leadership, Nate, flanked by his mother and father, clocked it all quicker than me and shouted above the din of chaos like he was calling a play. "Everybody, run! Follow me!"

No one in earshot could deny the command.

Ma scooped up Leek like a three-year-old. I dropped my prop football, covered them both, and followed Nate, along with most of our team, back to the field house.

Though whether the path forward led to safety was as much of a coin toss as any.

BRADY

The two bleacher bombs were triggered remotely, using gear and instructions Mr. Skinner provided, but Brady knew this next part needed to be hands-on for it to mean something, for it to generate the thrill he'd sought for some time now.

He sat on the field house roof with his legs dangling, the crate containing his remaining dynamite sticks resting beside him. He overlooked the path from the stands to the locker room as the wholly predictable happened. Many of the Sparks retreated toward him, thinking the locker room meant safety. It never meant safety for Brady, though, and he planned to give them a taste of their own medicine.

Grabbing a stick with a short fuse from the crate, Brady coached himself, "Wait. Wait."

The path was a wide corridor, fenced on one side, with various field maintenance equipment parked along the other side, creating something of a chute, like the kind cattle got directed through on their way to becoming T-bone steaks. The first to approach were some defensive guys who'd been on the sidelines closest to the field house when the explosions started. He spotted Brett—arguably the worst Moneybags—in the group. Nate trailed closely. Perfect.

The path flooded with the fleeing team, coaching staff, and Senior Night family members. In the midst Brady caught sight of Cade Webster and his family. A momentary pang of guilt speared Brady. He recalled when he'd liked Cade, but he'd come too far now. There was no us versus them, only Brady versus the world.

Behind Cade was a mix of stragglers: Sheila the communications lady, some of the band still toting their gleaming instruments, a few school administrators who'd made the unlucky choice of chasing a crowd. Brady lit the fuse with a BIC he'd purchased from the 7-Eleven, then chucked the sparkling stick in a far-high arc toward the slowest runners. He watched the stick flip end over end, then bounce off Taylor Maye's head like something from a blooper reel.

"Nate's not the only one with an arm," Brady mumbled.

The dynamite exploded near Taylor Maye's feet, tearing her and four others apart.

Brady lit another stick with a shorter fuse and dropped it straight down. It blew fast, sending vibrations through the building and killing some of the defensive line, halting the terrified stampede. Cade and his family froze like squirrels on a highway, unsure which direction was safe. Answer: none.

Brady grabbed another stick and stood for this moment. Wanting them all to see what they'd brought upon themselves.

"Hey, Sparks," he yelled, lighting the fuse. "How you like my shoes now?"

He prepared to chuck the stick in the center of the crowd.

But while Nate wasn't the only one with an arm, he was the only one who still had a football.

The quarterback had been running slightly ahead of the Websters and never let go of his decorative Senior Night football. He stepped back easy, arm cocked, a motion practiced to unconscious perfection. Nate threw the pass with everything on it. Velocity. Precision. Purpose.

It clocked Brady in the jaw like a missile, knocking him off balance. So close to the edge, with nothing to grasp, he fell off the roof, swiping first for air but managing to snag the edge of the dynamite crate, bringing it with him. If not for that, Nate's play might've been flawless.

Brady collided with the ground in a bone-crunching manner, shrieking in the way he deserved.

He still held the lit stick, though. The remaining sticks landed with him, too close to his broken body.

A pathetic, mewling Brady locked eyes with Cade Webster for a second, both of them understanding the moment. With reflexes that had made Cade famous all over the state, the football player dragged his family behind a riding lawnmower a second before the night's final explosion.

It wasn't fast enough.

Though the detonation of the remaining dynamite—a boom that felt like the earth tearing in two for those who survived it—was the end of any further carnage at Neeson Field, when it came to the horrors of that night, Cade Webster still had miles to go.

45

My ears rang. My lungs seized from the smoke and dust, triggering a coughing fit. The cloud swirling in the air made it hard to see anything but the ring on my hand, gleaming and unblemished.

I peeled myself off the ground, feeling my mother and sister next to me, prone. The way they weren't moving sent panic jolts through me. "Ma!" I screamed, though my voice seemed far away. "Leek!"

Working my way to my knees, something stabbed at my left pectoral. I screamed, the pain sharp. I looked down in the general area and nearly fainted at the sight of a ragged metal spike protruding from my chest.

It hurt, but a new adrenaline surge dulled the pain. What should I do? How far in was it? I shouldn't pull it out, right? Bracing myself, I touched the exposed metal, testing the extent of the damage. It simply fell to the ground. Less than a quarter inch of the sharp tip stained with my blood.

My shoulder pads! They'd kept the projectile from going deeper, turning what might've been fatal into a minor puncture.

My heart plummeted. My family hadn't been wearing any

protective equipment. Ma's and Leek's bodies were entangled with each other. The ground beneath them was a dark and alarming mud puddle. I wanted to believe it was only mud.

"Nooo," I shrieked in a stranger's voice.

I turned Ma over. A bloody trench gouged her skull from her forehead all the way to the back of her scalp, something like a part in her hair administered by a stylist who preferred a sword to scissors. She groaned, shifted; her eyes fluttered beneath the lids. Alive.

Leek, though . . .

When I turned her over, her left side was soaked almost black with blood. A charred chunk of wood had speared her just below her ribs. I could barely make out the word *Neeson* on the stake-shaped hunk. Her chest rose and fell the way it did when she was a baby, so fast it was frightening. Pop told me babies breathed like that and had fast heartbeats because they were so small and it helped them stay warm. Was she cold? Would warmth help? I peeled off my jersey, intending to cover her, but remembered in the movies they said you had to stop the bleeding, apply pressure, and there was a big hole in my little baby sister's side.

I balled my jersey up and pressed it to her wound. She SHRIEKED.

"Help!" I screamed, not knowing if there was anyone left to hear.

Everything was so still now.

Everything.

I twisted toward the field; running people were posed at gravity-defying angles. I glanced up: A plane miles above was perched on air. The only things that moved were me, Leek's fluttering eyes, Ma's steady breathing. And the ground.

It was less of a movement, more of a transformation. The bloody mud hardened, as did all the earth around me. Into asphalt. It stretched into road that ran all the way to the end zone behind me. In front of me it extended beneath Brady's dismembered parts toward the field house. When it touched the front of the building, the structure vanished, giving a view stretching into infinity, its sides bordered by swirling gray mist. The mist consumed everything around me, too. All that was left beneath me and my family was the road and the abyss beyond that.

I heard the engine before I saw it. A shrieking, howling muscle roar. Headlights grew as it drew near. The sterling chrome grille looked like teeth, and the black paint had a mirror's sheen.

The long body slowed and swung sideways as it parked on the chunk of road just shy of Brady's corpse. The driver's door opened wide and Skinner exited, his body tensed in mock concern.

"Oh no, Cade. This is horrible," he said. "But don't worry. I'm here to help."

46

Brady stood up, seemingly whole. His soul showed no signs of the damage his physical body had taken. The ethereal version of him appeared to scramble out of the earth, leaving behind the gory, singed parts that had been dismembered in the blast. I was seeing something I shouldn't—something no one should see this side of the divide between living and dead—and I quaked inside.

Brady was dressed as he had been on the roof, in some stupid surplus tactical gear like he'd gone to war instead of murdered people from a distance like a coward. *Weird*, I thought, *he's going to spend eternity looking like an unpopular G.I. Joe.*

He glanced around at the road, the car, Skinner, confused. He locked eyes with me and said, "Cade, what's happening?"

I glared.

He looked down at what was left of his body and flinched away, stumbling as he did, then crab-walking all the way to the edge of the road.

"Cade, Cade, I'm sorry," he called to me, then, "I'm scared."

Well, now I knew of one way to nullify my wish. My ring seemed to hold no sway over the dead. Didn't do me, or him, much good.

"Brady," Skinner said. "Come here, please."

Brady ran to the old man, terrified and hopeful at once. "Mr. Skinner, can you help me? I did what we talked about. I used what you gave me."

Skinner grabbed Brady by both shoulders, gently, sympathetically, and slowly turned him so his back was to the car.

"You used what I *sold* you, son," Skinner said. "It's time to pay up."

The car's hood cracked open silently, rose on its hinges, wide like a gator's mouth.

From where I crouched, I couldn't see inside, yet I somehow understood that if I had, I might've lost every bit of my sanity. The light emanating from where the car's engine should be was wrong. Orange and red, churning. A bouquet of gray-pale groping hands rose from that infernally lighted pit. Brady didn't notice.

He said, "You told me it was okay if I didn't have money."

Skinner nudged Brady until his hamstrings bumped the car's snarling grille. "I did."

"I sent a message like we talked about. They know better than to mess with Brady."

Skinner pressed his finger to Brady's lips, shushing him. "You've done good work here, and I appreciate it. But, son, I don't deal in untruths. No one's going to remember your name. Enjoy what you've earned."

Skinner shoved Brady into the waiting hands.

Brady screamed but was silenced by a pale palm clamped over his mouth.

Fingers crawled over him like bugs, boneless arms looped around him like tentacles. He bucked and moaned but could not break the infernal embrace. Brady soon looked like a mummy wrapped in flesh. He sank into the engine cavity, and I couldn't stop watching him go down, down, down, until that terrible light winked away and the hood closed almost gently with a soft *ca-chunk* as the latch caught.

Skinner rubbed his hands together like a workman shaking off the grime of a long day. "Cade, are you ready to talk terms so I can save your sister?"

"I—I . . ." What to say?

"Don't let what you just saw discourage you. Brady made choices that necessitated a certain . . . onboarding. We can discuss the time and manner in which you'd be required to pay your debt. If you want your sister to live."

"Of course I do," I said, defeated by the possibility of any other outcome.

Skinner walked to the back seat and opened the door. "Come. Bring her. We do this at the store."

That shook me. "You want me to get into that thing?"

"It's a car, my boy. That's all. For now."

"What about my mother?"

Skinner looked disappointed to give me good news. "She's going to be fine. Mild concussion. Now come on. Little Malika's prognosis isn't so positive."

If I was brave, if my wish worked on me, perhaps I could've rationalized that losing my sister was ultimately better than what was being offered. I wasn't, though. I'd just lost Pop, and I couldn't see letting Leek go, too. I scooped my sweet little sister in my arms and got in that car.

God help me.

47

It was a short but eventful ride.

All the gigantic faces pressing out of the mist, their mouths stretched in silent warning, made me want to squeeze my eyes shut. But suddenly having a seatmate made it so I could barely blink.

"Leek?" I rasped.

My sister was strong, alert, and confused sitting beside me.

My sister was injured, bleeding, with considerably slowed breathing stretched across my lap.

Ruin Road ran between life and death, as did Leek now.

She glanced at her body in my lap and showed no signs of fear. Good. If the wish still worked, she wasn't too far gone. Yet.

Skinner watched us in the rearview, unbothered by the second Leek. He knew the twists in this road better than I did. Perhaps my spirit realm sister was simply another familiar landmark.

"If she's splitting from her physical form like that, then we don't have much time, Cade. You should know that."

"What does 'should' and 'shouldn't' even mean anymore?"

"You may have a point there, boy." He rapped his fingers

on the steering wheel in a rhythm and said, "I have a confession to make."

He let it hang. I refused to bite.

He went ahead anyway. "That wish of yours hasn't done as well for me as I led you to believe. It was interesting seeing someone like you—relatively selfless, upstanding, real opportunities—play with my wares. My normal customer might've wished that their own fear be taken from them so they could go out and get into all sorts of trouble with no remorse. Something that would've undoubtedly gone sour. Your version . . . a mixed bag. Those cops I'd definitely log in the asset column. What your friend did to that unpleasant gang leader was impressive. Brady, he certainly put on a show for his final act. Yet . . ."

He trailed off again, but with a furrowed brow.

"What?" I said.

"The impact of the wish on your community has done more good than I like. Your people, absent of fear, are showing a great deal of ambition. Jacobs Court was never meant to inspire. The will to overcome hardships and pain and strife was meant to be the exception. What you've done has the potential to make exceptional the norm. I'll be happy to retire the experiment of your wish. In the eyes of my superior, it'll be like dumping a loser stock."

Other Leek said, "You need to watch how you talk to my brother!"

She also cursed. A string of profanity I didn't even know my sister was capable of.

Other Leek was a beast.

Skinner chuckled. "She is spunky. I can see why you want her to stay. Just a little more road and a little more paperwork."

The store became visible through Skinner's windshield. Then we were there, Skinner's headlights blaring on the packed display window.

Skinner exited the vehicle and held the door for us. Other Leek climbed out; I followed carrying Not-So-Good Leek.

Skinner walked us into his establishment, door chimes jingling.

The store was the store. Except this time Eddie wasn't on his perch behind the counter. He was on top of a tall stepladder, dealing with some inventory on a nearby shelf. He seemed neither surprised nor happy to see us.

Skinner barely spared him a glance as we traversed the center aisle and he rounded his counter, ready to deal.

"So," Skinner began, "I can definitely save the little girl's life."

I rested Leek's body on the counter. The Other Leek stood at my hip, head cocked, curious.

"For my soul?" I said.

Skinner rolled his eyes. Big we've-already-covered-this energy.

I said, "I get to pick how much time I get, and other benefits."

"No," Skinner said.

"What? When we talked before—"

"Yesterday's price is not today's price," he said, mocking. "The leverage I had over you before was the promise to break the wish . . . something I was willing to do anyway, just not for free. Now you want your sister to live. Those years you would've been granted go to her, and you will be on my time, boy. I'm not heartless, though. I'll give you ten years and a decent pro football career on top of the little girl's life."

My head spun. I'd thought more about the possibility of dealing with Skinner than I liked to admit but had never considered this kind of swerve. Leek's body lurched and she sputtered blood from her lips. Other Leek looked worried.

Slow down, Cade. Think. You can't make any mistakes here. The voice in my head was right. No surprise. It was Pop's voice.

I said, "What if—"

"My offer is firm." His fake charm was tucked away. He smiled with sharp teeth. "Take it or leave it."

My chest heaved.

Other Leek tugged on my hand. "Don't do it, Cade. Not even for me."

That alone nearly broke me. That meant I had to. "It's okay. I got this."

Then, to Skinner, "Where do I sign?"

Skinner opened a drawer and removed a yellowed piece of parchment. He placed my contract on the countertop, along with a quill.

"Read it," he said. "The terms are clear."

It wasn't a long or complicated document. I didn't suppose it had to be. As he said, the terms were clear. Beneath them, a signature line.

Skinner offered the quill to me.

I reached for it, but he jammed the tip into the hand I had planted on the counter, right at the webbing between my thumb and forefinger. When I screamed, he snatched it back.

"Sorry," he said, offering it to me for real, the tip wet with my blood. "It was dry."

Of course, this is the way the deal would be ratified.

I lowered the quill tip to the page.

"Cade, no!" Other Leek said. I focused on her dying body and not the wise entity warning me not to throw away eternity.

Eddie had come off his ladder but kept his distance, shaking his head in sorrow.

"Whenever you're ready," Skinner said, clearly anxious to close the deal.

"I know." The quill touched the paper, and I signed my first name in blood.

KINCADE

So.

Here's the thing.

From the time I came back to the store to discuss terms

of a deal with Skinner and understood what he was, that I couldn't beat him with my anger and grief, I'd considered scenarios. All were on my mind as I signed my last name.

WEBSTER

Rules matter. Laws matter. Contracts matter. Even in a space between the living, dead, dreams, and wishes. Skinner wouldn't run his scams the way he did otherwise. My father wouldn't have been able to beat him in court.

Pop taught me about contracts from the moment he recognized I'd eventually sign one that would change my entire life. You had to be smart when dealing with the powerful, all the way to the end.

There's power in this place. Eddie said so—I remembered now. Especially when there's shared blood. And shared names. So, I still made the final two slashes to finish the number. They just . . . didn't touch in a V. Because I was smart, and every smart man is a con man.

KINCADE WEBSTER III

And all hell broke loose.
Literally.

48

What happened wasn't planned or expected. How could it be? I didn't really *know* how selling your soul worked! I thought I was being slick and giving myself some loophole to work with later by, technically, signing the wrong name. But, when I completed the slash in lll, the quill and contract began to smoke, then a winking flame sparked on the parchment by the signature line and rimmed the entire document in magma-like light.

All the eager pretense Skinner projected dissolved into a ghoulish mask of rage. His head whipped from the contract to me. "What did you do?"

Darkness spooled from him like the ink a frightened octopus spews, a portal of some sort. Emerging from it were snapping, hungry mouths. No faces, no bodies. Just mouths. What???

I grabbed Leek's prone body off the counter, then shielded Other Leek with my own. As the darkness seeped from behind the counter to our side, threatening to engulf us, and those mouths hovered closer, I feared I'd played myself and my deception meant the entire deal was void, allowing Skinner to take me and Leek to whatever torment awaited us for the rest of time.

The parchment on the counter turned red, the air around it wavering, as hot as an open oven. Then from the display window at our backs, the bright light of approaching headlights. That got brighter still, like the stadium lights we left behind at Neeson. Then brighter still, like staring in the sun.

Me, Leek, and Eddie flinched away, unable to bear the sight. We heard door chimes, though. That blazing light cut out. Someone new had joined our party.

Pop.

He looked younger. Healthier. He was wearing the same suit he'd had on in the picture when he'd defeated Skinner in court.

He looked mad.

"My kids?" he roared, and charged down the aisle, a leather briefcase swinging in one hand. "MY KIDS!"

My father took a leap ten feet from the counter and cut through the air like a torpedo into Skinner's midsection, propelling them both into the darkness. Stones through oil.

Their battle was loud. Thuds, grunts, crashes. We couldn't see what was happening, but it all became less of a concern when the mouths aimed our way.

Eddie's hand fell on my shoulder. "We should move. The veil's thin now."

"Veil?"

"Between realms. I don't know what you did, but we're sitting in the middle of Ruin Road right now, and traffic is heavy. Come on!"

Where? The store was a little bigger than our apartment. Not much room to maneuver.

Eddie clapped his hands and changed that.

The store stretched in all directions, shelves and merchandise multiplying into several football fields of space and opportunity. I definitely knew how to use a football field.

"There's way more power flowing through here than I've ever felt. Even I can tap into it!" Eddie said, leading us and yelling over his shoulder. "Skinner's still the strongest, but we've got a shot. Find weapons. Tool up!"

Leek's body was already light, and in my adrenaline-fueled state, she felt weightless on my shoulder. I moved, spotting the handle of that old machete protruding from a shelf. I snatched it on the run, while Other Leek grabbed a bat farther down the aisle.

The chattering demon mouths stalked us.

"What are those things?" I screamed.

Eddie said, "Consumers."

He did not offer further explanation, but took a left, slowing to dig in his hip pocket. I caught him, could've passed him, but I didn't know this place. The dark portal Skinner summoned seemed to grow and spread, despite the store's expanded size, and I knew in my gut we had to be careful where we turned and when. To break through that darkness was game over.

312

The veil broke anyway as Pop was flung from the void into a shelf of small kitchen appliances. He hit with the approximate force of a meteorite, bowing the shelf and flattening toasters. He didn't look hurt, just angry, staring into the dark.

Skinner burst to our side, colliding with Pop, his fingers curled into claws, his jaw unhinged while he screamed curses. They tussled, delivering heavy but seemingly ineffective blows to one another.

I squeezed my machete's handle, rushed them, put every bit of my weight into a swing that should've taken Skinner's head. Pop hit him with an uppercut that lifted him five inches at the exact wrong moment, and I sliced the old monster's shoulder instead. He felt it, though. Howling, he spotlighted me with eyes where the irises had gone scarlet and were set in black. The wrongness mesmerized me. But I understood immediately that this was what more power did to a monster like Skinner who fed on it like a parasite. It showed his true face.

Floating teeth chomped toward my skull, but Other Leek yelled, "Down!"

My reflexes did what they do; I ducked in time for Other Leek to break those teeth with her bat. Jagged ivory flew like shrapnel, discouraging the attack. That Consumer retreated into the abyss it came from, but more gnashing mouths sailed our way.

"It's like demonic *Pac-Man*," Eddie said, freeing whatever had been in his pocket.

It was a road flare. He struck the cap against its top, igniting it with a hiss. The shelf we'd stopped by was filled mostly with home workout gear . . . dumbbells and resistance bands. There was a rolled yoga mat, too, with something like sweatpants hanging from its center coil. The pants were wet. Soaked and dripping. I smelled kerosene. Eddie's doing, no doubt.

He touched the flare to the fuel.

Pop and Skinner kept fighting while the entire shelf lit up and traced a fiery trail back the way we'd come. The creeping flame was strategic. The Consumers stopped their pursuit, flinching away from it. I said, "Eddie?"

"I told you, you made me brave enough to try something I've been scared to do before. I'm burning the joint down."

Okay then.

We kept running.

49

And running.

I don't know how long, but I was starting to feel it. This was fourth-quarter fatigue like I'd never known. Prolonged sprints down lengthy aisles, with Eddie sparking new fires that seemed to have little effect because the space had gotten *so big*. However far we went, Pop and Skinner's battle kept crossing our path. They burst through shelves, fell atop merchandise, crushing Skinner's cursed goods beneath them. I wanted to help, to tackle Skinner to the floor and hold him while Pop stomped him into nothing, but we had our own fight.

We turned a corner and two hungry mouths zipped at us from the far end. I swung my machete, splitting one through the middle. Other Leek squared up to swing her bat but clutched her stomach in a pained grimace and collapsed to her knees before she could strike. At the same time, the Leek I'd hoisted onto my shoulder began shivering violently, something like a seizure.

Eddie plucked the bat from Other Leek's hands and caught the attacking Consumer with a downward swing, pounding it into the floor while I knelt beside my ailing Other Sister.

"What's wrong?" I asked.

Through clenched teeth, she said, "Hurts."

"Can you keep moving?"

"Yes. It's hard, though."

Think, Cade!

Skinner, with his hands latched on to my father's lapel, rammed Pop through more shelving into a different aisle. I screamed, "Pop! We need you!"

He saw me, even entangled in Skinner's vicious attacks. He slipped free of the old man, got behind him, grabbed him by the scruff of the neck, and hurled him back into the dark portal that was never too far behind us. Pop came to us then, kneeling where I'd lowered Leek's weakened, convulsing body.

Another mouth appeared, greedily targeting our party. When it zoomed our way, Pop caught it by the teeth and stretched the jaws until something in it snapped. He kept stretching until the upper and lower jaws detached from each other. He threw the pieces away and rejoined us.

My vision blurred. I'd shed so many tears of sorrow since he passed, privately and at his funeral. Never once did I imagine seeing him again. Certainly not like this. Strong. His hand grazed my cheek, as warm as sunshine. He said, "I'm happy to see you, too, son."

He touched the unconscious, shuddering Leek's face while speaking directly to the Other Leek. "How you feeling, baby girl?"

"Not so good, Daddy."

"I know." Then, "You Eddie?"

Eddie nodded. "Yessir."

"You know this place. Can you get us to the exit?"

Eddie's jaw flexed, something unreadable there. "I can, but how are you going to get back up the road? You didn't come here through a dream. I don't know how any of this part works."

Pop said, "Me neither. But we better learn fast. Because—"

A body-sized portal opened over Pop's shoulder and Skinner stepped through, delivering a haymaker punch in stride. It caught Pop across the jaw with a sound like a gunshot and the shock wave tossed us all flat on the floor.

Skinner stood over us, enraged, and more frightening than I'd ever seen. His eyes were gone, the sockets dark hollows rimmed by veiny flesh. His coat billowed and bulged in places that a human body shouldn't.

"Enough!" he roared, and brought his clawlike hands together in a thunderclap.

The store contracted around us like a stretched spring suddenly released. Loose items flew off the shelves with the force of it. I dropped my machete and crouched over Leek's body to protect her from toppling inventory. A paperweight hit me behind the ear, triggering a bloody trickle. A golf club caught me in the thigh hard enough to bruise.

The store, back to its original size, was half engulfed in flame. Eddie's final act as shopkeeper. Skinner's head panned

317

back and forth, surveying the damage, infuriated. "I'll have your flesh torn from your living carcass every hour of every day for this insult!"

I didn't know if that was for Eddie, or all of us. Probably all of us.

Well, that old fiend was gonna have to earn it.

I reclaimed my machete and rushed him, juked his wild swing at my head like he was a defender on the field. As I ducked under his swiping hand, I pulled the machete blade across his ribs, opening up his coat, the garments underneath, and his flesh. He hissed from the pain, distracted enough that Pop caught him in the side of the head with a roundhouse punch, producing another shock wave and tossing more wares into the spreading flames.

My chest tightened from the smoke, but I didn't slow down. Reversing direction, I swiped the blade across Skinner's Achilles tendon, hoping to hobble him. It worked, dropping him to one knee, giving Eddie the opening to fire a bolt from the crossbow he'd snatched from the wall. It caught Skinner in the shoulder, then Pop was on him again, beating him with such force it drove him against the shop's counter.

The group attack was working. Whatever strength Skinner'd gained from the store, it wasn't enough to fend off multiple opponents. I aimed to finish it.

"Pop! Move!" I said, already in motion, the machete thrust ahead of me like a spear.

Pop rotated just so, giving me the angle. I drove that

machete through Skinner's chest and kept going until I felt it shatter a pane of glass in the display case behind him. I stared into his monstrous eyes, expecting the light to fade.

"No," Skinner said, blood staining his lips.

He shoved me hard, forcing me airborne before I crashed into the ground next to Leek's body. Other Leek was gone and I didn't have a moment to consider what that meant because Pop tried attacking the impaled Skinner, who flicked his wrist and opened four dark portals around my father. A demon mouth chomped from each, clamping on his arms and legs, affixing him in place like shackles. Pop strained but there was no give.

Eddie, so angry and unafraid, ran at his boss, intending to bludgeon him with the unloaded crossbow. Skinner swept up a handful of fire from the counter, forming a ball in his palm, and hurled it at Eddie. It hit him in the chest, setting him entirely aflame. He shrieked and spun in place. Skinner snapped his fingers and muted Eddie's screams.

Leaving me and Leek on the ground before him.

Skinner, coughing blood but seeming no weaker, grabbed the machete handle and tore the blade from his body. A slight gout of blood spurted, but nothing like the geyser I would've expected from such a wound.

Skinner said, "This is a place of cosmic energy. Energy I tap into simply by having my name on the door. I'm so strong here."

A deep hum reverberated through me. The pulsing energy

that Skinner spoke of. Beyond him was the checkout counter, the working area where Eddie used to do his thing, and the door leading to some unseen back room. At the same time, none of that was there. It all wavered like a fading projection, translucent enough to see through, a silk-thin illusion, a protective scrim between what was supposed to be real and actual reality.

I stared at something like a galaxy. It was the only way to describe it. An insane astronomer's infinite map draped over the world. A strange dark planet fixed in the expanse, surrounded by pinprick stars. A planet that opened its eyes to stare back.

ZAZEL. ZAZEL. ZAZEL.

"Arggh!" I winced at the horrid chant buzzing in my head.

ZAZEL. ZAZEL. ZAZEL.

A name. A curse.

ZAZEL. ZAZEL. ZAZEL.

A buyer and seller of pain. Suffering.

ZAZEL. ZAZEL. ZAZEL.

Those stars weren't stars. Each stretched, split, into grinning teeth. The disembodied mouths that tormented Eddie and chased us through the aisles of the shop were now set in twisted, desiccated faces. Recognizable ones flashed in my head in time with the chant. Corner Joe. Winton Jacobs. Treezy. Brady. Thousands of them.

ZAZEL. ZAZEL. ZAZEL.

This thing was what Skinner worked for, where he derived

320

the power behind the power behind the power behind the power . . .

ZAZEL. ZAZEL. ZAZEL.

I almost forfeited my soul *to that!*

Skinner spoke, solidifying the veil again. I wept with relief.

He said, "It could've been good for you. You could've had years with your family before I collected your debt. The little girl might've gone on to a bright future. Now . . . you're going into the pit. You and her. I'll use the time you would've been allotted to further my pursuits, extend my life, profit from the pain."

Skinner reached for me. "Prepare to meet *my* maker, Cade."

Bright light washed through the display window.

Skinner's head jerked up as the front wall smashed inward.

A chrome grille, glossy black paint, and a screaming engine barreled toward us. I had enough, just enough, juice left to do what I did. I grabbed my sister's body and threw us sideways, out of the path of the tires.

Skinner's hearse roared past me, Pop, Eddie in flames and smashed directly into Skinner, pinning him against his counter.

Scrambling to my feet, I cradled Leek's body, turning so I was positioned between her and the car. Had the vehicle come to life on its own?

No.

In the driver's seat was Other Leek. Behind the wheel and cheesing. She said, "I told you driving was easy."

Though I barely heard her over Skinner's screams.

He thrashed against the car's hood; spittle flew from his lips and splashed the paint. "I'll tear your souls apart! I'll take you to the depths, to the absolute limits. Zazel will reward me! I'll—"

The car's hood unlatched. Unholy light leaked from within.

Skinner became quiet. Concerned.

Afraid.

He locked eyes with me, his tone so drastically different from the moment before. "Hey, hey. Listen. There's still something we can work out."

The hood rose; the paint on the car's flank bulged outward in the shapes of hands, arms, and torsos. It was the same with the tires. Radial-belted limbs stretched up, seeking, seeking.

Skinner said, "I can fix your sister. No strings. You'll owe me nothing. Want to be the best the NFL has ever seen, I'll do that, too. I don't need your souls. Just—just back this car up."

I took steps forward, to see his face. "No deal."

I expected fury and threats, more expressions of his true self. He didn't have time. The souls he'd collected, and condemned, and ridden around for his pleasure had reached him.

Fingers burrowed bloodlessly beneath his flesh, triggering a horrid roar of agony.

They tore his body apart, then his ethereal essence, but every piece of that still seemed to be alive and quivering, and the dozens of groping arms worked with the fluidity of a spider spinning a web to reassemble him. Not correctly, though. An arm was plugged into his head, a leg shoved through his sternum, his spine knotted and wedged into his ribs until he was a horrific mound of wrong. Then they did it again. Fast. A blur. Over and over, the tearing and stitching of bloodless conscious chunks while dragging him into the car's infernal engine. Down and down and down and . . .

The hood latched on his screams, but I didn't know if I'd ever stop hearing them.

50

A coughing fit lurched me from my frozen horror. The veil between what was and what I never wanted to see again solidified completely and the fires spread to other parts of the store. With Skinner gone the flames that had consumed Eddie wicked away as quickly as they'd started, leaving him intact like he'd never been touched. The portals and mouths holding Pop in place winked away, freeing him. Pop opened the passenger door to Skinner's car and shouted, "Everyone in."

Through a cough, I managed, "We're taking this?"

"There's no other way."

We'd ridden in this thing before and we'd done fine. I would not think of what I'd seen this car's engine do. As horrible as it was, it wasn't as bad as what I saw behind the veil. Nothing was as bad as that.

I opened the back door and placed Leek's body on the seat. Motioning to Eddie, I said, "Get in."

"I can't, Cade."

"What do you mean? Skinner's gone."

"I'm bound to the store. Burning it all down, it was always going to be me, too. That's how I get free."

"But . . ." I was coughing again.

"You gotta go, man," Eddie said.

I wasn't foolish and wasn't torn. I got it. I was sorry this was going to be his fate, but I had Leek to think about. As I tried to climb into the car, Eddie's hand fell on my shoulder. "There's one problem, brother."

Brother? I became afraid. "What?"

He pointed at my right hand. "Your ring. Your wish. Skinner never broke it."

"I— But you're burning the store. I'll take it off and throw it in the fire."

Eddie's head shook. "As I am bound to this store, that ring is bound to you. Fire won't destroy it. You throw it away, it'll come back. Like it always has."

"What am I supposed to do?"

"If you take it back in the world, the chaos it causes will continue as long as you're alive."

My heart dropped. Then my lungs burned. The smoke was getting worse.

"I think there's a loophole, though," he said through his own coughing. "It always comes back to your hand. Maybe it can be destroyed if it has nowhere to go."

I looked at my hand, that ring like a swollen platinum knuckle. "I don't understand."

Only, I did.

Eddie crouched. When he stood again, he held the machete I'd dropped. "You've got a tough choice to make, Cade. Right now. I don't envy you."

"Wait. No. What if—" My mind whirled, and the smoke had me hacking the words. "What if I was careful? I only went around people who needed to be courageous. Even Skinner said what happened wasn't as bad as he thought it would be!"

I sensed a presence near. Pop, beside me. Having him close made me feel stronger. Not braver, though. Not for this. "Pop?"

"The harm will inevitably outweigh the good," he said. "I love you, Kincade. I can't force you to do this. It's not fair, I know it's not. Very little in this entire universe is."

My eyes welled. The alternatives spooled through my mind, but what was the point of going there? If I took the easy way out, then I might as well prepare myself to see Skinner in the pit eventually. I'd be no better.

ZAZEL. ZAZEL. ZAZEL.

My voice cracked when I said, "Do it fast. Please."

No more words. Eddie laid the blade in the nearest flames, and I chose not to watch its edge turn rosy red. He whipped his belt off and cinched it painfully tight around my forearm. My father stood behind me, not even pretending to comfort me. He was a brace so I wouldn't move and drag things out. He used whatever supernatural strength that had been infused in him to splay my arm across the car's hood, the wrist of my ring hand exposed.

The smoke was almost too thick to see through now, but maybe that was a blessing. My coughs were bad and forced my father to apply extra strength to keep me still, but I never saw Eddie retrieve the machete, or raise it. I turned my face toward the windshield, looked at Other Leek, who mouthed, *It'll be okay.*

Eddie was as fast as he could be, but that was never going to be fast enough. The pain was blistering and terrible but not eternal, and there was solace in that.

I passed out.

51

Darkness.

I was in the car, beside the version of my sister who was hurt worse than I was.

Darkness.

We were in motion, reversing from the smoke-choked storefront while Eddie stood stoic among the flames. He'd dropped the red-hot machete that he'd used to sever my hand and cauterize the stump. He tossed my hand, with Pat the Patriot still gleaming high on the ring finger, into the fire. The flames engulfed that lost piece of me, then him.

Darkness.

On the road, the abyss pressed on both sides, gray mist rising to the top of the universe. Leek, the injured one, only took breaths every fourth second. The sound hurt more than my wound. *I don't want you to go, Leek, but if you're in pain and it's too hard to stay, you do what you need to.*

Darkness.

Pop was in the back seat between us. When did that happen? He cradled our heads in his lap, stroking our hair gently. "You did good, kids," he said.

From behind the wheel, Other Leek said, "Thanks, Daddy."

I felt myself slipping into darkness again but willed my eyelids open. "Pop, I'm sorry I wasn't there when you died."

"Stop that. You were. A piece of you, and your sister, and your mom are always with me. Never worry about that again."

The pain at my wrist was immense. It took every bit of strength to stay conscious. "Can you help Leek?"

Other Leek said, "I'm doing fine."

I looked into my father's face as he stared at Leek's declining body and I couldn't read a thing there.

"Please," I managed before . . .

Darkness.

A mighty jolt jerked me awake, shooting white-hot lightning up my arm and throughout my entire nervous system. We'd come to a stop right back where the trip began, near the field house entrance at Neeson, the scene still frozen in the moment after Brady's death.

Pop leaned over me, opened my door. "Trip's over, son."

He shifted my weight as if I was as light as Leek and got me out of the car, onto the ground, next to Ma. He left me to retrieve Leek's body while Other Leek looked on from the driver's seat, her lip quivering. Pop lowered her body between me and Ma's, noticed how distraught Other Leek looked. "What's wrong, baby?"

She seemed almost confused when she said, "I'm scared."

My heart lurched. Brady's fear had returned after he died. Was Leek gone, too?

Her body still rasped. The breaths were ragged, but there. So that meant . . .

The ring was gone. My wish was broken. It better be.

Pop kissed my mother's forehead first, then Leek's, then mine. "I love you all, for all of time."

He turned his attention to Other Leek while he rounded the passenger side of the hearse. "What are you scared of, sweetie?"

"Where we're going," she said.

I couldn't see her from my low angle on the ground. Once Pop slipped around the bumper he was out of sight, too. The only way I knew he'd gotten in the passenger seat was from the way the car settled on its springs and the sound of his door closing. They'd be leaving soon.

Pop said, "We've been on trips before. You loved the one we took to Great Wolf. Remember?"

"I do."

"Do you remember what you told me while we were there?"

"I probably told you a lot of things."

"True. I'm talking about how much you wished your mom and brother were with us."

"Okay."

"And I told you it was fine for Daddy to get a little solo time with his favorite girl. Right?"

"Yes."

The next part happened fast.

The car shifted oddly on its springs, and the driver's-side

330

door swung open, giving me a full view of Other Leek, looking surprised. Pop had reached across her lap, shoved the door open, and was now shoving her.

Other Leek said, "What are you doing?"

"We'll have our time again, sweetie. After you live a long, great life that you deserve."

"Daddy! Wait!"

Pop did not.

He pushed Other Leek from the car, and in the short drop between the driver's seat and the ground, Other Leek vanished in a poof of smoke and stardust. A moment later, Leek's body arched as if struck by lightning. Her muscles spasmed and she cried in intense pain, pawing at the giant splinter still embedded in her side, but she was alive. Somehow.

"Take care of them, Cade," Pop said. "I'll be waiting for you all."

He slammed the door, revved the engine, and made a sharp turn on Ruin Road, speeding back the way he came, and with each yard he put between me and him, the road retracted. It vanished, became flat earth, and the entire mystical horizon faded, revealing the entrance to the field house.

The world jerked back into motion. We rejoined the tragic aftermath of Brady's attack perhaps a second after we left. With great effort I slid closer to my family, pulling my ailing sister and mother closer.

I went out again and didn't wake up for two days.

52

It was hard to remember.

I awoke to something cold running into my veins. It was the same soothing cool as a strawberry ICEE from Lim's, and if I got uncomfortable, I could push a button for more of it, but then I'd doze off. At first, those moments between summoning comfort and getting it jerked like rough edits. Jump cuts from day to night to day with the occasional sloppy frame of my mother sitting by the window crying.

Eventually I got used to whatever was being pumped into me, or the button wasn't giving me enough of it, and I stayed awake. My mother was there, and I said, "Leek?"

Ma left her chair, the bandages around her skull slightly pink where her head wound seeped. She clutched my knee. I braced for horrible news.

She said, "Leek's going to make it, but she's got a long road ahead."

That phrase triggered a flash of the longest road I'd ever seen. One so long it ran between ruin and salvation. I jabbed my button but got no relief.

•   •   •

When I was strong enough, mentally and physically, to have conversations, Ma held my remaining hand while a doctor explained the additional surgery I required.

"The damage to the limb was extensive. Do you recall how you were injured?" the doctor asked.

Bombs exploded. Debris flew. *How* was unimportant, though he clearly observed a difference in my injuries versus other survivors. I shook my head and claimed ignorance. He had no choice but to move on.

"Well, to remove the dead tissue and prevent the spread of infection, we had to amputate an additional four inches above the wrist."

Yeah. I'd noticed.

From above my elbow to the nub just below, a thick coating of white bandages concealed my new-look arm. He said other things about recovery time, physical therapy, and prosthetics. I barely heard a word. One thing was guaranteed: I'd have ample time to review the pamphlet. So to speak.

After some time in the ICU, the hospital moved Leek into my room. She was missing pieces, too. A kidney. Part of her spleen. A few chunks of bone from her hip. The miracle, Ma explained, was the amount of blood she'd lost.

"They told me," she said, choking back sobs, "they don't know how anyone survived losing as much as she did. She was just determined not to leave us."

I had a sense that was close, but not quite right. I flashed on that road again. Strained to remember what it was. So fuzzy.

Within a week the battered and bruised Webster clan was released. We returned to Jacobs Court. To a long, cold winter of change.

I never went back to Neeson Preparatory Academy.

The number of deaths, and the mystery of how "The Bomber"—the media wasn't saying his name and none of us were either—got his hands on hundred-year-old explosives still stable enough to inflict damage, essentially shut the school down. It was easy to think that the superrich somehow bought their way out of feeling what the rest of us did, but I saw a bunch of the footage on TV and the socials. The In Memoriams. The wailing parents, faculty, and classmates. Nate threw the pass of a lifetime when he stopped Brady, saved a lot of people—including me and mine. Just not himself. Some people were saying his father's going to put a statue of Nate in front of the school when it reopens. For much of the time I knew Nate, I didn't like him. I don't think I liked him much on the day he died. I wanted to see that statue, though. He put in work. He deserved it.

No one ever posted on the racist NeesonFriedChicken account again. Maybe the account owner was a victim of the bombs. Maybe they simply woke up the next day afraid in a way they hadn't been in weeks. They'd had a run, though. That kind of thinking was never without fans.

For the rest of my mostly wealthy classmates, I wasn't sure how it worked. I imagine they enrolled in different pricey schools here or abroad. For me, I'd done well enough in my coursework over previous years to have met graduation requirements. I was done with high school and had no real college prospects since the programs that had been recruiting me sent their condolences but no offers. They seemed to have little use for a one-armed wide receiver.

It hurt.

I wasn't talking about my phantom limb.

When the days got cold-cold, and I didn't have the escape of school or sports, I started getting cabin fever. The best part of my day was the PT sessions to get me used to life with a missing limb. I worked on becoming more dexterous with my left hand, learned that I need to balance differently to account for a different weight distribution. I got fitted for a prosthetic, though the cost of acquiring a good one was daunting. Ma assured me Pop's life insurance had us covered. But for how long?

I began reevaluating the ways I'd help my family long-term. Daily. Usually while walking the Jacobs Court streets in a deep funk.

That's when a new recruiter targeted me. Book.

It was January. I'd been home from the hospital for two months, and Leek finally had the energy to return to school. With Ma back at work, I found lonely days in the apartment oppressive. So, I walked. Ten degrees outside. Snowing. I didn't care. I strolled past Lim's and Pop's old office—the whole building got bought by developers with promises of *New Opportunities* coming soon. Whatever those opportunities ended up being, they'd already started the work by painting the entire structure an industrial gray. Only a single graffiti tag marked the redone facade. A warning to the neighborhood.

GENTRIFICATION HAS COME TO THE COURT

The old-man crew moved their daily conference inside the barbershop for the winter, so I often stopped in there just to have someone to talk to. They kept me up on Court gossip, reminisced about the bigger neighborhood milestones of the last fifty years, and generally did what they could to cheer me up. Eventually, inevitably, someone came in for a cut and wanted to talk football. That's when I had to leave. Too soon.

On one of those pained exits I crossed paths with my old friend and his new crew as they patrolled—or preyed on—the block.

My head had been down, I wasn't paying attention to anything but my own pain, so I bumped right into a One-Eight. He immediately bucked with the confidence of someone who had five other fighters ready to take me down if I proved to be too much.

Book waved them off. "Chill, chill."

The minions backed away, then kept moving when Book gave them the signal. He wanted to talk. I asked, "What's up, man?"

I hadn't spoken to him much since our group text died. His desire for a conversation struck me odd.

He looked different, though I was used to this change in people around me.

The brash confidence was gone. The Machiavellian schemer might still exist somewhere in him, but he was no longer the brave alpha ready to conquer the One-Eights, then the world. Yet it wasn't like he could step away, was it? He'd promised too much with his actions. The stress was showing.

Book said, "Um, listen. I know you got a lot of free time on your—"

He stopped himself, recognizing the insensitivity of the common phrase he almost used.

"You got free time, right? Want to make some cash?"

No. Not any way he was going to suggest. I was more wary of bad deals than I'd ever been. Didn't mean I wasn't curious. "How?"

He scanned both directions of the sidewalk like he was wary of eavesdroppers. "It'd be easy. There are a lot of snakes in the crew. Someone always looking for a come up. I need someone I can *really* trust to watch my back."

Book twitched as he finished the ask. Something like a scared forest animal. Waiting.

"I'm sorry, Book. That ain't me."

He couldn't hide his heartbroken terror, though he tried. "Man, I knew that! I was messing with you. What I'mma do with a one-armed bodyguard? No offense."

"It was plenty offensive, but whatever."

Book stuffed his hands into his pockets and rocked on his heels.

I said, "You talk to Gab lately?"

"She been busy. Doing the thing. She be singing at a couple of lounges downtown."

That cheered me up a little. Not much. "That's what's up. I'm glad."

If there was one good thing that came out of this all, it was Gabby's situation. Whatever fears came back after I did what I did, she wasn't letting them stop her. Maybe all she needed was a glimpse of what was on the other side of fear to get her going. A peek through the veil.

ZAZEL. ZAZEL. ZAZEL.

I shuddered so hard, Book put a hand on my back to steady me. "Yo! You good?" he asked.

"I'm fine. It's okay." I was talking more to myself than to him.

Whatever connection we'd rekindled over Gabby was gone. Book heavy-sighed, stared in the direction his crew went, and said, "I should go."

"Yeah. I know. You got things to do."

I extended my hand for dap, but he hugged me instead.

I held on a beat longer even as he tugged away. "Be safe, man. Please."

A short nod, then he was on his way and I was, too.

He was always the smartest guy I knew. Every smart man was a con man. He'd been running his gangster con on the One-Eights for a while and I hoped he found a way out before they caught on.

January became February. On Super Bowl Sunday, Ma announced me, her, and Leek had reservations at the stuffiest, quietest restaurant in the city, which, coincidentally I'm sure, had no TVs broadcasting the game.

I loved my mother a lot, but especially for that.

Life for the three of us had been . . . *grayer* since everything happened. I don't know a better way to put it. Trauma and tragedy drain vibrance. We woke up. We went through the day's routine, something that included a lot more medicine and nursing. Leek was finally gaining weight after all she'd lost after her injuries, but she still looked frail.

"How's that lasagna?" I asked.

She poked the mostly uneaten mound with her fork. "Fine."

I was still clumsy handling my utensils left-handed, and I gave up on my grilled salmon halfway.

Ma noticed the daily disappointments beginning to take hold and interrupted what was about to become a downer of a night out. "I have some news for you, Cade. It's good. I think."

"What?" I asked, nervous.

"Commonwealth University reached out to me. They want to honor your scholarship offer."

"CU wants to . . ." My face scrunched so hard I thought my jaw would cramp. "For football?"

Ma shook her head. The wig she wore to conceal the scar on her scalp shifted slightly. "Not exactly. Given the circumstances of how you—we—got injured, and how that event affected the entire community, the university is extending the offer as a kindness."

I pushed away from the table while she was still talking. "I don't need nobody's charity."

"You'd be welcome in the locker room. They're happy to have you assist with team management."

That hit worse than any tackle I'd eaten on the field. "I'd be their Brady."

Ma winced.

I got my phone out and tapped the screen. "I'm getting a Lyft home. Don't let me stop you from ordering dessert."

That night, I had a hard time going to sleep and was staring at the ceiling at 2:00 a.m. when my door creaked open like it had every night since moving on her own stopped hurting Leek. She tiptoed across the floor and I slid over, giving her room to crawl in under the covers. She sidled up next to me, nuzzled her cheek against my chest, but didn't doze off right away.

"Mama cried a little after you left. The people at the table next to us got all grumpy like we messed up their dinner." Then she called them a name that would've gotten her detention if she'd said it in school."

"Hey!" I might've told her to watch her mouth, but I had to stifle a laugh first. *She* wasn't laughing, though. That calmed me down. "I wasn't trying to make her cry," I said.

"Stop being so mean, then."

I shifted in bed so I was looking in her face even though it was too dark to see. "I'm not."

"You are. Every day. You don't talk to us. You don't want to be in the same room with us. That's mean. Daddy's gone and you're making yourself be gone, too."

"I—" I didn't know what to say.

"I remember *it*, you know."

I sat up. "It?"

"That store. That scary old man with the car. Daddy helped save us."

"Yeah," I said, seeing no good reason to do anything but confirm. "That happened."

"What did he save us for if this is how things are going to be from now on?"

She rolled over and was snoring almost immediately.

Unlike most nights when she snuck in, a comforting routine I'd come to cherish, I couldn't follow her into sleep. Her words had me rattled way past sunrise.

341

The next morning as Ma hovered over the stove, where bacon and eggs sizzled, I stood in the kitchen threshold and said, "Thank you for telling me about CU. You can let them know I'm grateful and I'll be there for training camp. I'll do whatever the team needs."

When she started sobbing, I went to her and curled my good arm around her.

"You're a good boy," she said. "Your father and I used to *marvel* at how incredible the kids we made are."

Leek, in the doorway now, said, "I'm more incredible, though!"

Chuckling, I waved her over to get in on the hug.

The three of us were like that awhile. Until the smoke detector went off and Ma scrambled to get that ruined bacon under some cold water in the sink.

The Websters. Incredible people. Bad cooks.

53

The warmth lasted long enough that we had to scramble to get Leek dressed, fed, and out the door to school. Ma got herself together and declared she needed to run errands, leaving me alone and exhausted, with nothing better to do than try and catch up on the sleep I'd missed last night.

I flopped face down on my bed, already feeling the crash. Fatigue hit me like a ray gun, and though the doze came fast, it wasn't peaceful. In the last second of wakefulness, for reasons I didn't understand, I made myself think of Ruin Road and . . .

I was back. Walking the road, the mist on either side swirling. The asphalt went on forever in both directions. The scale of it should have been terrifying, but I'd seen worse.

On a whim, I yelled, "Pop! Are you here? Can you hear me?"

Directly to my left the mist swirled into the rough shape of a man. As if emerging from a cloud, the shape stepped from the abyss to the asphalt, still connected to the wall by a thick cumulus column. Not my father. Eddie.

"Oh my god!" I went to him, to try to hug him, but it was as awkward as real life because my arm was still missing here in the dream. I overbalanced and fell right through him as if he were smoke, my head and torso thunking off the invisible barrier between the road and what lay beyond.

"Good to see you, brother," he said. "Don't do that again, though. It feels weird."

I backed up a step, taking him in.

He looked more like something that came out of an Eddie mold. He was Eddie's height and size, and I could make out the texture of the flannel shirt and jeans he'd worn each time I encountered him. But he lacked all the color of life, presenting in the same swirling gray of the mist.

I asked, "Are you going to explain why you look like you came out of a vape pen?"

He glanced down like he hadn't noticed, rotating and examining his hands. "Ain't that something. Remember how I said there was a bunch of weird stuff between life and death and dream? Well, there are whole worlds, Cade. Worlds!"

"I don't get it."

"I don't think you can on your side of it. You will one day. Just vibe for now."

I motioned to the wall. "Is my father in there?"

He shook his head, somewhat sad. Pointed down the road. "Your father took a long trip. To somewhere nice, I bet. I don't get to go that far yet. The things I did for Skinner— even though I didn't want to—I need to make amends for before I go farther. That's why I called you here."

"You didn't call me. I came on my own."

He stroked his chin, considering. "That's even better, then." He thumped my chest. "Must mean it's meant to be."

"What?" I didn't like the sound of that.

"Remember me telling you there are a lot of Skinners out there?"

"I do now."

"You want some get back for what him and his kind took from us?"

Yeah. Maybe. But when he said Skinner's "kind," my thoughts didn't go to the old man skulking through my neighborhood in his Cadillac. I thought of what backed him. The power behind the power behind the power . . .

Zazel.

I didn't dare say it aloud because what if it heard me? Didn't matter. This was a place of thought as much as action, and that horrible blank face formed in the mist above Eddie, as large as a billboard.

I stumbled backward, or the road tilted under me. Either way, I was going to be tossed from the dream. As before, Eddie whipped his arm forward, catching me. Keeping me.

Only he grabbed my amputated arm. The stump.

And. It. HURT.

"Hey!" I winced. "Let go! Let go!"

I dug my heels into the asphalt, attempting to pull away, but Eddie didn't let go. Instead, his misty arm stretched with me, administering hot agony that extended beyond where my flesh ended to where the missing part of my arm used to be.

"Eddie, stop! What are you doing to me?"

"You have to make amends, too," he said, but he didn't sound exactly like Eddie anymore. His voice was still there, but more overlapped. Dozens of voices. "You've engaged with a disciple of Zazel, but there are other disciples, other masters. You must stop innocents and the corrupt alike from making the same mistake you did. Destroy those who would lead people to peril for their own gain. What Zazel and its ilk have used for harm you may use to help! We have given you the tools."

The burning in my arm from the elbow to the stump to the hand and fingers that no longer existed drove me to my knees, as torturous as when I'd lost the limb. How could you feel this much pain in a dream?

"Fear not!" the entire mist wall seemed to say.

"Fear not!" the dozens of voices from Eddie's mouth said as his smoky tendril finally, mercifully, released me.

I collapsed on the asphalt that tilted near vertical and began rolling limp from the dream. In the moment before wakefulness I heard Eddie's voice, and Eddie's alone, say, "Go to the store, brother! We left you something! And remember . . . fear not!"

Snapping awake in my bed, drenched in sweat, raising my stump expecting to see a gnarled, crisped version of my arm reattached and smoking, I was relieved and disappointed that I was the same amputee I was before I fell asleep. Maybe.

I sat up and tugged on shoes and a sweatshirt from the closet, and a bubble coat. Because this wasn't like the last time I spoke to Eddie in the dream. I remembered everything.

I knew where I needed to go.

Fear not?

Easier said than done.

54

Snowflakes drifted when I got off the bus and started to stick by the time I passed the Knitmus Test. I made the turns, walked the walk as an icy wind bit into my face and I left mushy tracks in the rapidly accumulating snow. Never thought I'd come this way again, but my instructions were clear.

Not that I was beholden to whatever entities existed in that otherworldly mist. If it was just that, I might've ignored those voices out of spite, convinced I'd given enough. One thing they said stuck: *You have to make amends, too.*

They didn't elaborate because they didn't have to. The guilt ate at me daily. Brady might've gone dark side without a nudge from me eventually, but that's not the way it went down. I walked Skinner's and Zazel's power into the world. I might've claimed ignorance for a while, but once I knew, I didn't run into the woods and hide until some better idea came along. I tried to make it work because that's what felt best for me. I understood my sin. I'd seen where the worst sinners go.

So, I had to make amends. Somehow.

On the block where Skinner's Pawn & Loan used to be,

the burned-out husk of the store looked different than I expected on this snowy day. It looked older than it was, as if it had burned down a decade ago, wedged between two empty storefronts with their flanks singed from the heat of that night. The roof had collapsed, giving it the appearance of an empty diseased gum socket surrounded by healthier teeth. What was I supposed to do here?

My stump itched. I rubbed at it through the long flapping coat sleeve.

The snow was heavier now, blanketing the collapsed roof of the store in a uniform white sheet except for one small section that remained bare and moist. For some reason, the snow was melting there.

I squinted. A mound of broken cinder blocks and roofing tile protruded, damp with steamy wisps snaking into the air. The more I stared, the more my stump itched, and almost without thought I was maneuvering into the destroyed store's footprint, careful not to twist an ankle on debris. At the mound, the itch became unbearable.

Tearing my coat open and shrugging my right shoulder free, I gritted my teeth, trying to understand what was happening. The mound kept melting snow, and I kicked at it, dislodging the top layer of broken bits, exposing what was beneath.

A long handle, running to a longer blade. I winced away.

It was the machete Eddie had used to take my hand.

What?

My stump wasn't itching anymore. Angled toward that handle, it stretched. Not with new flesh, but with smoky mist swirling into the shape of a muscular forearm, a flexing wrist, an eager palm and grasping fingers! At the urging of the impossible manifestation, I lurched forward, wrapping those smoky fingers around the blade's handle, and yanked it free.

The metal was scorched black yet did not appear hindered. What I felt—and I didn't know how to explain feeling anything through an arm made of mist—was strength and purpose. I felt like that blade could slice steel. Maybe it'd have to, because I sensed motion from the corner of my eye.

At the curb, another familiar thing wisped into reality, at first mist, then real.

Skinner's car.

The gleaming black hearse my sister once drove in spirit form to save us sat at the curb. Instinctively I sank into a fighting stance, the blade on guard.

The car's door opened on its own, the interior empty.

We left you something! And remember . . . fear not!

I stood straight.

Approaching the car cautiously, I leaned for a peek inside. The radio dial glowed amber and old-school rap flitted from the speakers. 50 Cent.

It was difficult overriding the urge to run until I collapsed, but Eddie's words stayed with me. Other Leek drove this car once. It was a tool.

What Zazel and its ilk have used for harm you may use to help! Fear not!

I settled in behind the wheel. Laid the machete on the passenger seat and placed my hands—the real one and the one made of mist—on the wheel at nine and three.

The snowfall was heavier, but not a single flake touched the car. A key was slotted into the ignition, a fuzzy rabbit's-foot key chain dangling from it. I turned it with my mist hand and the engine roared to life. Literally. It sounded like screaming.

Flinching, I said, "Are you going to do that every time?"

What was happening right now? Three months ago, I was on my way to the NFL. But something told me the game I was about to play was way more important.

There are worse Skinners out there.

"The Checkered Game of Life," I said.

I wrenched the gearshift to drive and let off the gas. Let's get to it, then.

The destinations ahead wouldn't have made my vision board, but I needed to be a different kind of hero for Jacobs Court. Like Pop said, you carry your people with you even when you ride alone.

Maybe. Maybe everyone crossed paths with malicious merchants in their journey. At some point we all fought demons, and sometimes we won.

Not without scars.

EPILOGUE

GABBY

It was a snowy night in the city, much of everything shut down. The next school day had already been canceled, and plows trudged along deserted streets, pushing dirty slush piles to the curb. It was a good night for hot chocolate on the couch and a movie, but GeneBeatz insisted snow didn't stop parties. He warned everyone in the group that if they didn't show, they were out, so Gabby didn't get to relax. She got to sing.

To a nearly empty club, because GeneBeatz was wrong.

They were performing at a downtown spot called Catalyst, a place Gabby wouldn't have been allowed in if she wasn't with the band, GeneBeatz's dated, kind of lazy throwback of a group called the Vocab. Gabby was brought in to replace the former vocalist, Marissa, who got a job with an insurance agency or something. During a fifteen-minute break, she found herself crying in a bathroom stall because this sucked!

It took effort to get past the jitters to do what she did. Even for a slack audience of disinterested drunks. Those nerves felt amplified now, months past when they'd vanished completely. The short period of perceived invincibility felt like a drug she'd kicked cold turkey. The detox wasn't going well.

The lights flickered from the storm but managed to stay on while Gabby snatched squares of toilet paper and dabbed at her eyes, knowing she'd need to reapply makeup or get yelled at by Gene. Summoning what little energy she had, she stood, her eyes catching on some scratched-in graffiti on the stall door: THE HYPE BOX 4EVER!

The Hype Box. Why did that sound familiar?

It was a fleeting question. She didn't have time to dwell if she wanted her full pay—thirty-five bucks—for the night. Gene docked dollars for minutes, after all.

She shouldered the door open and nearly smacked some poor passing woman in the face.

"Oh, sorry, sorry!" Gabby said, meaning it.

The woman who'd dodged the door with the reflexes of a cat waved it off. "No worries." She beamed. "Hey, aren't you the lead singer of the band?"

Gabby nodded, returning a half smile. "That's me!"

"I'm so glad I bumped into you! I mean, maybe not in the bathroom, but I would've gotten to you eventually."

Gabby tensed. "Why?"

"I recruit talent."

Gabby reassessed the woman, taking her in fully. Tall, slim, with fitted leather pants over wide hips. She tapered at the top, though she wore her leopard-print crop well.

Her black lipstick and eyeliner were a bold choice but suited her under the club's party lights. She dug in her clutch and produced a business card that seemed to glow.

ZZL Investments
Belinda Raask

"Investments?" Gabby said. "You're not a record label."

"We have interests in all sorts of ventures. What we look for is talent and potential. You have both in spades!"

Gabby's face warmed. Who didn't love a compliment?

The club lights flickered again, a longer interruption than before, three seconds maybe. In the dark bathroom, only Belinda's teeth were visible, her smile a grotesque, disembodied thing that might've set Gabby running if not for Belinda standing between her and the exit.

The lights flared back on, and that momentary jolt of terror felt childishly ridiculous.

Especially when Belinda said, "I'd like to help you. If you want."

"Help me how?" Gabby asked, scared to hope for something good.

"Let's talk pie in the sky, sweetie." Belinda's smile widened. "What's your greatest wish? I'd love to hear it."

ACKNOWLEDGMENTS

Big thanks to everyone who traversed *Ruin Road* along with me:

Editor
Jody Corbett

Designer
Maeve Norton

Publisher
David Levithan

President
Ellie Berger

Production
Melissa Schirmer

Manufacturing
Katie Wurtzel

Sales

Kelsey Albertson
Holly Alexander
Tracy Bozentka
Savannah D'Amico
Courtney DeVerges
Barbara Holloway
Annie Krege
Brittany Lowe
Brigid Martin
Dan Moser
Nikki Mutch
Sydney Niegos
Caroline Noll

Jaqueline Perumal
Sarah Phillips
Betsy Politi
Kristin Rasmussen
Jennifer Rivera
Jacquelyn Rubin
Chris Satterlund
Terribeth Smith
Jody Stigliano
Sarah Sullivan
Melanie Wann
Jarad Waxman
Elizabeth Whiting

Publicity & Marketing
Seale Ballenger
Erin Berger
Greyson Corley
Rachel Feld
Daisy Glasgow
Tessa Meischeid

Library & Educational Marketing
Emily Heddleson
Maisha Johnson
Sabrina Montenigro
Lizette Serrano
Meredith Wardell

Scholastic Clubs & Fairs
Zoe Berman
Jazan Higgins
Rachel Schwartz
Mona Tavangar

Scholastic Audio
Lori Benton
Paul Gagne
John Pels
Melissa Reilly Ellard

Andrea Brown Literary Agency
Jamie Weiss Chilton

TV/Film
Jennifer Justman
Mary Pender
Jason Richman

Family & Friends
Adrienne Giles
Melanie Giles
Jaiden Taylor
Jacari Johnson
Clementine Williams
Britney Williams

Writer Crew
Kwame Alexander
Terry J. Benton-Walker
Preeti Chhibber
Dhonielle Clayton
Tiffany D. Jackson
Meg Medina
Ellen Oh
Jason Reynolds
justin a. reynolds
Olugbemisola Rhuday-Perkovich
Eric Smith
Raúl the Third
Jeff Zentner
The Hotel Bar (iykyk)

ABOUT THE AUTHOR

Lamar Giles is the critically acclaimed author of *The Getaway*, a YALSA Top Ten Best Fiction title and a Quick Pick; *Spin*, a *New York Times Book Review* Editor's Pick; *Overturned*, a *Kirkus Reviews* Best Book; *Not So Pure and Simple*; *Fake ID*, an Edgar Award finalist; and *Endangered*, also an Edgar Award finalist, as well as numerous middle-grade novels and comics. He is also the editor of the anthology *Fresh Ink*. Lamar is a founding member of We Need Diverse Books. He resides in Virginia with his family. Find out more at lamargiles.com.